THE CAT IN THE BOX

Andrea James

For my Bastine.
Thank you for always being my strength.

A special thank you goes to the Scott Editorial team for helping me turn my little idea into more than I ever thought it could be.

First published in Great Britain in 2022 by Scott Editorial

www.scotteditorial.com

A CIP record of this book is available from the British
Library.

Chapter One

I was pouring soup, then all I did was blink, and my entire world changed. I was no longer looking down into the bowl. Instead, my mum was looking down at me. Harsh fluorescent lighting and bare white walls framed the concern and worry pouring from her gaze. I drew in a long breath to question, but the taste and smell of something clinical made me internally berate myself. How the hell had I managed to put myself in hospital by making soup?

I inched up the bed with a wince. 'What did I do?' I asked, but like a nail bomb had exploded inside my head, searing agony blinded me.

'You're in hospital, sweetie.' My mum leant in and ran her hand down the right side of my face. It was such a lovely gesture.

'I gathered that, Mum.' Apart from feeling bruised in various places, every part of me that should move, could; so naively, I believed nothing serious had happened.

The queue of questions was ready to be unleashed, but I caught sight of something that pushed an unexpected addition to the front. 'What the hell are you wearing?'

'Do you like it?' she asked sweetly, looking down over her pink woollen skirt suit. I had never seen my mum in anything other than jeans, black trousers, or on special occasions, a black skirt.

A bit of decency kicked in, and I was about to respond with a polite lie, when other things made their way past the dazzling pink. Her hair which should be straight, brownish grey, and four inches long, sat in wavy blonde curls upon her shoulders. She was thinner, tanned, and her usual slapdash, 'that'll do' makeup was immaculately contoured.

I looked to my dad for a bit of normality. He hadn't changed his overall style since the seventies. It was seeing my northern dad, the man who wore jeans to my grandad's funeral, in a pair of chinos that started the panic.

'Oh, breathe sweetheart. Just breathe,' my mum said in the voice she used to mock posh people.

'What the fuck happened? Why am I in hospital?'

'Language, darling.'

With Mum's help, I slowly sat up. My back ached, and my head swayed slightly, but the pain was bearable this time and, from what I could tell, coming from behind my right ear. Before I could investigate further, something dark cascaded over my shoulders, distracting me. Squinting, I assessed the deep chestnut brown, loose curls and touched what should be a straight blonde bob.

'There was an accident, but you are okay.' My mum stroked my arm while I checked I wasn't wearing a wig.

'No. No, I'm really not.' I shook my head, but the room seemed to move with me, and I nearly threw up.

'Relax sweetheart,' my dad said, tapping my right foot.

'Did you dye your hair?'

Dad reached up self-consciously and smoothed his hand over his slick jet-black hair. 'I have for years. Why, what's wrong with it?'

My mum assessed him from a few different angles. 'It looks the same.'

I ran my hand over the rough bedding, trying to steady my breathing. Choking back tears, I asked, 'How long have you been dying your hair?' I may not have known what the hell was going on, but I knew I had never seen my dad with black hair.

Realisation slackened my dad's face, and it took everything I had to hold it together while I waited for my answer. 'About five years.'

Every part of me went numb from shock, and it was the only reason I was able to push my next questions out. 'What happened? Shit. Dad, what year is it?'

My mum's back straightened, and the door to my left opened to my dad saying, 'Oh shit.'

A tall, slender doctor walked into the sideward, wearing an overly happy expression. 'Fantastic, you're awake. And how are you feeling?'

Before I could answer, or he could say anything else, my mum said, 'She just asked; what year is it?'

His smile slipped, but he had the type of rounded face that even when relaxed, had a jovial expression. Wisps of white hair jutted out of his ears, matching what was speckled across his head and jawline. A massive nose occupied the centre of his wrinkling face, and a name tag, pinned to his white coat, said, *'Dr Warburton'*. He was also the messenger about to incinerate my world.

'It's 2022,' he said softly. 'Freya, what year do you think it is?'

I wanted to answer, but the edges of my vision were darkening, and I was starting to hyperventilate.

'Freya, breathe,' Dr Warburton said softly. Reaching forwards with a plump, age-spotted hand, he shone a light into my eyes. My mum grasped my hand, and my dad stepped back. His eyes widened like he was about to watch a car crash, knowing there was nothing he could do to stop it.

My breath was trying to move as fast as my mind. So many questions came to me, but I couldn't put them together to create a consistent thought. All I could push out was, '2015.' My dad took another step back, and my mum inhaled so loudly I thought she was going to join me in hyperventilating.

I watched my mum, hoping to find comfort in her inability to catch her breath, but instead, I saw something pass across her face that made me shiver. We had been close my entire life, and I knew something had just occurred to her. The rose colour in her cheeks dulled, and I actually watched the blood drain from her face.

A dark-haired woman in pink scrubs entered while the doctor tried to get me to follow his finger, and asked questions I couldn't hear past the blood pumping in my ears. I couldn't look away from my mum and the growing horror in her expressions. She wasn't looking at me. She was internally replaying the last seven years of my life. From the look of devastation on her face, I wasn't sure if I wanted to know.

Something twitched my left hand, and a wave of calmness settled over me. My breathing slowed, and my endless list of questions evaporated. Sitting back, I saw the nurse leave the room, carrying a little silver tray with a hypodermic needle lying upon it.

'You were in a car accident,' Dr Warburton said. I looked towards my dad to my right. He was holding his face in his hands, his eyes only just peeking over his fingertips.

'Was anyone hurt?' I heard my own voice, but there was something subtly different about it. I put it down to whatever was in that needle and waited.

Dr Warburton moved in closer, wafting the smell of chlorine over me. 'The driver of the other car was badly hurt, but they are here and stable. You were alone in the car with your dog. Who is also okay.'

'You saved their life,' my mum said softly. Tears freely flowed over her perfect makeup. 'The driver of the other car. You saved them.'

'Whose fault was it?' I asked apprehensively.

'Theirs,' my mum answered, but my dad interjected with, 'Preliminary findings are that there was a fault with their brakes.'

4

I ran my fingers over the grey blanket to try and ground myself to when and where I was. It was then I saw it, or the lack of it. My lefthand ring finger was bare. The doctor's words replayed in my head. *'You were alone.'* Tears pooled in my eyes, and I blinked so they would fall. It would appear there had been no significant life changes over the last seven years. I was apparently now forty-four, and instead of a doting husband at my side, there were my parents.

'Will they come back? My memories?' I asked the doctor through a dry throat.

He lifted an orange plastic cup next to me, and I gratefully accepted it. The cold liquid sliding over my throat made this strange alien environment feel more concrete.

He stepped back, taking the smell of his morning swim with him. 'The brain, unfortunately, is not an exact science. You received a nasty knock to the head, and we had to operate to release the pressure.'

I reached up with my free hand and touched soft gauze just behind my right ear. Thanks to the contents of that needle, the pain was gone.

'What is the last thing you remember?' my mum asked.

'Soup.' I could see it. I was standing in my little blue kitchen, pouring tomato soup from a can into a bowl. I tried blinking in rapid succession to see if I could get back there. The pain behind my eyes returned, and I stopped, swallowing past the nausea. '24th November, 2015. I can tell you the bloody date.' A giggle I didn't know was coming escaped, and I giggled again at giggling. Whatever was in that needle was lovely.

'At the flat,' I added. As calm as the drugs were making me, I was freaked out by how clear that last memory was. I could've told them what was on the TV in the background, what the weather was like outside. I could still smell the soup and taste the ready salted crisps I was snacking on, before dumping them into the bowl. I was single, that was considered acceptable behaviour.

There was so much sympathy in my mum's eyes when she said, 'It's the 6th of July, 2022.' The accuracy killed my buzz a little, and I shivered.

They continued asking questions, but I couldn't pull forth anything between those dates.

'Everything is healing well,' the doctor went on. 'We just need to wait for the swelling to go down. Although I cannot say with certainty that your memories will return, there is a strong chance that when the swelling reduces, they will. We will know more over the next twenty-four hours, but Freya, this is very important.' He stopped to make sure he had my full attention. 'You have to keep your blood pressure down. I know everything is confusing and scary, but you are safe here, and you just need to stay relaxed, for now.'

The once smiling doctor now looked like a straight-backed drill sergeant, and all I could do was nod in reply. I wasn't going to press it. I actually didn't want to know. Life hadn't been that fantastic for the thirty-seven years I did remember, so I highly doubted it had gotten that interesting over the last seven. Perhaps if I had paid more attention to how quiet and pale my parents were, I would have been more prepared to deal with what my life had become.

After more lights were shone in my eyes and I took another trip to the CAT scan, I was left alone. My overly doting parents were nowhere to be seen, but before I could question their uncharacteristic behaviour, the door opened, and a short olive-skinned man in green scrubs walked in with a tray of food.

'Hungry-yy?' he stuttered. The silver tray shook a little, and he nearly lost the glass of water. 'Sorry. Sorry,' he exclaimed. His cheeks reddened as he carried the tray over, and the cutlery rattled a little tune. Behind him, the door was closing slowly, and from somewhere in the corridor, I was sure I heard my mum crying. The only other time I had heard her cry like that was when her father died. A shiver ran up my legs until my scalp tingled.

'Today is duck. The chef's speciality.' There weren't many things he could have legitimately said that would cause me to forget the sound I had just heard from my mum, but that was one of them. I looked at him first to see if he was joking, but there was just the same nervous smile and red cheeks as before. When I saw the food, I was nearly as befuddled as seeing my mum's makeup.

'I'm going to go with I'm in a private hospital,' I mused, observing the perfectly cooked sliced duck breast, covered in a plum glaze, accompanied by a selection of oriental vegetables.

'That you are,' he said, looking away from me. 'Can I get you anything else?'

I looked back at him with a smile and a soft shake of my head. There was something strange in his expression, and I openly stared at him, trying to work it out. The massive smile and wide, excited eyes made him look slightly deranged.

'Are you okay?' I asked warily.

He swallowed loudly. Composing himself, he said, 'Yes. Thank you. I hope you feel better soon. Thank you.' With one last piercing look and a flinch of his hand towards me, he turned and left.

'Okayyy,' I said to my food. It looked delicious, but my stomach was in knots. Even though I felt hungry, I wasn't sure I could swallow it.

My thoughts slipped over to the driver in the other car. I had been somewhat distracted and forgot to ask if 'stable' meant 'okay'. Whoever they were, I wished them well and pushed the table away. Looking around, I found the remote control and what would hopefully be a distraction, but all I got was static on every channel. The 'call' button was next to me on the bed, so I pushed that instead.

In less than ten seconds, a nurse rushed in. 'Is everything alright?' she asked soothingly.

'Yes,' I answered, a little spooked by her eager assistance. 'I just wanted the TV on, but I can't get it to work.'

She shuffled from side to side and looked at the floor. 'It doesn't work. I'm sorry.' Without making eye contact, she just left.

'It's not me!' I said to the blank TV.

My dad walked in as I was about to hit the 'call' button again. 'Dad, the TV's not working.' I even pointed at the fuzzy screen for emphasis. His gaze followed my finger, and then he looked everywhere other than at me.

'I'll get it looked at,' he said, carefully placing himself in the seat next to me. Straight-backed, his hands were tightly held together in his lap. He looked around, squinting every now and then as if searching for cobwebs in the corners.

'Dad, you once took my ice cream back out to the van because you thought the guy had scrimped on the sprinkles.'

'Well, he had,' he said with an assured nod.

'Well, my TV's not working.' I waggled my hand towards it again to really get my point across.

'That thing will rot your brain. You need rest.'

'Can I not rest and watch the TV? They kinda go hand in hand.'

'No,' he said while rising. 'No, you need rest. Sleep.' With a kiss on my forehead, he switched off the bedside lamp and plunged me into darkness before leaving.

With little else to do, I leant back, and sleep found me without effort. When I awoke, the little clock on the beeping machine next to me told me it was 3am. In need of the bathroom, I sat up and moved my head around. I felt stiff, and there was a throbbing where the gauze was, but apart from that, I didn't feel that bad. Slowly, I got out of bed for the first time. It only then occurred to me that I hadn't seen myself.

At the end of the bed was a door that I assumed was the bathroom. When I pulled the cord on the inside, a lavish washroom with harsh lighting was before me. On the far wall was a floor-to-ceiling mirror, but before I got there, I needed to relieve myself. In a mad dash, I just made it to the toilet. Apparently, in the last seven years, I had lost quite a lot of bladder control.

Rising, I let the hospital gown drop to the tiled floor and walked over to the mirror. I was expecting the change in my hair. It was a style I had in my twenties, so it wasn't overly unfamiliar. The shock came from the fact that I looked better than I did in my twenties. It would appear that, at some point, I'd joined a gym.

For the next twenty minutes, I scanned and touched every line and curve of my body I could reach. I was still relatively slim, and my bum had only drooped a little. The same went for my breasts, but I felt softer, more cared for. There was a bit of a sag to my stomach and four stretch marks, two for either hip. My face was thinner than I remembered, and my lips a little fuller, but my green eyes with flickers of gold were a familiar sight that was nice to see.

While trying to see my back in the mirror, I caught sight of a small black suitcase on the side. Opening it, I found two sets of cotton pyjamas, one blue and the other green, a pair of fluffy white slipper boots, and a large orange wash bag. Assuming they were for me, I slipped into the blue pair, put on the boots, and then went back to the mirror for one last look. Overall, it was me. With a resigned shrug, I left the bathroom.

I shuffled over to the window to my left, but all I saw was a wall opposite a small alleyway. 'Where am I?' I asked the wall. Thankfully, it didn't answer, so I opened the sideward door and stepped into a brightly lit corridor with three doors on each side. The one opposite mine had a gold-plated sign that said, 'Family Room'.

'Ha. Tv.'

I walked-slid in my slippers, over to the door and quietly opened it. Spotlighted by the light that came in with me was a large TV on the far wall next to a window. It was on but silent, playing a black and white film that looked familiar. Next to it, on a little shelf, was a remote control.

I let the door close behind me, and the lights scattering the sky outside grew brighter. From where I was, I could see the tops of buildings and the open sky, which meant I could probably answer the question of where I was.

The first thing I saw when I got to the window was the Shard. 'Okay, I'm in London.' I was reaching out to pick up the remote when I heard the rustle of material and a light cough behind me. I spun around to see someone on one of the sofas to my left.

'I'm so sorry,' I said quietly.

I placed the remote back on the shelf, but as I started walking towards the door, a croaky male voice said, 'No. No. It's okay. Are you okay? Do you need anything?'

The unexpected sincerity in his voice made me stop. Then I realised that was probably the question you asked a patient wandering around a hospital at 3am. 'No. Thank you,' I said, still whispering. 'I didn't think anyone was in here. Sorry.'

A little light clicked on next to him, but it wasn't bright enough to fully illuminate him. With a baseball cap low over his forehead, all I could make out was a chiselled jawline covered in a dusting of fair stubble. Below that, a bulk of muscle spread over his broad shoulders and down his chest. I smiled apologetically and made to leave again.

'No, please. Stay.'

There was a faint sense of desperation in his voice. If I had been anywhere else, it would have been strange, but I supposed in a hospital, the comfort of a stranger was generally welcomed, even coveted.

'The company would be nice,' he continued. 'It would be good to talk to someone who isn't a doctor, technically speaking in another language.' He lifted his arm, which was bigger than most people's thighs, and signalled to the sofa opposite him.

There was something so soothing about his voice that it made me want to stay. As soon as I sat, he slid forward in his seat, passing cushions over. With the first wince I made in placing one behind me, he rose. All six-foot-five of him loomed over me, blocking out the light like an eclipse. I should have felt disconcerted that a stranger, especially one this big, was building me a pillow nest, but the closer he got, the warmer I felt.

'Thank you,' I said when he stood back to assess his work. Leaning back, I smiled my appreciation.

He stayed standing a few feet in front of me, swaying ever so slightly, as if he was fighting against a bungee cord attached to the wall behind me. Even though I couldn't make out any details through the dim light, from the way his shoulders slumped forward and his legs—that on a good day looked like they could hold up two small buildings—almost bowed under his weight, there was a strong chance he could have fallen asleep standing up.

Taking a deep breath, ladened with what sounded like physical pain, he rolled his shoulders back and dipped his cap further over his eyes. Walking around the sofa towards the window, he left behind the smell of lavender, of all things.

Wanting to give him a little privacy, I remained facing away from him, but after only a few seconds, he appeared back in front of me.

'While I'm up, would you like a cup of tea?' There was a slight choking in his voice, like he was trying not to cry. Perhaps he did need some company.

'Yes, please.' Before I could say anymore, he was out of the room. A cold sensation ran over me when the door clicked closed, and I nestled back into the pillows.

Just as my thoughts returned to the TV, the door swished open, and he walked back in, carrying two white steaming mugs. There was more light around him now, and even with the baseball cap, it was blatantly obvious who he was. Before I could stop myself, my mouth humiliated me. 'Oh my god.'

With a little chuckle, he said, 'No, just Matt with tea.' He let the door close behind him and held out a mug.

I took it, and instead of saying, *'Thank you,'* I humiliated myself again by repeating, 'Oh my god, you're Matt Lord.'

My eyes had adjusted a little more to the dimmed light, and I could make out his expression. For a second, I thought I had offended him. His forehead was scrunched, but there was a glimmer of bemusement there, and even though his lips were tightly pressed together, a flicker of a smile lay just beneath the surface. Sitting back down opposite me, he said, 'I am, yes.'

Casually, lifting his foot, he rested it over his knee, and with his eyes fixed on mine, he blew across the top of his mug. In a low but soft voice, he asked, 'And you are?'

I wanted to jump around and squeal like a teenage girl. I didn't. I was in my forties. So, while internally I just screamed like a deranged fan, I said, 'Freya Patrick,' in a squeaky voice.

His smile slipped, and when it returned, it no longer met his eyes. I supposed it was hard to keep up the pretence of being happy when you're sleeping in a hospital waiting room.

We sat there for a few minutes in silence while I drank comfort from a mug. I was completely oblivious to the fact I was staring at him until the smile returned to his eyes. Embarrassed, I averted mine while trying to casually hide my blush behind my mug, but in all fairness, Matt Lord had to be used to women gawking at him.

'I'm sorry, I don't mean to stare. I'm having a very strange day,' I stuttered out and looked towards the door.

'You're fine,' he almost whispered.

While I drank my tea, I took him at his word.

Without looking at me, he removed the baseball cap and ruffled his hair. He, like everyone else I remembered, looked different, a little older. His eyes were still a deep cobalt blue, and grey was yet to invade his short, well-groomed, blond hair. His chiselled jaw led up into high cheekbones with a lightly tanned, wrinkle-free complexion. The only fault that could be found was the small dent just below the bridge of his nose. Somehow, the consequence of a smack in the face had made him even better looking. Considering my gap, he had to be somewhere in his late thirties.

It took everything I had not to physically swoon, and I was so disappointed with myself. I should have known better than to be won over by a pretty face at my age. However, Matt Lord was the actor who could play a Greek god without the aid of the makeup department. There was also a slight air of sophistication, mixed with a 'give him an axe, and he'll build you a house' vibe.

'Are you hungry?' he asked, breaking my trance.

'I'm fine, thank you.' I wanted to laugh. This was all too surreal. One of Hollywood's finest British imports was trying to run around like a butler for me.

A slight clink of something on his mug drew my attention away from wanting to laugh, to a gold wedding band on his left hand. I felt my cheeks redden, and my stomach filled with acid. I didn't know a lot about the world of celebrities. I couldn't pick a Kardashian out of a line-up, but I knew who Matt Lord was. I wasn't a fan, so to speak, but he had, with no knowledge of doing it, saved my life. Seeing that ring made something inside of me shatter.

In the world I remembered, I was a writer. I'd published one thriller, but then when my boyfriend, who was also my publisher, asked if a strap-on could join us in the bedroom, and I declined, he broke up with me and essentially dropped my book.

My relationship after that one took me in a white dress down an aisle. An aisle I should have never gone near. My once loving husband then spent two years beating the hell out of me. Fear kept me in line and in his house. So, I wrote to escape. I created a world of warriors and magic but also threw in a little humour and whimsical wackiness, so it wasn't cliché.

Within that world, there was a character called Bastine. He wasn't the main character or even the hero. He was a general on the wrong side, but I made him strong, resilient, and formidable. He also looked like Matt Lord.

I had never taken anything or anyone from the real world into that fantasy world, apart from Matt. I couldn't say at the time that I thought any more about Matt Lord than I did any other celebrity, but there he was every time I sat down to write. On a random lazy Sunday afternoon, I had watched him play the unbreakable hero in a Viking fantasy film. Decked out in gold, war-battered armour, he had unblurred the image I had of Bastine.

Then one day, my husband was screaming at me, and next to him, I visualised Bastine. I knew he wasn't real, just a consequence of a writer's imagination. He looked at me and nonchalantly said, 'I could just snap his neck. That would shut him up.' Then he yawned.

When it became clear that my choices were leave or die, I borrowed the strength I knew Bastine had in abundance and got out.

Sat in the hospital's family room, I was about eighty-five percent sure the man sitting opposite me was real and fifteen percent sure I was on a day pass to a parallel universe. I was dying to poke him.

'People generally like to ask me questions.' His tone was relaxed. The light British accent felt familiar and comforting, and I only wanted to ask questions to hear him speak.

14

'Umm. I suppose the big one is, what you been up to for the last seven years? Made anything worth watching?'

He choked on his tea.

'I'm sorry,' I said quickly while blushing profusely. 'I didn't mean it like that. I'm sure all your films are worth watching. I just mean, you know? I'm sorry. I have no memory of the last seven years.'

'What's that like?' he asked sympathetically. His eyes swept over my face like he was trying to see the answer before hearing it.

'I thought I was the one who was asking the questions,' I said playfully. 'It's weird. No one will tell me anything because I have to keep my blood pressure down, or I'll die, so I feel like I'm a cat, and Dr Schrodinger shoved me in a box.'

He shook his head. 'No. You're Schrodinger. The cat in the box is the only one who does know if the poison has been released. Schrodinger is the one who has no idea if the cat is alive or dead.'

'Ok, so yes, the cat is my life,' I said, laughing at the absurdity of it all.

'Just think though, people can tell you what great books you've read, and you get to reread them. That's a plus.'

I beamed at him. It was so sweet hearing him try to make me feel better. As a mere mortal, he shouldn't be able to see me through the veil of celebrity, let alone interact with me. The insatiable urge to giggle returned, my heart was jumping around like a sugar-fuelled toddler, and every other part of my body was either quivering or sweating.

I wasn't the only one with an anxious edge to their movements. His posture was relaxed, and he had a comforting presence, but every now and then, his hand shook when he lifted the tea to his lips.

'You're an actor. Shouldn't you be promoting films, not books?'

15

He shrugged. 'I'm a sucker for a good book.'

I was about to fall into the writer's niche topic of conversation when he sat up a little straighter on the sofa and uncrossed his legs. 'What would you like to find in the box, you know, the one with your life in it?'

The light-hearted conversation had taken a turn towards personal and serious, but there was something about either his manner or just the environment that made me want to answer. It was also hard not to feel comfortable in pyjamas and fluffy slippers. If someone I knew had asked, I would have lied. I wouldn't have wanted to see the pity in their eyes for the rest of my life.

'A family.' It was slightly cathartic telling the truth.

He recrossed his legs with a bounce back into the seat.

'Anything else?' he asked, glancing towards the window.

I didn't need to think about it. 'Anything else is surplus.'

He looked down into his tea and gave no reply.

'Do you watch everything you're in?' I asked not to change the subject to something lighter but simply because it felt natural to do so.

He chuckled, and I had to give myself a little internal shake. Glancing over at his ring, I settled back into the cushions.

'Yes, I have. *Doomed* is my son's favourite film, so I've seen that a few times.'

'*Doomed*? When was that made?' I asked to cover the pain of hearing he had a son. When there was just a wife, there was the hope I could get her out of the way, but with children involved, that was just foul play.

'Sorry. Yes, three years ago. It's a light-hearted comedy about an explorer in the desert.'

'I'll be sure to check it out. How old is your son?' Before he could answer, an awful thought occurred to me. 'Oh god, he's not the one here, is he?'

16

He shook his head and placed his empty mug on the table between us. 'No. My wife,' he said solemnly. Looking away from me towards the door, it seemed like he was trying to see through it to her.

'I hope she's okay,' I said, and to my surprise, I genuinely meant it.

'Thank you.'

'How many children do you have?' I didn't really want to know, but I wanted to keep him talking.

He brightened at the question and reached into his pocket. Pulling out a phone, he pressed the open button and displayed a picture of four children as a screensaver. A girl and a boy who looked to be the same age, maybe five or six. A smaller boy of about three, and between them was a baby that looked to be somewhere just below one. They were a mix of blond and mousy brown with either green or blue eyes. I could see their dad in all of them.

'Would I know your wife? Is she an actor, like you?' I don't know why I asked. There was a strong possibility the answer would make me want to throw myself out of the window.

'She's in the gaming industry.' The way his face lit up at the mere thought of her ripped a hole through me. I sat back, making it look like I was trying to get comfortable. It was ridiculous how jealous and hurt I was getting. To me, Bastine and Matt were never the same person, so this reaction was absurd.

'Are you okay?' he asked, seeing me grimace.

'Just a little uncomfortable.'

He got up and came over to me. At that moment, there was nothing I wanted more than to reach for him. I was scared and alone, and I needed the comfort from his familiarity, but that would have obviously been weird. He leant over to adjust the cushions. Feeling his warmth so close was almost enough to quench the desire to bury my head into his chest. With his arms

17

wrapped around me, it would have hidden the uncertainty of everything else.

'Is that better?' he asked, sitting on the sofa beside me. Along with the lavender, I got the lingering essence of a woody aftershave. He was so close that I could see every line on his face and the small red blotches around his eyes. Even the whites of his eyes were veined with red. He looked exhausted, yet I had his undivided attention. The excitement I was holding in constantly tried to plaster a goofy smile across my face.

'Yes, thank you.' Before I could say anymore, the door opened, flooding us with light, and a large nurse in her early sixties appeared.

'You should be in bed.' She swept her arm through the doorway, signalling my way, and I rose with another wince.

Standing up, Matt held out his hands as if to catch me if I fell. 'Thank you,' he said but hesitated for just a second before continuing. 'For the company. It was… exactly what I needed.'

'You're welcome,' I said with a small smile as I passed. 'I hope you're not here for too long,' I added from the doorway, and I meant it. I had enough emotional hell in my life, and I was also fairly certain I knew who I had saved in the accident.

I crawled into bed, fluffy slippers and all, and curled into a ball. I didn't need to open the box to know there was a dead cat in there.

I bet he's a knob,' I heard Bastine say in my head. I hugged the pillow, feeling a little less desolate.

'Well, at least that is something you have in common,' I replied sarcastically.

Chapter Two

At some point, I fell into a dark, dreamless sleep that I was pulled from by the sound of clicking knitting needles.

'When did you start knitting?' I asked my dad, sitting in the chair next to me, with half an orange blanket in his lap. He was finally wearing jeans again, and his hair was slightly messier. It helped a lot to see something familiar in him.

He shrugged like it was completely normal for a Preston-born man in his late sixties to be knitting. 'A lockdown thing.'

His reply was almost as baffling as him knitting. 'Lockdown? What?'

He stopped knitting and looked at me wide-eyed. 'Nothing to worry about. There was a global pandemic. A bit like a real bad case of the flu. All's good, don't panic. We all got vaccinated, but while it was at its height last year, they made everyone stay at home for a few months. Some people baked, others exercised. I learnt to knit. It curbed the desire to kill your mother.' He looked up to see my mouth hanging open. 'It wasn't the black death or anything, nothing for you to go worrying about.'

'Where's Mum?' I asked, wanting to change the subject to something I could get my head around.

'You've got me today,' he said with a fake but comical smile.

My dad was a terrible liar. 'That's great. Lovely to have you here, but where's Mum?'

He stopped knitting again and thought about it. 'She's just sorting a few things out at home.'

'Home? My over-protective mother has gone back to Cornwall?'

'No. We don't live in Cornwall anymore. We live about an hour or so outside London.' He started knitting again as if the conversation was over.

'Why?'

'To be closer to you. Now stop asking questions and rest.' The knitting needles sped up, and I knew getting anything else out of him would be hard, but I had a question I needed to be answered. It went against all the evidence I had, but I just needed to hear the confirmation.

'Am I still a writer?'

He looked up, contemplating an answer. Mum had clearly given him strict instructions about not overwhelming me. 'Yes.'

I sighed, and he frowned. 'So, I don't work in the gaming industry then?' The little girl inside of me, holding a book of fairy tales, made me ask.

'What, like board games?'

I rolled my eyes. 'Probably video games.'

He shook his head. 'You write books.' His eyes glanced towards the monitor connected to the blood pressure device attached to my finger. 'That thing is rising, and by pain of death, I have to make sure you keep your blood pressure down. So pack it in and rest.'

Through the window, I could see sunshine pushing its way down between the buildings. As casually as I could, I asked, 'Where do you go to smoke? Do you still have to get about half a mile away from the hospital?'

My dad shook his head and kept clicking the needles. 'No, there's a roof terrace.'

I gave it a few minutes so he wouldn't sense the connection.

'That knitting is annoying. There's a family room opposite. Go clatter those things in there.' I tucked myself back down into the bed to make it look like I was getting ready to sleep. He looked

20

over his needles a little more sceptically than I would have liked but then nodded.

'Fine, but rest.'

I gave him a small salute and then lay down, waiting for him to leave. When I heard the door opposite close, I got out of bed and headed down the hallway, past the empty nurse's station, towards a sign that said, 'Roof Terrace'. I just wanted some fresh air and to feel the sun.

The door opened onto a small set of stairs with another door at the top. The bruises and minor aches made me wince as I climbed, but I couldn't bring myself to go back to bed.

Momentarily blinded by the afternoon sun, heat washed over me, and I stood at the entrance to the terrace, letting it soak through me. Breathing felt easier away from the dry air of the perpetual air-conditioning downstairs.

Opening my eyes, I blinked rapidly, hoping what I saw before me was a mirage. Facing me but looking at his phone was Matt Lord. Even dressed in scruffy jeans and a creased white t-shirt, he looked angelic with the sun radiating behind him. I almost turned and walked back down the stairs, but from this height, we were above the city skyline, and all around the terrace, there were plump chairs and sun umbrellas. I wasn't ready to go back to the artificial air and lights yet.

I moved to the left, towards a small cluster of chairs in the corner, trying to stay out of his eyeline. The wall around the terrace was about five feet high, with another few feet of Perspex above it, and even though I couldn't see down to the ground from this vantage point, I could hear music. I strained my ears to listen and caught what sounded like Dolly Parton, singing about a sparrow and an eagle. I was just about to stand on one of the chairs to try and get a better look when another sound caught my attention.

21

'Daddy, when is Mummy coming home?' The little girl's voice was soft and sad. I kept looking at the sky while lowering myself into one of the chairs, bringing my knees up to my chest.

'Soon, sweetheart, soon.' Matt's voice was almost a coo that was covered in sadness.

Another voice joined the mix, a little boy's. 'Dad, Isabella saw the news.'

'Oiy,' the little girl protested. 'You saw it too.'

'Only cause I was standing behind you.'

'I've told you two before to stay away from the news.' Matt's tone was a little sterner, but there was a quake in his voice.

'I know. I'm sorry, Daddy,' she said softly. 'But.'

'But what, darling?' His voice was so gentle and caring.

It was the little boy who answered. 'They said Mummy was seriously injured and might be… dead.'

Matt sighed loudly. 'And that is why you are not allowed to watch the news. Mummy was hurt, but the doctors and nurses are taking really good care of her, and she will be home in no time.'

'Do you promise?' both children said together. There was something in the pleading of their voices that made me look subtly over my shoulder. Matt wasn't looking into the phone, he was looking straight at me. Tears welled in his eyes. I guessed it was just too hard to look at his children.

'I promise.' His voice shook, but his eyes remained on me. I smiled sympathetically and turned back around, to give him some privacy. 'Now put your grandmother on the phone and go play like normal children.'

'Okay, Daddy,' the little girl said, laughing.

I heard the terrace door open, and in the corner of my eye, I saw Matt walk through it just as a woman said, 'Hi love, is everything alright?'

With Matt gone, I was now alone and could still hear the music from below. It drew me out of my seat and onto it, and I pushed my face against the Perspex, trying to see down. I didn't need to stretch too far to see what was happening. There were people everywhere, either standing or sitting. Candles were scattered across the ground next to flowers, and in a large cluster to the right, there were News cameras and vans with towering aerials. It wasn't hard to guess who they were there for.

'Tea?' I jumped at the sudden intrusion, and a hand reached forward and lightly grabbed my arm, lowering me off the chair. I looked up to see Matt holding out a mug of tea in the other hand. The warmth of his touch made my stomach drop. A sense of calmness washed over me, and breathing suddenly felt easier.

'How are you feeling?' he asked while I curled myself into the chair. His hand was still gently holding my arm as I took the mug. When it glided away, coldness smothered me, and I visibly shivered.

I wanted to say that I was lonely, sad, unloved, scared, and a teeny bit horny, but I settled for, 'A lot better today, thank you. Still no memory of the last seven years, though.'

He nodded and lowered himself into the chair next to me.

'How is your wife today?' I asked out of politeness.

He looked straight at me, and with the same adoration I had seen when he spoke about her the night before, he said, 'A lot better today, thank you.'

I smiled weakly and sipped my tea. He did the same. 'I take it the mass gathering down there is for her?' I hadn't meant it to sound petty.

'Yes.' He nodded with a proud smile. There was still a weariness to his overall demeanour, but the redness around his eyes had faded, and he seemed a little less rattled.

'What are your children's names?' I only asked to steer the conversation away from this woman, who I was quickly beginning to dislike.

Spurred by an enthusiasm I was yet to see from him, he sat up. With a natural smile, he began. 'Jack and Isabella are six in a couple of months and twins. Then there's Dylan, who is nearly three, and the youngest is Charlotte, who is nine months old.'

With a polite smile, I sipped my tea, letting him continue.

'Jack and Isabella are amazing, their mother's children to a tee. Intelligent, quick-witted, and lovingly manipulative.' He chuckled at a memory and then went on. 'Dylan is the most placid child I have ever known. He loves everyone and everything. I have only ever heard him cry when he was hurt, ill, or scared. He adores the twins, which we're not allowed to call them. My wife hates them being referred to as the 'twins'. She thinks it takes away their individuality.'

I nodded in agreement. I had always thought it was cruel referring to two separate children as a set.

'Charlotte, on the other hand, is the devil's child. She screams just because she can. In the middle of the night, when Charlotte is rattling the house, my wife always says, "I knew we should have stopped at three."' He laughed again, lighter this time.

'So, no more then?' I joked.

He shook his head. 'Nope. Snipped. I wanted five. Always did.'

'But Charlotte changed your mind?' The conversation was light and easy and utterly unexpected. I hadn't spoken to any celebrities before, but I was surprised by how much of his personal life he was revealing.

'Jack, actually.' He shuddered and put his mug down on the little table. 'When Charlotte was about six months old, we took them all to Legoland. Big family day out. It was a great day. Perfect weather. Kids loved it. Even Charlotte kept the screaming to a minimum.' He slipped into the story, slowly telling me about his perfect family. My chest heaved, and I wrapped my arms around myself as casually as I could. 'Then, in the car on the way

24

home, I was feeling a little broody. I reached over, stroked my wife's knee, and said, "How about one more?" I even gave it the little wink and smile.' He re-enacted the gesture for me, and I nearly cried with longing.

With his eyes fixed back upon the memory, he continued. 'She looked back over at me, completely unfazed by my flirting, both eyebrows raised, and just as she was about to speak, there was this guttural sound from behind me. Then a wave of green liquid came at me from behind.' He swished his hands over his shoulders like a flight attendant during the safety speech.

'It covered the windscreen, steering wheel... me. It literally went everywhere. Jack groaned, "I don't feel well." Isabella was dry heaving at the smell of the vomit. Dylan was screaming because he had just seen his brother pull off something that looked like it was from the exorcist, and obviously, Charlotte was bellowing and drowning them all out. My wife said nothing. As I was trying to pull the car over, she just sat there with a wicked smile on her face.'

I couldn't help smiling with him as he recollected the messier side of family life. Even if it meant being covered in vomit, I would have given anything to be part of that.

'I should also point out,' he continued, 'it was a brand new Bentley. I'd ordered it months before. I like my cars,' he said with a casual shrug. 'Luxury that can fit a family of six isn't easy. It had arrived while I was working away, and I had to wait weeks before I could drive it. The inside was meant to be grey, not luminous green.'

I don't think he appreciated me laughing.

With his eyebrow still raised indignantly, he went on. 'Well, after we cleaned everything and everyone up as best we could, with my wife laughing the entire time, we got back in the car. The smell was atrocious. She didn't need to say a word. As we started driving again, I said, "I'll book a vasectomy appointment tomorrow." She just nodded with wise agreement. One of the most horrific times of my life.'

'The green vomit-covered road trip, or the quick snip?'

'Both! But it wasn't a quick snip. My left ball swelled up to the size of an orange. Most painful thing I have ever experienced.'

I spat my tea out through laughter, trying not to choke on what was already halfway down my throat. He reached over and patted me on the back as I tried to catch my breath.

'I'm sorry,' he said, laughing himself. When I was once again breathing properly, instead of lifting his hand away, it glided over my back and off my shoulder.

'We lead a quiet life, really.' I was surprised to hear him say more about his family. I didn't know what else to do, so I listened as casually as I could. 'The whole celebrity/fame thing, it plays such a small part in our lives. Most of our days are about the normal things. We have a small estate away from the city. Lots of open fields and a large vegetable patch that keeps the kids away from the TV... most of the time. We have chickens, horses, and even a couple of reindeer.'

'Reindeer?' I sniggered. 'Yes, that sounds very normal.'

He beamed at me, and I swallowed my desire. 'Isabella and Jack's first Christmas, my wife went a little, all out. I was told that we were fostering them. That was five years ago. Morris and Maureen.' He looked down at the table and laughed again at a recollection I was not privy to. 'Obviously, the kids think Morris and Maureen are Dasher and Comet in disguise. So, every Christmas eve, I have to move them to the top field where the kids can't see them. Then, when they're asleep, I have to go and get them.

'You can see the stables from the kids' bedroom window, so instead of them looking for full stockings in the morning, to see if Santa has been, they look to see if the reindeer are back. Last year, I completely forgot. My wife and I woke up naturally, wished each other a Merry Christmas, and then realised we should have been up hours before with small children in the house. We bolted out of bed.' With a soft laugh, he exhaled. The hospital was a long way from this happy recollection. Hiding his pain behind a fake smile, he retreated back into the memory.

'I got to the kids' room first, and they were all sat huddled in the window seat, red-eyed and sniffling. Isabella looked at me through her tears and said, "Daddy, I think something bad has happened." Oh god, my heart broke.'

'What did you do?' I interrupted.

'I made some excuse about perhaps I didn't leave the gate open. Ushered them away from the window, and then in my boxers and slippers, with my dressing gown flapping open, I pegged it up to the top field to bring the reindeer back down.'

'You saved Christmas.'

Sitting up straighter, he steepled his fingers under his chin. The strained smile lifted into something that looked mischievously jubilant. I felt his eyes bore into me. 'I'm sorry, can you say that again? I missed that.'

My eyebrows dropped in confusion, and his smile flooded his eyes. He had clearly heard me, but I repeated it out of politeness. 'I said, you saved Christmas.'

'I thought you did,' he said with a serious nod of his head. 'My wife did not agree. She told me I traumatised the kids. She was semi-joking, but she still refers to it as the year I nearly ruined Christmas.'

I wondered where I had been last Christmas. As he was chasing reindeer, I was probably opening my third bottle of mulled wine.

'I'm going to grab some food. Would you like more tea?' he asked, breaking my reverie.

'Yes. Please.' I wasn't ready to go back inside yet. The sun was warm and soothingly massaging the back of my neck, holding me captive.

27

'I'll be right back.' He leaned forward and then jolted a little. I looked at him, slightly taken aback, but with his eyes low, he took my empty mug from my hands and left.

'Oh, Bastine, what have you done to me?' I said to the fresh air, then curled up in the chair and closed my eyes to the sun.

The rustling of plastic roused me, and I blinked past the warm beams to see Matt arranging food onto plates. There was something so humble in the action. A movie star unwrapping a sandwich and spooning salad onto a plate should have caused me to question my reality, but delusion or dream, it was just so nice to have someone looking after me. My body was getting stronger, but there was a fragility in my mind that was weakening by the minute.

'So, we've got a chicken and falafel sandwich. Brown bread and a tomato salad.'

'Thank you,' I said, taking the plate.

We ate in silence, and I was starting to get the sneaky suspicion that his wife was in some form of coma. Unable to care for her, he was using me as a substitute.

'So, what *do* you know about yourself?' he asked when all the food was gone, and I was tucked up in the chair with another cup of soothing tea. I stared at him, not knowing how to answer that question. 'I mean,' he continued, seeing my confusion, 'no one changes that much. Fundamentally, the person you were seven years ago is probably the person you still are.'

I thought about that for a few seconds before answering. 'I like being outside. A country girl at heart, not scared of a bit of mud. I like tea,' I said, lifting the mug to show my gratitude. 'I do a bit of rock climbing, well, I used to.'

'Not scared of heights then?'

'No. There's something so freeing about being high up, closer to the clouds than the ground. The noises are different. More natural. I love to read. I am apparently still a writer, which is nice.

I am a typical woman in the sense that I like to shop. Love shoes. I come from a close family. One brother, one sister. My sister's the eldest, then me in the middle. I have—' I stopped to do the math. 'An eighteen-year-old niece and a sixteen-year-old nephew from my sister. Last I remember, my brother was nowhere near settling down, so I don't know what's going on with him. I like jazz and good food, and wine, red, not white.'

He leant forward and blew on his tea. 'It sounds like you know a lot about yourself.'

I raised my eyebrows in an absentminded gesture. 'Yeah, just missing current events.'

'They'll come back,' he said with a decisive nod. I almost believed him.

We both sat back quietly for a while, just enjoying the summer afternoon lightness of the air. Ignoring the smell of smog drifting up from the city and the lingering scent of disinfectant that clung to me, I pictured the rooftop somewhere far more exotic. Imagined cocktails, and Matt in just a pair of shorts, lounging by a pool. I couldn't remember ever feeling this content. That was until a petite female nurse in her twenties walked through the door and approached Matt.

'Hi-ii,' she stammered. Her eyes flicked back and forth between us. 'Uhh, Mrs, uhh, Lord is looking for you.'

I felt like she'd slapped me. I even flinched upon impact.

Looking from her to Matt, I saw in all its glory how happy her words had made him.

With a 'Sorry' and an 'Excuse me,' he bounced out of his seat, speeding up into a light jog by the time he reached the door.

Sadness crushed me. I finished my tea, lay my head back against the cushion, and closed my eyes.

When I opened them again, I was back in my bed. The room was dark, and I had no memory of how I got there. There was nothing new in that, so I gave it no more thought. Turning my head into my shoulder to wipe away the tears gathering, I caught the hint of lavender, with undertones of the woody aftershave I'd smelt in the family room. I moved my head again, but it was gone, and so was he.

The door opened with a swish, spilling light in from the hallway, and Dr Warburton walked in with my mum behind him. Neither was smiling, and my mum was no longer immaculately dressed. She looked more like I remembered her in jeans and a jumper.

'How are you feeling?' the doctor asked, flicking on a light next to the bed. I squinted at the brightness and rubbed my eyes. The truth was, I was tired of feeling discombobulated. I had been trying to ground myself in this new reality, but it was impossible to do so when I didn't know what that reality was. I was so scared to open the box and see the state of the poor cat, but what choice did I have?

I looked first to the doctor and then to my mum before saying, 'The twenty-four hours are up. I'm ready for answers now.' I plumped my pillow and straightened my blanket like a child getting ready for a bedtime story. He looked to my mum, and they shared a silent conversation of raised eyebrows and pursed lips.

Dr Warburton folded his arms and assessed me before saying, 'Your vitals are good, and the swelling has reduced, but I would still like you to take it easy.' Then reluctantly added, 'But, of course, you deserve to know things about yourself.'

I looked at my mum. She held my eye contact for a while. Her gaze was serious, and for a second, I thought she would refuse. With a sigh, she sat on the chair next to me. 'Okay,' she said while taking a deep breath. Untucking the curls gathered behind her ears, her eyes lowered to the floor. I watched her force herself to lift her head and meet my eye. 'But,' she said, straightening her resolve and clicking into mum mode, 'I know what you are like. You've always been the same. You want to know the ins and outs of a duck's arse. I will give you the bullet points for now, and then more can come later, when the doctor agrees you are fully out of the woods.'

'Can I ask questions?' I pushed.

'No.' My mum wrung her hands and stared straight at me. I waited, knowing she was considering where to start. 'You sold your books, the series you had been writing.'

I inwardly hugged Bastine. We'd done it. I'd finished the series, and Bastine was out there in the world. His response was to push me away by my forehead and say, *'Bloody took you long enough.'*

'They sold okay,' my mum continued. 'You bought a house in the countryside, and when the sea air started playing havoc with your dad's chest, we moved closer to you. Your sister and brother-in-law, yes, still Lance.' My mum sighed. She had never been a fan of Lance. He had a lighter perspective on life compared to the serious way my mum looked at everything. 'They moved up as well. Lance now works closely with your dad. He mainly does renovations, and your dad does building work when required. You have a dog called Wisp. A big mastiff.' My mum rolled her eyes. She wasn't a fan of any animal, really. They were too messy for her liking. 'And a cat called, Cat.'

I smiled at that. I didn't remember, but I knew he would be a ginger tomcat, like the one from *Breakfast at Tiffany's.*

'You don't have a boyfriend, and you spend every spare moment either writing or tending a garden to keep the writer's block at bay. Your brother is a nightmare, as always. Still works in finance. Still drinks and smokes too much and refuses to settle down. No one has died recently. You have a few friends. You and Laura are still good friends, but now she lives in the States, so you meet up occasionally, but mostly talk online. She got married and had a couple of kids. You were maid of honour.'

The tears overflowed, and I didn't want to stop them. They were a mix of every emotion I could think of. I was ecstatic for Laura. I'd known her since the first year of secondary school. She'd been an incredible friend to me and deserved to get everything she ever wanted. I was happy that no one had died and that I was a working writer. It was nice to know I had made enough money to buy a house and pay for private health care that fed you duck and housed movie stars.

I just couldn't get past the sadness. She hadn't used the word, but I knew she was trying to say I was alone. Well, apart from the dog and cat. Wrapped around all these emotions, the most prominent was grief. Seven years ago, I had hope. There was still time for a family, but now I had blinked, and time had left me. Left me alone.

'Right, that's enough,' my mum declared, clapping her hands lightly together. 'I'm going to run you a bath. We'll get you all cleaned up and then back to bed.'

'My TV doesn't work,' I said with tears in my eyes as she walked into the bathroom.

Through the echo, I heard her reply loud and clear. 'Your dad told me.'

I looked at the doctor. 'Any chance of getting the TV working?'

He stood up and brushed his hands over his white coat, straightening out the non-existent creases. 'I'll get someone to bring you a selection of books.'

'Where's my phone?' I asked my mum as she walked back in from the bathroom.

'It was broken in the accident. I'll get a replacement ready for when you get out.'

The doctor silently left, and my mum laid out a fresh pair of pyjamas for me over the chair. 'Right, in the bath you go, smelly.' She clicked her fingers and swung her arm in the direction she wanted me to go. Reluctantly, I rose and walked towards the running water.

While my mum fussed over towels and the contents of my washbag, I climbed into the bubbled wafts of eucalyptus and jasmine, and when she left, I cried. It was crazy to think I was sobbing with grief over something I had never had, but I didn't want to stop the tears. I wanted to feel the sadness. I wanted to feel sorry for myself. I also no longer wanted to ask any more questions. The box was open. The cat was dead, and I had no intention of doing an autopsy. The cat had died because of a lack of love, and that was the end of it.

Chapter Three

Over the next twenty-four hours, I did as I was told. After another CAT scan and possibly what may have been an MRI, I let people shine lights in my eyes and tend to the small wound on the right side of my head. I asked no more questions. Spoke only when spoken to and lay quietly staring at the bathroom door at the end of my bed. My dad took over from my mum and continued to knit. Then my mum returned. My dad left. I stared.

For most of the time, my mind was blank, but occasionally, it would torture me with images of Matt Lord and his family. I got to envisage them all on Christmas morning opening presents. Taking summer walks around their estate. I watched the children I had seen in the photo play. Imagined Matt's arms enveloping me from behind, pulling me into a warm, comforting embrace.

Such a large part of me wanted to get up and wander the hallways looking for him. Some masochistic part of me also wanted to see her, but I remained heavy under the grief.

A knock on the door turned my head but not my attention. With what sounded like apprehension, my mum called out, 'Yes?'

The door opened slowly, and Matt stepped over the threshold. The sheer size of him filled the doorway. 'Can I come in?'

I had been holding back the tears all day but seeing him was almost too much. I wiped across my eyes, pretending it was to remove sleep, and offered the most welcoming smile I could.

'I was at the shop, and they had a film collection, so I got you a few that I think you will like.' He held out a selection of DVDs that took two hands to hold. 'Apparently, even though you can't get TV channels, the DVD part should still work.'

I sat up and didn't have to force a smile. It was a wonderfully kind gesture. He lightly scattered the DVDs across the bed next to me, and I looked from them to him.

Rubbing one hand across the back of his neck, he put the other in his pocket and cleared his throat. A thin veil of perspiration covered his forehead and blushed cheeks.

'Any you would recommend starting with?' I asked to relieve what I could only perceive to be nervousness.

'You asked about *Doomed*, so that is in there. Obviously, anything with me in is going to be great,' he joked. His shoulders relaxed, and his deep blue eyes seemed to lighten, but it still looked like the redness of crying was trying to dominate.

'Is there anything else in there with you in it?' I had actually forgotten my mum was there, but the seriousness of her tone had me looking over at her, a little embarrassed. Was she accusing him of showing off?

'No, that is the only one,' he answered without looking at her. My mum was glaring at him.

'I'm sorry. Matt, this is my mum, Francis Patrick. Mum, this, as I'm guessing you know, is Matt Lord. We met in the family room the other night. He makes a great cup of tea.' Matt laughed but kept his eyes on me.

'It's lovely to meet you,' my mum said in a tone that told me she actually wasn't that thrilled about the introduction.

Matt finally looked over at her and extended his hand. 'Thank you. It's nice to meet you as well.'

Mum half rose and offered her hand weakly in reply.

'So, start with *Doomed* then?' I asked, rifling through the boxes. Looking at the unfamiliar casings, I pondered how many of them I had already seen.

'Of course.' He shrugged with a charismatic casualness.

The palm of my hand slipped over the coarse blanket and grasped onto nothing but loneliness. I swallowed the pain and just tried to enjoy his company while I could.

'Well, it is your son's favourite, so I'll give it a go,' I said, pushing past the lump in my throat. My mum choked on what I could only assume was air. 'You okay?' I asked, reaching over to her.

'Yes. Yes-ss,' she stuttered. 'Just tried to breathe and swallow at the same time.'

I shook my head slightly and went back to the DVDs. Lifting *Doomed*, I offered it back to him with a sweet smile. 'Care to do the honours?'

He nodded and took it over to the TV. I found the remote and switched it on to the right channel. It was lovely to see a picture appear after so long of only seeing my blackened reflection.

'There's a spare seat if you want to watch.' It was out before I could stop myself. As much as I needed him to leave, I desperately wanted him to stay.

His smile was so endearing, and the whisper of a swoon escaped before I could stop it.

'I'll let you watch this one alone. I have seen it far too many times. Come find me when you get to the third *John Wick* film,' he said with a wink.

'Okay.' The smile on my face was huge. I was so happy. If these little moments were all I was allowed, I was going to enjoy every second.

'See you soon,' he said, a little sadder than I was expecting. Without looking back at me, he left.

'Cup of tea to go with the film?' my mum asked, but was already halfway out of the door before I could reply. Settling back into my pillows, I ignored the weirdness and just basked in the excitement that I would get to see Matt again soon.

My mum returned with a mug of tepid tea, but I didn't care. I had an unobstructed view of Matt Lord, shirtless in the desert.

'You've got to admit, Mum, he is seriously hot,' I said over the top of my mug. My knees tucked up to my chest.

'He looks like he'd be a pain in the arse,' she said without looking away from her book.

'Okay,' I said with a giggle. That wasn't overly out of character for my mum, and it was reassuring to see.

Doomed finished, and I immediately put on the second *John Wick* film. I looked for the first in the pile, but it wasn't there, and thankfully, I'd seen that one before my memory blanked out. My mum tutted when she saw my choice but also smiled into her book. Ten minutes in, there was another knock on the door. Electrified by anticipation, I watched it inch open.

A bashful looking Matt poked his head in. 'I'm bored. What you watching now?' His expression turned slightly mischievous as he craned his head around to see the TV.

'The second *John Wick* film.' I gestured to the chair next to me on the left. The pitch in my voice gave away my attempt at hiding that this was the most exciting thing that had ever happened to me. He walked in with a broad smile that dropped into a polite nod when he looked at my mum.

'I brought you popcorn.' He threw the bag lightly into my lap and winked. It was a mix of salt and sweet, my favourite. Until that moment, I never knew I could get so turned on by someone bringing me a snack. My mum fidgeted around her seat, quietly huffing.

For the next three hours, I sat in the definition of bittersweet. I was ecstatic that he had sought out my company but having him close enough to touch was self-torture at its finest. I didn't see a single second of any of the films. I had the perfect viewpoint. His chair was level with my knee, and when I turned onto my side facing the TV, all I saw was him.

My mum lost interest in the film within minutes, retreating to the window to continue with her book. Unsupervised, I inspected and committed to memory every line, bulge, and movement he made. For a while, his chest rose and fell with heavy breaths. He crossed and recrossed his arms and legs, but every time he turned to me to offer a small smile, he seemed to relax a little more. Each time I feigned interest in the film and then went back to watching the only actor I had any interest in.

The jealousy I felt towards his wife was tipping towards hatred, and I couldn't believe I was considering pulling the plug on someone I had never even met.

Just as the third *John Wick* film finished, the door opened, and my slightly less sullen doctor entered, dousing the room with the smell of chlorine again. 'Okay, so I have looked at the results from your latest CAT scan.' He paused to look up at me but then caught sight of Matt.

'I… Uhh…' His eyes darted between Matt, me, and my mum.

Matt ran his hands wearily over his face, and through a pained expression, he said to no one in particular, 'I'll give you a minute.' Raking his fingers through his hair, he looked at me with an agonised expression and then left.

After a couple of seconds, the doctor still hadn't said anything, so I patted down the blanket.

'Yes,' he said as his attention returned to me. 'The CAT scan. All is looking well. We still need to keep your blood pressure down, but you are definitely out of the woods.'

My mum cried lightly, and I reached out to take her hand. There was only one question to ask. 'When can I go home?'

He looked at my mum, but she was busy blowing her nose into a handkerchief. 'Umm. I would like to keep you in for a couple more days for observation, but after that, I see no reason why you can't be discharged.'

My mum's shoulders rocked as she tried to push back the sobs. I leant over the edge of the bed and pulled her towards me. 'I'm okay. It's going to be okay.'

She sniffled and blew her nose once more before composing herself. 'I know. I know. It's just been… It's been a bit scary.'

'I'll see you later. But, for now, lots of rest, and keep that blood pressure down.'

I nodded in agreement. As the doctor left, I saw Matt standing by the nurse's station. He had his back to me, his hands raised to his head. Every muscle strained and tensed, pulling against the fitted thin blue jumper.

'Oww, sweetie, my hand.'

'Sorry, Mum,' I said, letting go.

I waited, but Matt didn't return, and I didn't want to watch any more films without him. I was back to staring at the bathroom door. Mum left at 9pm, and I was all alone. Something I needed to get used to.

The thought of leaving the hospital was an inviting one, but leaving Matt was not. It felt absolutely ludicrous. I knew he was just using me as an innocent distraction. Being a small ward, his choice of companionship was limited. To me, he looked like an old friend. He looked like the person who had been there for me when I needed strength, and with the thought of returning to my 'absent' life, it was something I was running low on. What made it worse was Matt Lord was everything Bastine wasn't. There was a softer, more caring side to Matt, and I was not only out of strength, but in desperate need of a little old-fashioned TLC.

'Are you having a fucking laugh?' I cringed, hearing my internal strength vocalise itself. I kept my eyes closed, not wanting to see Bastine standing at the end of my bed in all of Matt's glory. It did nothing to shut him up, though. *'Pull your shit together. You're a published author, probably thanks to me, but still. You own your own home. There's just no bloody pleasing you.'*

He was right, but it did nothing to change the fact that I would swap it all for what I really wanted to find in the box.

For the rest of the night, I lay on my side and stared at the moonlight cascading down the wall opposite. I tortured myself with thoughts of things that could never be, and by morning, my eyes were red and painful from the torrent of tears I had unleashed throughout the night. My throat was hoarse and dry, and I needed more than anything to get out of the hospital.

Before breakfast arrived, I was showered and dressed in a pair of jeans, a blue hoodie, and of all things, a baseball cap. All items that had appeared in the little black suitcase the day before. I couldn't recall ever wearing a baseball cap in my life, but I put it on in an attempt to hide my red eyes.

My plan was simple. I was going home.

At some point in the middle of the night, it had occurred to me to look at my notes hanging from the bottom of my bed. I found a lot of jargon and stuff I already knew, but on one of the insurance documents at the back, I found my home address, or as it was labelled, my 'billing' address. I had hitchhiked across half the world in my younger days. I was sure I could pull off an hour or so up the road.

Before the day staff came on, I snuck out of the room. The fluorescent lights swarmed me feeling like silent alarms, but my mind was made up. Lowering the tip of my cap, I shuffled quietly down the corridor. Scanning left and right, I expected someone to come along and foil my escape, but all I could hear over my rapid breathing was the beeping of heart monitors and the occasional cough from a patient as I passed their room.

The exit was just to my left, but my eye caught on the 'Roof Terrace' sign. It was still early, and the chances were he wouldn't be up there, but I still found myself opening the door and climbing the stairs.

My heart sank when I found it empty. He was probably tucked up in a little bed next to his wife. Where he should be. I lost a little of my motivation, and I felt the energy drain out of me. In the distance, I could still hear faint music, and over the edge, I could see that more News vans had gathered.

Glancing down to the sofa Matt and I had sat on, I replayed the ease of our conversation. He had made me laugh at a time when I thought that would be impossible. Agonisingly, I already missed him. He wasn't there to say goodbye to, so I said goodbye to the memory.

Before reaching it, the door burst open, and Matt breathlessly rushed through. He took one look at me and dropped his hands to his knees like he might throw up. I stood there puzzled, but then an image of my mum finding me gone crossed my mind. With an internal, exasperated sigh, I imagined her rallying everyone on the ward into finding me.

He straightened himself up, gave me a disapproving look, and then tapped at his phone for a few seconds before slipping it into his pocket. When he looked back at me, I took it as my cue to speak.

'The doctor gave me the all-clear last night, so I'm off home. I just wanted to say goodbye.' I smiled politely, but he looked back at me like a child who had been caught in a lie.

'The doctor said you could go home? They're discharging you?' He folded his arms, and instinctively I did the same.

Defiantly, I replied, 'No. He wants to keep me in for a couple more days. I'm the one saying I'm off home. And, well, seeing as I have no one to answer to but myself, it's pretty much my decision to make.' It was nice to see I was still stubborn and a little petulant.

His expression darkened, and every part of my body prickled. Shuffling his legs, he readjusted his jeans. 'I think you should stay.' His voice was firm but playful, and my response was to stutter out a weird squeaky noise. Unwrapping his hands from around his chest, he placed them in his jeans' back pockets. The material of his blue jumper again pulled across his chest, and I completely forgot what we were talking about.

Desire, like nothing I had ever felt before, consumed me. My body even pulled towards him enough to shake my balance. I staggered forward slightly, and his hands reached out to my sides to steady me. Heat surged inwards, and every inch of me burned with an unbearable yearning.

I placed my hands on his forearms to push him away, but as they touched, I felt him quiver. My heart heaved against my chest, catching my breath. When I raised my eyes back to his, my own desire was reflected back at me. I was sure that if he hadn't been holding onto me, I would have fallen.

Somewhere in the back of my mind, I heard my own voice point out that I had already fallen. The same voice then went on to remind me that his wife was downstairs, possibly fighting for her life.

I let go and stepped out of his hands. Cold pulsed through me, and I shuddered. 'I have to go.' Lowering my head, I passed to the side of him. I desperately wanted him to reach out and grab me, but he was frozen to the spot. I was unsure if he was even breathing.

Opening the door, I forced myself not to look back.

'Before you go, can I tell you a story?'

I stopped and slowly turned around, cursing myself. 'What's it about?' I asked in what came out as little more than a whisper.

He slipped his hands into his front pockets and drew his shoulders upwards. His eyes locked onto mine. 'It's about the first time we met.'

My eyebrows bunched together as I asked, 'We've met before now?'

He nodded slowly with a flicker of apprehension coating his expression. 'Yes, about seven years ago, in a café.'

I looked over my shoulder down into the cold, dark stairwell. I was pretty sure he was stalling until someone else came to try and stop me from leaving, but I was intrigued.

'Can I tell you the story?' He took his right hand out of his pocket and gestured back to the sofas.

I had already proven myself to be a masochist, so with a sigh, I followed. 'You can tell me whatever story you want. I'm leaving this hospital today.'

He didn't answer, just blankly sat down opposite me, on the very edge of the seat. Leaning forward, he perched his elbows on his knees.

For a moment, he just stared at me, but then a look of resolution crossed his face, and he began his story. 'The first thing you should know is my family is mad about quizzes.'

I had to admit it wasn't how I thought the story would start. 'Okay,' was all I could think of to say, but I sat back into the sofa and gave him my attention.

'Yes, massive. And, every Christmas from Christmas eve to New Years' day, we've all got to answer ten trivial pursuit questions. The one with the most right answers wins. Simple. But, obviously, we're not all together over this period, so we randomly call each other to ask the questions. If you don't answer the call, you forfeit the point.' He stopped to laugh at a memory, but before he could continue, I jumped in.

'Look, I know you're stalling, but please get to the story.' I glanced over to the door, waiting for my mum to shoot through it.

He sat back and folded his arms. 'I am telling the story. Shhh. There is also another element to the game. If you don't know the answer. You can pick left or right, and then ask someone, anyone who is either to the left or right of you. If they get it right, you get the point.'

'Okay,' I said. 'Sounds fun.' I crossed my arms and settled in to listen as instructed.

'It is. It can also get a little crazy. My wife is the reigning champion. She's even stopped traffic before now to get to someone she thought might know the answer.' He winced and paled slightly but continued.

'I had been dumped quite publicly by my girlfriend the month before and decided to get out of London between Christmas and New Year. So I went to Cornwall, for a bit of sea air. On the 28th, I stepped into a coffee shop, needing to thaw out. Just as I was walking over to a table, my phone rang. I dove into the first seat I could find to answer it.

'My elder brother, sounding a little tipsy, shouted, "It's question time." The question was: In the song, *Me and My Bobby McGee*, on what journey did Bobby McGee share the secrets of Janis Joplin's soul?'

'Ahh, did I help you get the question right?' I smiled fondly, but he shook his head.

'No, I asked the guy on the other side of me. He was older than you; I was hedging my bets. Which was a bad move because not only did he not know the answer, but looked at me like I was crazy. I ended the call and was just sipping my coffee when you stood up next to me. As you were packing your book back into your bag, quietly and for only me to hear, you sang, "From the Kentucky coal mines to the California sun, there Bobby shared the secrets of my soul." I glanced up over my coffee, knowing I was being mocked. Lifting your head from your bag, you said, "You should never underestimate a blonde." With a playful little wink, you walked away.' He stopped to chuckle and shake his head at me before continuing.

'It was one of those cafes that could pass for a mini maze, and less than ten seconds later, you were walking back towards me. I realised what you had done, and I have to admit I was ready to be all smug and get my own back, but just as you passed me, you said so casually and without embarrassment, "I wouldn't ask one for directions, though." I spat my coffee everywhere, and with a smile and a shrug, you headed towards where the door actually was.'

He looked up at me, and I pursed my lips, feeling a little proud. It sounded like something I would say. I couldn't help wondering if he had the wedding ring on then, and if he didn't, what would have happened if I had not walked away?

'Thank you for telling me that. It's the first actual story I've heard from my missing time.'

I made to stand up, but he reached forwards and stopped me. 'I came after you then, and I'll come after you now. Please hear me out.' This voice was soft and pleading, and to begin, all I could do was gawk at him.

'You came after me in the café?' I stuttered out incredulously.

The smile that alighted his face grounded me to the seat. 'The guy who got my question wrong said to me, "If you don't go after her, you're an idiot."'

'Huh,' was all I could say. I dug my fingers into the sofa cushions, gripping tightly to what felt real.

'I caught up with you, and we talked. We walked and talked and then found various bars, and we drank. We drank a lot… and then.' He stopped and raised both his eyebrows at me. As he watched the dawning grow on my face, a wickedly mischievous smile arrived, sitting below a proud glint in his eyes.

I was so pleased and disappointed with myself at the same time. Inwardly I screamed for not being able to remember.

'Great, I'm a slut,' I joked. He wasn't my first one-night stand, but I wasn't going to tell him that.

'Oiy, that's my wife you're talking about.'

Confusion stunned me. I replayed the last part of our conversation in my head, and no matter how I thought about it, I couldn't see how we were talking about anyone other than me.

Exhilaration crept in at the chance that it could be possible, but it was too insane to even consider. Then panic threw itself into the mix. Each emotion clambering for precedence pushed against my lungs making it hard to breathe. My eyes searched for his hand and saw the gold band. They moved to my own bare finger. I tried clinging again to the cushions, but my hands were numb. There was nothing to grab onto as my mind stumbled through the dark. Breathing in deeply through my nose, I tried to ground myself in the familiar smell of him, but the breeze shifted, and all I got were car fumes and the potted tulips next to me.

He leant back on the sofa and reached into his pocket. Pulling his fist out, he opened his hand in front of me. Laying across his palm were two thin gold bands, with a perfectly round diamond attached to one.

'Is this what you're looking for?' My eyes moved from his hand to his expression. Tears pooled in his eyes, and when he blinked, a solo tear from each eye dropped onto his jeans. I felt my body pull towards him again, but fear had now joined the babble of emotions, and it was welding me to the seat. 'They had to remove them for the CAT scans and MRIs.'

He reached out and took my hand. Turning it palm up, he let the rings tumble free. They clinked lightly together as they hit, and the sound and weight of them in my hand made my breath catch. The reality I had been constructing for the last few days shattered, and every thought that tried to push to the surface became muffled and blurred.

Needing to do something, anything! I stood up, but the blood in my head didn't accompany me. Before I could lower myself back down, my vision darkened, and all I heard were the rings chiming against the concrete floor.

Chapter Four

I opened my eyes to the familiar sound of the beeping machinery and the smell of disinfectant. Every muscle in my body throbbed with tension, and thoughts jumbled like puppets in a hurricane. I was lying flat on my back, petrified that if I moved, the multitude of emotions would overwhelm me.

Concentrating on the unfathomably real, I scraped my nails across the woven blanket. There were thirty-one ceiling panels within my peripheral vision. A box of latex gloves in a blue holder by the bathroom door. A small sink and a tissue dispenser by the window. Outside I could hear a doctor being called over an intercom. The whoosh of an automatic door, and next to me, a man lightly snoring.

I took a shaky, deep breath and turned my head to the right.

He was lying on his front on a small bed, his arms folded above his head. The blue jumper was discarded upon the chair next to him. In its place, a faded black t-shirt clung to his back with the rise and fall of soft breaths. Asleep, he appeared more plausible. More human.

Taking a chance, I sat up. Folding my legs in front of me to keep them within the safety of the blanket, I swivelled to face the peaceful form beside me. His lips were parted slightly, and his eyes moved beneath the lids, following a dream. The gentle, rhythmic pace of his breathing calmed me, and for a while, I discarded every other overwhelming thought and just enjoyed watching what the rest of the world didn't get to see.

My eyes lowered to my left hand, and there they were. The only things I wanted to find when I first woke up. I moved them around, feeling the cold metal against my clammy finger. Their quiet tinkling echoed off the pale bare walls. I shook my head in disbelief. It was too absurd.

Holding my hand out so I could see Matt and the rings together, I turned it to the left, to the right, and back again. I moved my head to observe them from differing angles, but no matter how hard I looked, I couldn't connect them. A wicked little voice in my head, did though point out, *'You can touch him if you want. Legally.'*

Cautiously, my hand stretched out until the tips of my fingers touched his back. He didn't stir, so I let them drift upwards, over the cotton towards his shoulder. A smile crept onto his sleeping face, and he shifted slightly towards my hand. I inched closer and lay my palm on his shoulder. Even this minimal contact was enough to warm me.

Adrenaline pulsed, but the heat traversing my arm kept the panic under control. Bravely, I allowed myself to consider what wearing a wedding ring meant. I got no further than the realisation that we shared a bed, when the brittleness of my mind didn't just shatter; it exploded. Within the debris lay an image displayed on a phone.

I doubled over, unable to stop all the air rushing from my lungs. My mouth filled with saliva, and I was seconds away from throwing up. Wrapping my arms around me, I pulled as much air in as I could, swallowing the building nausea.

As soon as I could breathe, a desperate need for clarification erupted from me, a lot louder than I expected. 'Oh my God, you've got kids!'

Matt's eyes shot open, and he bolted upright. I nearly laughed, but my breathing had gotten insanely erratic at the word 'kids'.

'You have kids,' I repeated just as loudly, before he had even stopped assessing the room for a threat. Realising it was me, his shoulders relaxed, and he rubbed his palms over his face. With a soft intake of air, he took my hands, while I sat there, paralysed with shock.

'We have kids,' he whispered.

Everything went numb. I couldn't feel his hands in mine, but he must have pulled one of them free because his phone appeared before me. It was alight, and I could see the picture of his... our children. 'I've been putting together a video and photo timeline for you; when you're ready.'

My mind repeated over and over, *Our children.*

'Please don't faint again. You scared the shit out of me on the roof.'

I wasn't going to, but I was going to cry, and I did. It was all too much to even think about processing.

The sobs came out loud and fast. Matt dove forwards, doing the one thing I had been aching for. He wrapped his arms around me and pulled me into his chest. I wept out of happiness and relief, confusion and frustration.

I stayed there crying for a long time, using his warm, solid mass to stop me from completely falling apart.

While he soothingly stroked my hair and kissed my head, the most calming thought flooded me. *He's mine.*

'I want to go home,' I finally said when I could stop crying for long enough to get the words out. I needed to see this life that he was trying to convince me was real.

At first, all he did was pull me closer, and I breathed in the smell I knew to my core was home. 'You will. I promise, but—'

I shifted out of his arms, wiping my eyes on my hoodie sleeve. 'No, now. I want to go home. I meant it on the roof. I need to get out of this room. I feel like I'm drifting, and I have to concentrate so hard on not floating away,' I blubbered and croaked, desperately trying to hold it together.

His eyes locked onto mine, firm and resolved. 'I'll be your anchor. I won't let you float away. I'm here, and I'm not going anywhere. But—'

'Please. I need to go home.' I almost begged. The thought of there actually being children was making me desperate.

'Freya, sweetheart, there is so much you still don't know.' The agonising look that crossed his face told me it was rare for him to deny me anything.

'Can't you tell me about it all at 'home'? Somewhere it stands a chance of feeling real.' If it hadn't been for the red blotches below his eyes, I would have pointed out that I had an address and legs.

I reached up, wanting to touch his cheek. To connect with him, make absolutely sure he wasn't a mirage. My hand shook, and I almost pulled it away, but with a soft, knowing smile, he stayed still, never taking his eyes from mine. My fingers grazed his jawline and my chest pulsed with the confirmation that he was real. I expected him to flinch away, but instead, he closed his eyes and moved into my hand, relishing the touch. All the tension I was holding subsided.

With an exasperated sigh, he opened his eyes and looked past me at something on the bedside cabinet. Leaning around, he picked it up, and I saw it was the blood pressure monitor.

'Okay. If after I tell you this next bit, you can keep this thing from beeping like a burglar alarm on steroids, I'll get on board with you leaving here.'

I nodded and held out my finger. What could he say that was bigger than I was married to him with four kids?

'Right.' Taking a deep breath, he stood up and walked over to the TV. Reaching around the back, he did something that made a click sound and then pressed the power button on the front.

Facing me, he said, 'I want you to think about what you could hear and see from the roof terrace.' Behind him, the TV came to life.

'What? How did you do that?' Out of everything that was confusing the hell out of me, the suddenly working TV threw me.

'There's a bloody good reason why we've kept you away from the TV,' he said, lifting the remote to change the channel.

On the screen, a male News presenter in his thirties, standing outside a hospital in front of row upon row of candles and flowers, began speaking.

'It's been four days now since award-winning screenwriter and author of the *Occurrences* series, Freya Lord, was involved in the car accident, that saw her being rushed here to St Michael's. There is still no word from Lord's team as to the seriousness of her condition. All we know is Matt Lord was seen entering shortly after she was admitted and, from what we can tell, has not left since.

'We can only assume that Freya Lord is in a critical condition behind these walls.'

An immaculately dressed female presenter from the studio appeared on a split-screen. 'We've had reports of the crowds growing further outside the hospital today. Can you confirm this, Jim?'

'Yes, absolutely.'

The camera moved away from Jim and over the crowd. I inhaled at the sight. There had to be at least two hundred people.

'Many have left flowers and notes wishing her well.'

The camera zoomed in on the carpet of flowers and plastic wrapping gathered along a long metal fence running the length of the hospital.

'What the fuck?' I stood up, and the blood pressure monitor started beeping frantically.

Matt muted the TV, then lowered me back onto the bed. 'And that's why you are staying in.'

My hands drew down my face, acting as a shield and scaffolding.

'How the hell?' I said over the top of my fingertips. The beeping continued in rapid succession.

'How about we get you back into bed?' Matt tried to gently coax me back.

'No. No,' I said, pushing against him. There wasn't a chance in hell I was getting back into that bed. The boxed room was making me claustrophobic. I needed to get away from the sterile smell and constant beeping.

Taking a deep breath, I shook out my shoulders. 'I've got this.' It came out a lot higher than I expected and Matt didn't look convinced. He was still trying to lightly guide me back towards the pillows.

I pushed out the sight of the crowd holding candles and crying into each other's shoulders and pictured the mundane things that came with any life. Doing washing. Cooking food. Cleaning a house. My breathing slowed, and the monitor ceased its incessant beeping.

I stopped trying to grasp onto reason or logic and just concentrated on the denial being coaxed forward by self-preservation. 'So my books sold well. I married a movie star.' I pointed to the screen that was showing people sobbing. 'That stands to reason.' My voice was still higher than normal, but the blood pressure machine only betrayed me with a few infrequent beeps. I was trying my best to keep it down, but if I didn't get out of here soon, I was going to have a full-blown tantrum.

'Sweetheart,' he said, smoothing his hands down my arms. I only then noticed I was shaking my head, and it took a lot of effort to get myself to stop. 'Your books didn't just sell well. You sold more books last year than any other author. You have two Emmy award-winning TV shows under your belt, and the *Occurrences* series is up to its second film. The first sold more at the box office over its first weekend than any other film in the last ten years. You are one of the most famous women in the world, and that's just the tip of the iceberg.'

He surveyed the traitorous beeping machine, waiting.

I heard every word, and I desperately wanted to hyperventilate and pace the room in a frantic mess, but my only concern was getting out of the hospital. The hot, smothering, recycled air was stretching my skin and tightening my lungs, tortuously suffocating me with every breath.

I thought again about the children, picturing them playing in the vegetable patch. Opening presents on Christmas morning. Walking through open fields in the sunshine. There was a peace there that made everything else seem inconsequential.

'I'll freak out about all that another time, but right now, I want to go home. Please.' I even shocked myself with how calm my voice sounded, and I almost started laughing. The kind of hysterical laugh that saw you in a padded room, but by fixing the image of children front and centre, I kept it at bay.

He smiled warmly, clearly impressed with how well I was taking everything. Let's face it, I wasn't. I was on the brink of a complete breakdown. There was only so much one person could handle, and I thought four children under six and a husband were enough for one day.

'Okay.' He drew back and assessed me before continuing. 'But one thing at a time. Isabella, Jack, and Dylan are at my parents', and Charlotte is with your sister. Come home first. Get settled in, and then we'll get the kids home. Okay?'

I wanted to immediately disagree, but then the weight of what I was doing truly dawned on me, and I nodded.

'Where's my mum?' For some reason, I looked around the room for her.

Matt's lips perked up a fraction at the corners. 'She had to go around to your sister's for a bit.'

'Is everything okay?'

His lips twitched again. 'Yes, absolutely fine. Your sister just needed a bit of… support. I spoke to your mum after you fainted. She went bat-shit crazy at me for telling you and was about to run over, but.' He stopped. Lifting his hand, he brushed his fingers over my cheek. 'You're my wife, and I'm meant to be the one looking after you.'

My chest pulsed, and the mini traitor beeped once. The word 'wife' followed into the word 'mother'. Their meanings were trying to scrape away my veil of denial, but until I got this thing off my finger, I was keeping my mind in a vegetable patch digging up carrots.

'Are you sure you're ready?' Matt asked, still trying to inch me backwards.

For the 'ready' he was referring to? Absolutely, unequivocally, no! But, there was only one thing that was making me hesitate.

'What if I can't bond with them?' They were children I didn't know. Even if they had come from me, I had no recollection of that. How was I meant to be a mother to children I didn't know?

Matt stroked the side of my face, and like he had, I leant into the warmth of the touch. 'They are bonded to you, and you are an incredible mum. I promise you, it was something that came so naturally to you then, and it will again now.'

There was only one way to find out. 'Yes. I'm ready. I'd like to go home.'

He assessed me and the little traitor, and then with a deep inhale of breath, he kissed me lightly on the forehead. 'I'll go sort the paperwork, and you need to get yourself ready.'

'For what?'

'Them,' he said, pointing at the TV and the mass crowd gathered outside holding candles. I felt the blood drain out of my face and go all the way down to my toes.

'What do you want me to do?' I asked, absolutely petrified he was going to say, walk amongst them.

'Not me. Your publicist. She wants me to go out and look at the flowers, then take some flowers off someone. Thank a few people for their support, and tell them I'm taking you home to rest and recover. Then I come back to the entrance, where the car will pull up, and you will walk out. I will give you the flowers, you smell them, smile, and then we get in the car. The windows will be blacked out, but most cameras with a good flash can get an image inside, so when you're in the car, hold the flowers and lean into me.'

I just stared at him, and he laughed. 'Oh, this reminds me of the day you figured out you were famous. It was about a year after everyone else knew it.' The laughter stopped, and before me, I visually watched him loosen every muscle across his shoulders. With a heavy but almost silent sigh, he said, 'Mrs Lord.'

He was searching my eyes. To start, I thought he was looking for my reaction, but then I realised he was looking for her. Trying to call his wife forth.

There was so much love there, and I was desperately trying to ignore that I was a poor substitute for the wife he wanted to see. Hearing that title made me remember the precise second, I gave up all delusions that there was a chance I was Mrs Lord.

'The nurse, she came and told you on the roof that Mrs Lord was looking for you.'

Before he answered, I watched his expression fight between happiness and sadness. 'My mum, bringing my clothes.' He lightly grazed his lips across my cheek, and I stopped breathing. 'I will never get pleasure from your pain, but I couldn't tell before then whether you suspected, or wanted it enough to think you

55

were my wife, but it looked like her words physically hurt you.' He brought his face close to mine. 'I was so happy.' He kissed me on the cheek and then walked out.

I ran my hands over the rough bedding. It didn't help, but while Matt was out of sight, I took off the traitor and slipped it under my pillow.

Chapter Five

I was watching the sunlight flicker on the wall outside the window, trying to stop my head exploding, when the image on the TV changed, catching my attention. There was no longer a presenter but what looked like a CCTV image.

It showed an average road empty of traffic, and I was just about to reach for the remote to unmute it when a car flew in from the left and collided with a Range Rover. The speeding car spun off to the right and flipped once, twice, and then on the third flip, it rested on its side. The Range Rover spun off to the left and collided with a lamppost, but from this angle, I couldn't see how much damage there was.

No one stirred from the car emitting smoke, but after a minute, the driver's side door of the Range Rover opened, and a woman stumbled out. A large dog clambered out behind her.

I stood up and walked to the TV to get a better look. Before I saw a clear image of her face, I knew it was me.

On the TV, I walked down the side of the Range Rover, holding onto it for support. This close to the TV, I saw it was raining heavily, and my feet were slipping over puddles. When I got to the end of the Range Rover, I looked around, and upon seeing the car on its side, I rushed over, stumbling slightly. The dog followed, staying close to my side.

I moved around the car. Then it shocked me to see myself clamber up and prise the front door open. I watched as I slipped inside the car, but for another minute, nothing happened. Then, so quickly that I almost missed it, the car's already dented sunroof flew off and skirted across the road.

I crawled out backwards through the hole, dragging an unconscious man. Then behind him, a little girl shuffled out.

I leant over the man, tilting my ear to his mouth. When I pulled back up, I immediately started chest compressions. After ten, I dropped down to give him mouth to mouth. The little girl came towards who I assumed was her dad, and while pushing into his chest, I twisted around towards the dog, who trotted over obediently.

I reached for the remote and unmuted it. The presenter was giving a narration of the scene.

'We now know from Mr Morris's family that Lord called her dog, Wisp, over and asked Laila Morris, who sustained only a few cuts and bruises, if she could look after her dog, while she looked after her dad.'

I was watching as he spoke. The little girl picked up the dog's loose lead, and after one more round of mouth to mouth, I said something, and the dog trotted off across the road, the little girl in tow, towards a covered bus stop.

'Mr Morris is still in St Michael's, but we have been informed this morning that he is awake and on the road to making a full recovery.'

It was a relief to hear he would be okay, but I tuned out the presenter, absorbed with what I was seeing.

I hadn't seen anyone else in the image, but suddenly two ambulances appeared from each side. Two paramedics carrying bags rushed to my side and immediately took over from me. I leant back against the car, and another paramedic came to me, but I shook my head and pointed to the little girl. I said something, and the dog trotted back across the road with the little girl still holding the lead.

The paramedic looked over the little girl, and I tried to stand, but halfway up, I collapsed. Another paramedic rushed to me and blocked my view.

'Scariest film I've ever seen,' I heard whispered from behind me. I had been so transfixed I hadn't heard Matt come back in. I turned to him, and the pale, agonised expression I saw made my breath catch.

'I'm okay,' I said with a breezy smile, but I softly cried, basking in the joy that I was important to someone, and he was making no attempt to hide how scared he had been.

I reached for him, and he stepped into my arms. Silently, he sobbed against me, and it made me feel stronger. I wasn't the only person this was happening to. I had lost my memories, but essentially, he had lost his wife. There was a comfort in our shared grief.

'Right, come on.' I patted him on the back and looked at him with mock seriousness. 'Suck it up buttercup, and let's do this.' I deserved an Oscar. I was absolutely shitting myself!

He wiped his arm over his eyes and kissed my cheek.

'Smile and smell the flowers. I can do that,' I said with a shrug. A little of the hysterical laughter tried to escape, but I pushed against it just in time. My mind started repeating over and over, *'Carrots, carrots, carrots.'*

Perhaps the padded room wasn't the worst idea, but for now, I was done with hospitals, even if it did mean dealing with a craziness I couldn't even begin to comprehend.

Matt shook his head and laughed. 'No, smell the flowers, then smile.'

'Yeah, I'm screwed.' And I meant it.

He picked up my bag and pulled me into a side hug. 'You're good at all this, I promise. You gave a talk to a couple of thousand people a few weeks ago. You've even given interviews on live TV.'

Passing me the baseball cap, I slipped it on and let out a heavy breath. 'Let's start with smelling the flowers and smiling,' I said, walking out of the hospital room, I hoped I would never see again.

'There you go. You've got it,' he teased, holding me tighter.

The scene around the nurse's station was a little more crowded than I was used to seeing it. Doctors, nurses, and porters gathered, and they were all smiling. The masquerade was over. I knew the truth, and they knew it. I passed through them, following Matt's lead in thanking them for looking after me.

We stepped into the lift, and when it sealed us within, I counted the indents in the metal doors. Listened to the slow turn of the cogs, metal gently skimming against metal, and Matt breathing lightly next to me. Reality was creeping in at the edges, tapping at my resolve but the sterile smell that had been keeping it at bay still clung tightly to me. What lay beyond was still too blurred to fathom.

The doors squeaked open, and I had an urge to hide behind Matt. With the influx of light, my heart leapt, and I coughed back the anxiety. Matt's hand slipped into mine, squeezing it reassuringly. His warmth flooded my arm, consuming me, and my breathing slowed.

I was greeted by not only the same scene as upstairs on a larger scale, but two men in dark blue suits. They were so big they made the six-foot-five muscular mass that was Matt Lord, look normal. Matt nodded to them, and as we stepped out, they fell in line next to us.

The almost silent crowd of about forty people on each side of me slowly got louder. A couple even screeched. Camera phones flashed, and I lowered the tip of the cap over my eyes. I'd been upstairs watching myself perform CPR on TV when I should have been applying make-up.

Instead of heading straight to the exit, I was ushered into a small waiting room with the two suited mountains. Matt kissed me on the side of the head, and with a wink, he left me there. I knew as soon as he had stepped outside because the noise was deafening.

'Fuck,' I said under my breath. Then paced the little room to calm my nerves while the two men looked everywhere but at me. Concentrating on the squeak of my rubber-soled boots against the tiled floor, I tried to block out the screams penetrating the concrete walls. The air was just as suffocating in here as it was upstairs, but I wasn't sure I wanted to go outside anymore. That little hospital room was starting to seem more like a sanctuary than a prison.

A few minutes passed, and then the taller dark-haired mountain, with an array of little scars all over his face, said, 'We can go now. This way.'

The blond-haired, gentler looking one nodded and opened a door on the other side of the room.

'Smell and smile,' I said out loud.

'You've got this, Freya,' the blond one said as I passed. When I looked up at him, he gave me an encouraging, friendly smile, and I realised I was meant to know him.

I guessed feeling like I'd been dropped on an alien planet was going to be common for a long time.

'Thank you,' I said shakily.

The other one quickened his pace, so he was out in front, then held out his hand to halt me. 'Just waiting for Mr Lord to reach the car. Five, four, three, two, one.' He opened the door, and over the black town car, I could see the rows of people. I stepped outside into the warm sunshine, and they burst into applause, whoops, and cheers. All around me, cameras flashed, and people called my name.

'Just breathe,' Matt said, coming up next to me, holding out a bunch of pink roses. I lifted them to my nose and breathed in before smiling up at him.

Leaning around me, Matt opened the door, and I climbed in, with him close behind. As soon as the car door closed and he took my hand, the significance of what it meant to be in this car hit me. The sudden change from public to private. The smell of the polished leather, and fragrant roses, all contributed to reality, obliterating my wall of denial.

I tightened my grip on his arm, searching for an anchor.

'You okay?' he asked affectionately.

I nodded apprehensively but said, 'Tell me the rest of the story.'

The car moved through the crowd, and I lowered my head towards the flowers, trying to block out the photographers clambering over the car, calling my name.

'So, things went a bit downhill the next morning.' He smiled ruefully.

'Did you run out on me?' I asked jokingly.

With a slight nod and what looked like a wince, he said, 'Yes.'

My stomach lurched, and I had no idea how to respond.

Leaning over, he kissed my cheek, and I relaxed, just a little. 'It showed me early on what a little fire demon you can be.' He buried his head into the side of my neck, and I felt him just breathe in the scent of me before raising his eyes back to meet mine.

Seeing his desire for me had me paralysed with both shock and lust. A soft groan escaped, and he continued. 'We ended up in that little restaurant overlooking the bay, in possession of a dodgy bottle of tequila that led us to another bottle of tequila at the hotel bar.' He ended with a chuckle and shiver.

'Hang on, this was all on the same day we met in the coffee shop?'

'Yes. I did everything I could to stop you leaving.' He turned his whole body towards me, and like he had on the roof, he stared straight into me. My stomach responded with a customary flip. 'You know that feeling you get when you are tense as hell, and you take that first large sip of alcohol, and your body inwardly relaxes?'

I nodded. Alcohol sounded like a fantastic idea.

'That's what being around you felt like. You thought I wanted a bit of fun and then to run off back to Hollywood before you woke up.'

'But that's what happened, right?' Somehow, I managed to swallow the hurt so he couldn't hear it.

He nodded with a sigh. The slight blush in his cheeks paled.

'One shot in at the hotel bar, and they had a change over of staff. A new waitress came over carrying drinks. When she saw me, well, she screamed and accidentally dropped the tray in your lap.' He was laughing at the memory, and even though I couldn't see it, his laughter was contagious.

'You shot up, totally stunned. The waitress was so apologetic, but before you could say anything, the manager was over in a shot. He was about to fire the waitress on the spot when you stood up for her and said it was all your fault. You said you had accidentally knocked her elbow. He didn't believe a word of it, but the look on your face made it clear, that you would not be impressed if he sacked her.' He ran his hand down my leg and swallowed hard. 'Fuck, you're hot when you get all serious. You had me hours before then, but that officially sealed the deal.

'You were about to head for the toilets when the manager offered you a complimentary room where you could clean up, and said he would have a change of clothes sent to the room asap.' He looked down at me with a boyish, triumphant grin. 'I came with you…. More than once.' He finished with a wink, and I blushed, taking a deep, shaky breath.

'So, I'll happily go into details another time, but when I woke up the next morning…. There's no way to sugarcoat this next part, but what you saw when you woke up, was me literally running out of the door. It was still early, and you waited for a couple hours, but when I didn't return, you left.'

'Mr Lord, I have an Amanda Preston on the phone for you. She says it's urgent,' the driver called over his shoulder.

63

Matt sighed and pressed a button on the handle of the door. 'What is it, Amanda?'

'Matt, Finally.' An American accent carried through the speakers above the doors. 'Been trying to reach you all afternoon. We need to start talking interviews.'

'Amanda, no,' Matt interjected sternly. 'We've spoken about this. It won't be happening.'

'Matt, we would be crazy not to capitalise on this. Book sales are up thirty percent. We need to keep this rolling. We can stage the questions and prep Freya with the answers.'

Hearing my name jolted me. Even though I knew they were talking about me, it wasn't real till I heard that. My breathing quickened, and I buried my head into Matt's side.

'Carrots. Carrots. Carrots.'

'Absolutely not. There will be none. Work is on the backburner. Play on the mystery of it all. Be creative. That's what we pay you for.' Matt hit another button, and the car fell silent.

'Thank you,' I said, curling into him. My eyes closed, and I drifted peacefully to sleep.

'Freya? Sweetheart? We're home.' Matt's voice soothed me awake, and I opened my eyes to darkness. I blinked a few times, and when he opened the door, the car lit up, stunning me. It wasn't until I was out that I saw where we were.

Chapter Six

The car drove away, and we were left standing outside a large ink blue double door housed between two white columns. Spotlights dotted around the circular, gravel driveway pointing towards the house, illuminating the tanned, Georgian mansion. I stood stoic on the terracotta-tiled path, trying to find something familiar in the brightly coloured flowerpots, standing like sentries up the pristinely painted, white gloss steps.

'Welcome home,' Matt said a little apprehensively. I took a deep breath and walked towards the door that wouldn't look out of place on a bank. 'Here you go.' A silver key appeared in front of me.

I took it and slowly slipped it into the lock but just held the key in place.

Perhaps I wasn't ready for this. Denial couldn't walk through this door with me. It wasn't just about accepting this polar opposite life I couldn't remember. When I had planned my great escape that morning, I hoped the smell and presence of my home would return my memories. I had a lot riding on the next few minutes.

Matt's left hand rested in the centre of my back, and I felt his warmth standing next to me. I wasn't the only one with hopes and fears.

I turned the key, and the door opened with a soft sucking sound. Stepping over the threshold, I took a deep breath in through my nose. My memories did not instantly return, but there was a familiarity in the smell of floral washing powder, something citrus, baby powder, possibly a little warm dog, and of course, lavender.

'Are you okay?' Matt asked softly next to me. All I could do was nod and look around. I was standing in a large foyer. A mahogany, beige carpeted staircase curved up the left wall, leading onto a balcony that stretched out to the right, over large double doors into a dining room. The foyer was a subtle yellow, and hanging from the towering ceiling was a soft glowing tiered chandelier. Apart from a large painting on the wall, there was nothing else in the room except a vibrant green and yellow circular Turkish rug.

'If you're not liking anything you're seeing, you should know, you decorated the house.'

It was a stunning foyer. To my left and right were closed white painted wooden doors. Ahead of me over the dining table, floor-to-ceiling windows spread across the back wall. The soft glow of garden lights beyond them illuminated yellow rose bushes.

I heard the front door close, and then warmth engulfed me when Matt closed his arms around my shoulders. Whispering into my ear, he said, 'I'm going to let you just wander around and get your bearings. I'll be in the kitchen, making tea.'

'And where would that be?' I asked, genuinely wondering if I would find it in this place.

'Exactly where *you* would expect to find it. As I said, you designed the house. Everything is where you would want it to be.' He released me, and I ambled forwards into the dining room.

The table was beautiful, highly polished, dark wood, and could easily sit thirty. A simple four-stemmed, brushed silver candleholder sat in the centre upon a hexagon piece of light green silk. Dimmed spotlights overhead made it look warm and inviting. I let my hand run over the rounded backs of the chairs, trying not to think about all the dinners I couldn't remember.

When my eyes scanned away from the aching lack of memories, I caught sight of the dresser across the left wall and stopped breathing. My whole body shuddered.

Scattered around a multi-coloured Venetian glass vase full of wildflowers, were around ten framed photos, and I was in a lot of them.

There it was; my life. There were holiday photos of Matt and me with the twins. We were sun-soaked, and either sat around a crisp white table in the evening, or stretched on towels across crisp white sand.

To the right, was a large landscape picture of about twenty people wearing Christmas jumpers. I recognised half of them as my family. The rest I assumed, were Matt's family because I didn't have the foggiest idea who they were. A man who looked like an older version of Matt had his arm draped over my shoulder, and I was laughing at something he had said.

A baby of around six months was on my knee, and two children of about three were at my feet. I stared at my face, but it felt like I was looking at a ghost, or worse, a snapshot from a parallel universe. One I could never visit. I wanted to reach into the picture and turn her head, so I could look into her eyes. I wanted to know if I could see into her. Travel through her eyes and possess her. Perhaps I was the ghost.

Searching for another way into her, I scanned the rest of the pictures, looking for one where I was facing the camera. I found one of Matt and me at the *Doomed* premiere. I knew it was such because the word 'Doomed' was dotted behind us, over a fake black wall.

My hair was still blonde and sat in loose curls upon my shoulders. I was wearing a long, pale green dress. The skirt was layers of organza that led into a thick corset, with a tapestry of cream flowers that stopped just below my boobs. Matt was next to me in a black suit, with a dark green tie. His hair was a little longer, and he was clean shaven. For the first time, I saw what Matt looked like happy. We were both facing front on, but I couldn't find a way in. There was something fake about her. Like

67

I was seeing a replica of myself. The real me, hiding behind her somewhere, just out of reach.

In the centre, and the largest of them all, was mine and Matt's wedding photograph. I picked up the intrinsically designed metal frame, but unfortunately, I wasn't looking at the camera. It was one of those photos that get captured between the ones you pose for.

All around us was a stone veranda that looked out over countryside soaked in an orange and pink sunset. Our foreheads were lightly touching, and Matt's hands rested on my hips, while mine were on his arms. Both of us had our eyes closed, looking perfectly contented. I set it down lightly in its place.

I could have spent the whole night just looking at those photos, and as much as I wanted to explore every inch of this house, there was one room in particular that I wanted to see. Apparently, from the window, I could see reindeer.

Chapter Seven

Going back on myself, I headed for the stairs. Climbing, I gazed up at the massive oil painting of either a French or Italian villa and vineyard. It was a stunningly beautiful piece of art, but something about it told me there was another reason for its central presence.

At the top, I turned right across the balcony. It led into a wide cream coloured corridor with more framed photos scattering the walls. These were less formal than the ones downstairs. There was one where Isabella was blowing a raspberry into the camera. A few of babies, either on rugs or propped up, dressed as woodland creatures. I couldn't tell who was who. The thought sickened me, and I turned away from them.

I thought about what Matt had said. If everything was where I wanted it, where were the children's rooms?

At the back, I had always felt that was safer. When I opened the door at the end of the hall, the smell of the house changed to include a mix of something sweeter, with undertones of PVA glue, paint, and the unmistakable baby powder laced scent of children. Tears flowed out of sadness and happiness.

I flicked the light on and stepped in, wiping my eyes on my sleeve. When my vision cleared, I couldn't help gasping. It was a spectacular sight. An array of fantasy worlds in elaborate detail were painted over every available wall space.

Connecting Hogwarts to Middle Earth was a yellow brick road, that went on into Wonderland and Neverland. A giant peach was being inspected by a friendly looking giant, and a cat was tipping his hat to a lion standing beneath an old-fashioned lamppost in the snow. Then lastly, on the far wall was a little section of a world I didn't recognise at first, but upon seeing the little houses in the trees, I found a world Bastine would be familiar with. I took a deep, steadying breath, desperate not to allow the building emotion to overwhelm me.

Around the room were bookshelves and little tables. Miniature art easels. A small pool table. Beanbags and a variety of toys in all shapes and sizes, but to the left was an open double door. I walked over and switched on the light. This was the room I was looking for. Three beds dotted the edges and in the middle was a grey faux fur beanbag that was bigger than my first flat.

The bed to the right was Isabella's. A little further up on the left was Jack's and in the top right corner was Dylan's. The multi-coloured cushions lettering the walls above each of their beds told me so. There was an individuality about the spaces around their beds. Jack's orange and white spotted bedding was military procession straight, and the only thing on his bedside cabinet was a blue, weirdly shaped lamp.

Isabella was the complete opposite. Her cartoon fish-themed bedding was crumpled and in disarray. Stickers of unicorns and fairies were stuck to everything on her side, bed and wall included, and cushions in every imaginable colour covered the bed and the floor around it.

The little bed at the end was pale blue, and although there was a teddy for every children's character I could think of, it didn't quite look like someone had put their stamp on it yet.

I just walked around the room for a while, opening drawers, touching cushions, and smelling pillows. I needed to see them so badly.

Eventually, I left the room in search of where I would find my baby. I did find it slightly amusing that she wasn't in with the others due to her apparent inclination to scream, but then realised I was her mother and winced at the thought of what it meant to have a baby. It was like two people were jostling for space inside of me. They weren't fighting. They were trying to get comfortable.

I'd seen another door to the right in the playroom and headed towards it. As I passed, I looked out the window, but it was too dark to see the reindeer.

A pink and yellow cot with a matching cabinet sat in a smaller room. A large, comfortable-looking, pale blue rocking armchair sat over by the window, and cuddly toys occupied every shelf. The walls here belonged to the Hundred Acre Wood. It was lovely. I ran my fingers over the edge of the cot, aching to reach inside and pull her to me. There was a very strong smell of lavender in this room, laced with baby powder.

I opened a door, expecting to find a closet, but it revealed a large, squared hallway with a staircase to the left.

Another large sash window hovered next to the stairs, too dark to see anything through, but to the right and ahead, there were three other doors. I opened the second one, and when I clicked on the light, I involuntarily squealed. It was a gigantic walk-in wardrobe.

All across the right were a multitude of colours and materials hanging inside an open-faced space. Ahead of me was a sight almost as beautiful as the children's bedroom.

Eight rows of lit shelving displayed my shoes. I saw Valentino, Jimmy Choo, Gucci, Manolo Blahnik, and my hands clutched my heart. I wanted to run over and try them all on but what lay across the left wall stopped me. That was Matt's side.

I inched over to the hanging suit jackets and brushed my fingertips down the sleeves. Being amongst his possessions made me feel a little like a celebrity stalker. I backed away and turned to my side. The same designers as my shoes stared back at me and many, many more.

Around the corner, there were more fully stocked open wardrobes. I scanned the less formal attire like a nosey guest. The wardrobe I remembered owning consisted of around ten hangers. The chances were I wouldn't find a connection to who I was in here. I was about to leave when what Matt said came back to me.

With a knowing smile, I headed to the very end of the hanging splendour and brushed aside a dark woollen coat. Underneath, pushed back to the far left, I found the only thing in the house I was sure was mine. Crouching down, I rested my face in my hands and stared at the dust covered, khaki coloured rucksack.

It was fraying at the corners, and sown on by an untalented hand were cotton badges. Scattered between flags representing every weird and wonderful place I had explored, were memories I could actually recall. A sigh that relaxed my shoulders escaped when I saw the one of a blue tent on fire. That tent taught me that even though some brands of vodka do not burn—some do! Another depicting a bottle of rum with a white stitched label that said it was called 'No' made my stomach turn. I had fallen from the back of a motorbike on a beach in Antigua, cracked a tooth on the bottle of rum I was drinking from, and have never touched the stuff since. A bright orange parachute sat in the top corner, larger than the others. I had screamed from the second I left the plane until my bum skidded across the billowing dry mud of an airfield in Kenya. It represented such a carefree side of myself that I hoped still existed.

Instead of pulling the rucksack from the wardrobe, I climbed in and sat crossed-legged, holding the bag to my chest. Fully aware of how strange that was, I closed my eyes and squeezed the bag. The lingering smell of sweat and campfires brought tears to my eyes.

Clothes hung around me like reaching hands trying to console me, and I let them while I gripped tightly to the shoulder strap of the backpack. This bag had followed me in sadness, despair, excitement, and exhilaration. Wherever I went, my hand was wrapped around this strap. Lovers would be left behind, but this bag would not. If this was where this bag called home, then so did I.

I was a long way from building a bridge between my past and present lives, but at least I knew where to start construction.

'What'ya doing?' Hearing the familiar character in my head, I realised how much I would need his help getting out of the wardrobe. Somehow, seeing, holding something that connected these lives had disintegrated the last of my denial, and it was having a very debilitating effect on me.

I opened one eye at a time and visualised the golden armoured warrior looming over me. His arms were tightly wrapped around his chest, and he had a slightly humoured look on his face.

'You get that at some point, he is going to come and find you curled up in the wardrobe,' he said, looking towards the door, not bothering to try and hide his amusement.

'It's a big house. It'll take him a while,' I replied flippantly.

That earnt me a stern look. *'Get the fuck out of the wardrobe Freya. You look like a right prat.'*

I steadied my breathing and carefully placed the bag back in its corner. Crawling out, I rested my forehead on the thick slate-grey carpet and breathed in something that smelt better than the rucksack.

'This is bloody insane,' I said, lifting onto my knees. 'Count to three, and then get up.' A nervous giggle escaped, and I counted to three in my head. Rising shakily to my feet, I ran my hands roughly over my face. 'Just go with it. You've got this. Freak about how it all came to be later. For now, just enjoy it.'

Without looking at anything else, I left. Promising to return and try on everything.

For now, apparently, I had a date in the kitchen with my husband, Matt Lord. That last thought did it. Enough had finally sunk in, and I did a little jump around on the spot, excited dance, with a squeal, but then my head hurt, and I calmed it down. Closing the wardrobe door, I opened the one next to it at the end.

Windows adorned the left-hand side, but when I walked in, I found my/our bedroom. It was as big as the nursery, and up against the wall to the right was an enormous oak-framed bed with plump, navy blue bedding.

On the bedside cabinet closest to me, sat a man's watch and a framed selfie photo of Matt and me, lying across a double sun longer. Me in a white bikini and him bare-chested. His arm was around me, and I was tucked into the side of him, laughing while he kissed my temple. The blood rushed from my head, and I had to lower my hands to my knees to steady myself. My heart was thumping so loudly in my chest that I thought it would dislodge itself.

Stumbling across the room, I held onto the bottom of the bedframe for support. On the other bedside cabinet was a family photo from when I was about ten. We were all on holiday in Spain, and it had sat next to my bed since then. The house was like nothing I was used to, but finding another little bit of 'me' in such a personal space eased my breathing and clinked another piece of the bridge into place.

The bed itself refused to be ignored any longer. It was too big, and it had a presence that scared the hell out of me. I couldn't help imagining all the things we had gotten up to in there.

Brushing my hands through my hair, I took a quaking breath. It was an exciting thought to know Matt Lord was mine, but to know I would be getting into that bed with Matt Lord, petrified me.

'Yeah, you're on your own with that one,' Bastine said bluntly, and for a second, a smile flickered over my face.

I moved quickly through the room to the door at the far end, while I still could, and found myself facing the kids' playroom. I went back the way I came in search of the kitchen. I was hoping I could find more than tea in there.

Chapter Eight

Reaching the bottom of the stairs, I turned right through open double doors into an already lit room. Rustic oak flooring was surrounded by pure white walls adorned with landscape pictures from all over the world. Snow-capped mountains, burnt orange deserts, and oceans as blue as the front door occupied the left wall. To my right was a snow leopard peeking over a jagged rock, ariel shots of redwood forests, and erupting volcanos.

Two massive blue sofas sat opposite one another, with a white and brown coffee table between them, and next to them was a large, ornate fireplace. It all looked a bit formal, and I found it hard to imagine four small children running around.

I scurried through the room and into a red-tiled foyer, with a staircase running up the wall to my right. Up ahead, I could hear sounds coming from what I hoped was the kitchen. I shook myself all over, trying to expel the weirdness of the surreal, and opened the door.

Before I could take in the room, a huge dog jumped at me, trying to lick my face. Obviously, I screamed but recovered quickly when the dog jumped down in a hurry.

'Oh, I'm sorry, Wisp?' I was quickly forgiven, and the large, tan coloured Mastiff trotted back to me, wagging his tail. I gave him a scratch behind the ear, and he fell to my feet, belly in the air.

'You found me then.'

I looked up and saw Matt leaning over a massive, cream and grey marbled kitchen island, smiling. My stomach jumped. It was going to take me a while to get used to that. As incomprehensible as everything was, the most unfathomable was how the hell had the woman, who at one point, could fit everything she owned in that rucksack, married Matt Lord?

'Just about. There are a lot of doors in this house.'

'That's cause there are a lot of rooms in this house.'

I gave him a 'don't be a smartarse' smile, and I got another knee-shaking smile in reply. Quivering all over, I gave Wisp a quick belly scratch and then walked fully into the room to look around.

I was immediately very aware I had designed it. Pale green cabinets sprawled across the left wall with a black, eight spider-ringed cooker in the middle. Herbs grew out of wicker baskets hanging over the island Matt was leaning on, and above it was a green-tinged glass ceiling.

Over the other side of the room was a farmhouse-style table, nestled into the bay window. A cushioned bench curved around it, matching high-backed chairs on the other side. It could comfortably seat ten, and I was sure that was where we spent most of our time.

I padded softly past the island and Matt. My arms instinctively wrapped across my chest. The sense that I was an intrusive guest returned, trying to stop me, but Matt was watching me, seemingly as intrigued by my exploration as I was.

The dining room was to the right, but to the left was an open arched doorway leading into a glass-walled room with a door at the end. I was about to walk towards it when Matt spoke from behind me.

'Did you find your wardrobe and decide to leave it for another day?'

I looked back at him, a little shocked. Someone, who I barely knew, knowing me so well, was also going to take some getting used to. 'Yeah.'

He gestured his head towards the door. With a hint of humour in his voice, he said, 'You might want to do the same with that one.'

I looked at the door and then back at Matt. I could feel the size of the smile growing across my face. 'Why? What's in there?'

Matt laughed. 'The library.'

My smile dropped, and I gasped. 'When you say library, what we talking?'

His face lit up at my enthusiasm. 'Thirty-foot bookcases. Sliding ladders. It's also your office. So, when you are really ready to learn all about *you,* spend some time in there.'

I eyed the door. I was so tempted, but it had been a very long and overwhelming day, and my energy levels were depleted after my walk around upstairs.

'Tea?' he asked.

'Yes, please.' I came back into the kitchen and sat on a stool next to him at the island.

He moved over to the kettle, flicking it on, and I enjoyed watching him go. I only just managed to avert my eyes before he turned and caught my perverted leering.

Coughing away my longing, I scanned the room. 'So, give me the lowdown. What else is in this house? What's down the stairs by the wardrobe?' I nearly said, by our bedroom, but the thought of saying it out loud made me want to throw up.

'Cinema and Daddy's games room.'

I shook my head playfully. 'Really? How old are you?'

His voice rose an octave when he answered. 'You built it.'

'Oh, okay.'

He made my tea and brought it over. 'Thank you. So, where's the swimming pool?' This was my dream house, it had a pool.

He leant around me, pointing through the dining room, and I nearly quivered off my stool at the sudden proximity. The intoxicating sweet, woody scent that belonged to him coated me, and I had an insatiable urge to bite him. 'It's next to the gym and sauna. There is also an outside pool on the other side of the house.'

'Wow. It really is the perfect house,' I said, quietly laughing at myself and my urges.

'It's a big ass family home for a big ass family. Speaking of which.' He leant over to the counter and picked up a white binder. 'This is the baby bible. We've always had to have nannies. It wasn't a choice with both of our work, so you wrote a manual. One of our nannies went off recently to have a family of her own, so it was fully updated a couple of months ago for Jane.'

I hugged the binder to me, so grateful for the over-protectiveness I obviously inherited from my mother.

'You've got till noon tomorrow to read it. I've spoken with my mum, and she will bring them back in time for lunch, and then I spoke with your sister, and she is going to bring Charlotte over the morning after.'

Before I could argue against that, he hurried on. 'I know you want Charlotte here, and it is killing me to keep you two apart. But, you are her mother, and of course, she will be brought home if that is what you want. Charlotte does though, demand a lot of attention, and you have three other children. Spend the first night with them. Let it be relaxed. As relaxed as it can be anyway. Enjoy them. And also, they have been so worried about you. Let them be with you.'

'Is Charlotte really that bad?' I was starting to get a little scared of my youngest.

'Yes,' he said without hesitation, but then added, 'We were just really lucky with the other three. They are dream children. Charlotte could just be normal.' He shrugged and sipped his tea before going on. 'I do love my youngest daughter, I promise. She's my baby girl. She just doesn't like sleep.'

Something that had baffled me from the first night suddenly made so much sense. 'Is that why there is a strong smell of lavender everywhere?' I laughed.

'Yes. You grow it. Wash everything in it. There's bunches of it hanging from the ceiling in Charlotte's room. It does sod all, but it smells nice.'

'Okay. I'll go with whatever you think's best.' No matter how hard she was, I was dying to see my baby, but Matt was right, there were three others, and I wanted to see them just as much.

'Would you like me to run you a bath? Get the smell of the hospital off you.'

'Do I smell?' I said it jokingly, but it was hard not to feel self-conscious. I was sat next to my husband, but a large part of me felt like I was on a first date.

'No.' He chuckled affectionately.

'Yes. That would be nice, thank you.'

He stood up, and on his way past, he kissed the side of my head. 'Room next to the wardrobe, when you're ready.'

My breath caught, and way too much blood flooded my head. The room next to the wardrobe was our bedroom. Before panic could fully take over, I remembered seeing another door in the hallway that I hadn't opened.

He left, and as the panic subsided, I drank my tea and opened the binder. The first thing I saw was a medical page. Thankfully, there wasn't a lot on it, just their personal details, like dates of birth, insurance details, and a report on Jack, who apparently broke his arm a couple of years ago. According to the record, he fell out of a tree. I closed it for the time being. I would read it in the morning.

Left with only silence, I let my eyes wander. 'Home sweet home,' I said to myself, but there was an apprehension in my sincerity. As happy as I was, deep down, I couldn't shake the feeling that this was all too good to be true. There was also an acute awareness that things were being hidden from me. I only knew all I did because I had backed Matt into a corner on the roof. It stood to reason that anything bad would be concealed.

I wasn't the most trusting person, and essentially, Matt had lied to me from the second we met, hadn't he? My mum's statement that I didn't have a boyfriend came to mind. Technically, no one had lied to me. Instead, they were playing with the truth as they saw fit. Which made everything feel scarier; they thought it was justified. So, the question that refused to be ignored was; how else was I being blindsided?

I left my mug on the side but took my fears with me in search of a little bubble therapy.

Chapter Nine

Matt was nowhere to be seen when I arrived in the bathroom. Instead, I was greeted with a large square tiled bath in the centre of the room. Half a rugby team could have fit in there.

Over to the right, there was a walk-in shower, and to the left, a double sink and mirrors. With the small blue tiles covering the floor and half the walls, there was a vibrant Moroccan air to the room that emitted tranquillity.

Matt had lit towering church candles all around the room. Their reflections shone against the glazed blue tiles, bathing the whole room with a pale blue hue. I closed the door but felt it would be a little rude to lock it. Getting undressed, I quickly scampered into the bubbles and steaming water.

It was exactly what I needed. Lying back, I tried to use some old meditation techniques I had picked up during my yoga days. Concentrating on my breathing and the feeling of the warm water, I forced my muscles to relax. The knots in my stomach were just loosening when there was a light tap on the door before it opened slightly.

'Can I come in? I brought you something,' he said through the gap in the door. There was an edge to his voice that made me want to hesitate. This situation was as strange for him as it was for me, just in completely different ways.

'Yes, of course,' I tried to say casually while making sure the bubbles were arranged enough to cover me. I knew he had probably seen every inch a thousand times, but it was all very weird.

He walked in, holding out a large glass of red wine, trying to look over me and not at me.

'Thank you.' I smiled warmly and took the glass. He kept his eyes level but nodded and turned. Before he was out of the room, my head did a bit of random math from something I had seen in the binder. Isabella and Jack were born on the 27th of September 2016, and Matt and I met on the 28th of December 2015.

'Matt?'

'Yep?' He turned and finally made eye contact.

'How long were we together before Isabella and Jack were conceived?' I already knew the answer deep down. I also knew it would chip away a little of the perfect world I was starting to hope this was.

'First night.' He gave me what I thought could have been a proud smile and left.

I wanted to cry. One thing that was becoming very clear was that Matt and I had initially gotten together because I was pregnant. He had said it himself in the car on the way home. He had run out on me the next day.

There was obviously a lot I was missing, and we had clearly made it work due to the fact we had two more, but I couldn't shake the feeling of unintentional entrapment.

I didn't stay in the bath for much longer. After that revelation, I couldn't relax. Over the railing by the sink, I found white shorts and a vest top with tiny flowers dotted over them. Whatever was going on, he was sweet and attentive, and it was just what I needed.

I got dressed and stood in front of the mirror. It was time to go to bed, and I was petrified. My mouth was dry, my hands were shaking, and my breath was coming in short pants.

'Suck it up, you silly cow,' I said, shaking the anxiety out of my shoulders. With one last deep breath, I left the bathroom. I felt a little more at home, barefoot and in pyjamas.

The bedroom door was open, and my heart fluttered, making my breath hitch. Trailing my hand across the wall for stability and grounding, I walked in to find Matt leaning over the bed, wearing nothing but a pair of dark blue pyjama bottoms. It did nothing to ease my nerves. I wasn't sure if I wanted to jump him or run from him.

He turned, holding a pillow at his side when he heard me enter, and I was presented with the most luxurious thing I had seen in this house. His broad, tanned shoulders fed into rippling muscles down his chest and onto a toned stomach.

As devastatingly delicious as that would all be on its own, there was a softness to the overall effect. It made me feel like if I fell into him, I wouldn't just be hitting a solid boulder, but something I could mould myself into. Something comforting.

My cheeks flushed, and my blood was pumping so fast past my ears that I couldn't hear if I was even breathing. I thought about stepping forwards, but I was acutely aware that I couldn't feel my legs. I couldn't feel anything. Well, that wasn't precisely true. There was a throbbing between my legs, which was the cause of every anxious reaction my body was going through.

'I don't want to make you feel uncomfortable. We clearly have more than one bedroom in this house. I'm happy to sleep somewhere else, if it would make you feel more at ease.'

The coward in me wanted to agree, but I wanted my life back, and to do that, I needed to let go and embrace it. 'No. I'm fine.' I lied.

His face lit up, and he exhaled what looked like relief. 'Okay.'

With a little nervous bounce, I headed over to the other side of the bed, my eye catching on the family photo. 'Right then, to bed, we go.'

He laughed at me, but I could tell he was as nervous as I was. We both slipped under the duvet, and with just the addition of a blanket, our dynamic changed again. I felt my body pull towards him, but I held back. We were lying on our sides with about half a metre of empty space between us. I didn't know where to look, or what to do with my hands. Everything was just so confusing.

'We were so happy.' His whispered words crossed the divide, but they seemed to increase the distance between us, and I saw the gaping hole that existed between his world and mine.

Nervously, my hand reached over the chasm, needing to see that a physical connection could exist between the worlds. When my fingers brushed lightly through his hair, a searing pain coursed through my chest that was both excruciating and exhilarating.

He melted into my touch, and all my anxiety and panic slipped away. All I could feel, all I could see was him.

'I really had loved you, hadn't I?' My eyes were already closed by the time I finished the sentence, and I wasn't awake long enough to hear if he replied.

Chapter Ten

I awoke the next day to a strange sensation. Something small and soft was poking me in the face. My eyelids were heavy, and as I tried to prise them open, I heard a little voice say, 'Mummy, are you awake?' That did it. My eyes shot open, and I was suddenly more awake than I had ever been before.

We just stared at each other, but he looked a little scared. I must have startled him with how quickly I opened my eyes.

'Hi Jack,' I said, not lifting my head from the pillow. He was leaning over the bed on his elbows, and at this angle, we were face to face. Mere centimetres separated us. A smile spread over his face, and my heart thumped. He had his father's smile, cobalt blue eyes, and blond hair, that looked almost white against the morning sun cascading through the window.

'Are you still poorly?' he whispered.

'Only a little bit,' I whispered back, choking on the emotion. 'But nothing a hug couldn't fix.' His smile broadened further, and he launched onto me, arms stretched. I pulled him in tightly and forced myself not to cry and scare him. He smelt of lavender and coconut, and the scent's familiarity relaxed me enough to make sure I kept breathing.

'There you are,' Matt said, breathlessly running into the room. He was wearing the same pyjama bottoms as the night before, with the addition of a red hoodie that matched the colour of the circles around his eyes. 'I'm sorry. There's more of them than I have arms, and this one got away from me.' Matt made no attempt to move. He looked like he didn't know how he was meant to react.

'I'm making Mummy better,' Jack announced and squeezed me harder. I nodded to Matt agreeing with Jack. Both mine and Matt's eyes filled with tears, and a lump formed in my throat, threatening to choke me.

'Mummy!' another little voice hollered, coming in behind Matt. Before I could take in more than a bouncing pair of pigtails, she saw Jack hugging me and launched herself into the mix. I wanted to look at them, examine their faces, but I couldn't let go.

Isabella was covering my right side and Jack my left, so I failed to hear the last little voice in the house come into the room, but I felt him clambering over his siblings to get to me.

Matt came around to his side of the bed and lifted Dylan off so I could sit up. Oblivious to the fact that they were being looked at by their mother for the first time, they sat back and smiled at me.

I examined each of them in turn as they told me about what they had been up to at granny's and grandad's. Dylan wasn't as eloquent, but he got his ten pence in with the occasional shout about the fair, floss, and sticky apples. I was mesmerised by them.

Jack was Matt's, there was absolutely no doubt about that. He was his mini doppelgänger. Isabella was a little darker in skin tone and hair. She was more like me, and I could see a little of my brother in her when she rolled her eyes at something Jack said. Up close, Dylan looked like neither of us. His face was rounder than his siblings, and although he had green eyes like mine, his were as bright as two little emeralds.

'Coffee?' Matt asked.

'Please,' I responded appreciatively. 'And, thank you.'

'For what?' he asked, looking a little confused.

I looked to the chattering kids scrambling around over my legs and back at him with a watery smile.

'Best gifts I've ever received or given,' he said, and I expected him to lean over and kiss me, but for the first time since I had known who he was, he didn't. Just rose from the bed and addressed the kids. 'Come on, you little bunch of misfits.' Isabella and Jack giggled at the insult. Matt lifted Dylan by the back of his teddy bear onesie and carried him out of the room, which incited a rupture of laughter from Dylan.

Isabella and Jack dove off the bed to follow, but Jack turned around and said, 'I'm glad you're not in hospital anymore, Mummy.' He had such a serious look on his face, and my heart broke for the little boy. I might not remember carrying him, birthing him, or loving him, but the sheer intensity of what I felt when I looked into his little blue eyes, was all the assurance I needed.

'Thank you, baby,' I said warmly, and with a bounce and a smile, he dashed off after his dad and siblings. I took a second to just sit back and revel in the moment.

Sunlight streamed in from the window to the right, where the curtains had been left open, putting me both half in and half out of the shadow. The room was warm, and the bed had moulded to my shape, holding me in comfort I found hard to leave.

It was only a fraction, but this morning it felt a little more like home.

The sound of giggles coming from downstairs got me up, and I slipped into a fluffy white dressing gown, I presumed was mine, and headed towards the smell of coffee.

When I reached the end of the balcony, instead of walking down the main stairs, I kept going. There were stairs by the kitchen, and my sense of direction told me the top of them would be straight ahead. More pictures of my missing memories adorned the walls, between four doors on each side. I ignored them and kept going. I could see light up ahead.

The corridor opened into a circular landing. To my left was a floor-to-ceiling curved panelled window that looked out over empty green fields beyond the driveway. The passage went on to the right, but I had found the top of the stairs.

When I got halfway down, I could hear Matt's voice coming from the kitchen. I stopped at the sound of a woman's voice. She was not happy with him about something. I thought it might be a call about interviews again. I didn't want to get talked into anything, so I hung back to listen.

'I can't tell her today. She has literally just met her children for the first time. She hasn't even met Charlotte yet.'

There was a slight hesitation, and then in what I thought might be a Scottish accent, the woman said, 'Matt, she deserves to know.'

'I know,' Matt said with a resigned tone. 'I just don't know how she's going to take it.'

'You have till Wednesday to tell her about us, and then I'm coming over to tell her myself. Got it?'

'Yes. Yes. I will tell her.' Matt sighed loudly. 'I've got to go. Things are seriously messed up here.'

'I get that.' The woman's voice softened. 'You know I love you though, right?'

'Yeah. I love you too.'

The room fell silent, and then I heard Matt tap the phone down on the side in the kitchen.

My legs went from under me, and I dropped onto my bum in the middle of the stairs. The mansion that only moments ago seemed massive suddenly felt too small. I rubbed my palms over the carpet's soft pile. All I had wanted was for everything to feel real. I should have been more careful with what I wished for. My marriage had disintegrated, but at least I wouldn't have to be tortured with the good memories.

'Daddy, I'm hungry,' Jack announced, and two other little voices joined in. 'Me too.'

'What would you like? Did Granny give you any breakfast before she dropped you off early?'

'Toast,' Jack said, and I took a deep breath. This was what I wanted and what I was missing. I could pretend for one day, while I got my head around the fact my husband was having an affair.

If things seem too good to be true, they usually are. The facts were; I had fallen pregnant the first time we slept together, and he had tried to run away, but then he got trapped. I sickeningly wondered if Dylan and Charlotte came from me trying to keep him. But, the little things he had said about us all as a family didn't fit with him not wanting to be here. I didn't know what to think anymore.

I wanted to run back to the comfort I had felt in bed and sob out my confusion, but the sounds of the family I longed for walked me down the last few steps.

With all the strength I could muster, I entered the kitchen. Matt greeted me with a smile that didn't quite reach his eyes and a cup of coffee. I took it with a fake smile of my own and went over to see the kids at the table.

'How about a cheese omelette?' he called over, and all three kids shouted back, 'Yes.'

'Freya?'

'Umm, sounds good,' I said, only half turning back to him. I couldn't bring myself to look him in the eye.

From behind, the clinking and clattering of pans produced the smell of food. In front of me, Jack and Isabella chatted about people I didn't know, and Dylan sat contently in his highchair playing with bits of Lego.

For a moment, I considered crawling back into the wardrobe with my rucksack to weep like a little girl, but there was a numbing shock settling in watching the children. I was utterly captivated.

There was a plausibility with regards to Matt and me. There had been men in my life before him, but these three little people had come from me. They were part of me, and for some reason, that made them feel more alien.

Jack had a tendency to rake his hands through his hair like Matt did when he was exasperated about something. Isabella scrunched up her face when Jack said something she disagreed with; in that, I saw me. I still couldn't find anything overly familiar in Dylan, until Isabella tickled him, and Dylan burst out laughing. He had my dad's dirty laugh.

'I'm not the cook in the family,' Matt said, placing a half-burnt, misshapen omelette in front of me. Other plates arrived for the kids, and the table fell silent.

'It looks… edible.'

Jack nodded in agreement, and Isabella shrugged. Matt leant over my right shoulder to pass out cutlery, and as he moved back, he whispered in my ear, 'You said that once about something else I presented you with.'

His voice was dripping with innuendo, and when our eyes met, I desperately wanted to see the same look of desire I was so sure I had seen the day before. For a second, it was there, I was sure, but then something changed, and he looked a little forlorn, dropping his eyes to his coffee.

It broke me inside more than I already was, but it gave me hope. Before I found out in the hospital that he had a son, I was fully prepared to do whatever it took to take him from his wife. Wasn't taking him from his mistress an easier task? I choked back a sob and buried my face into my coffee cup.

'What are we doing today?' Jack asked through a mouthful of eggs.

'It's an outside day today. Veggies need sorting, horses and reindeer need mucking out, and that bloody peacock is harassing Cat again, so we need to sort out his pen.'

'Where is Cat?' I asked, looking around the floor. Wisp was asleep by the dining room door, but I couldn't see a cat.

Isabella answered while laughing. 'He moved into the stables when Charlotte came home.'

'Ah,' I said with a knowing smile, but then realised Isabella had explained something I should know.

Matt must have seen the confusion on my face because he said, 'I've told them that things are going to be a bit jumbled for you for a while, so to tell you stuff. See if they can... unjumble everything for you.' A look of desperation followed his words, and a torturous voice in my head pointed out that, with how quickly after the accident his mistress wanted me to be told about them, there was a strong possibility that I already knew about the affair.

He could have been days into a new home with his mistress, the domestic bliss he truly wanted when I had the accident, and he was only here for the kids.

I sighed. My imagination had apparently made me rich, but it had turned into my own personal torture device. The frustration at not being able to remember made me want to scream, but the chattering table reminded me that it wasn't just about me.

The conversation continued between them about outside jobs to be done, but all I could do was sit and listen.

'That reminds me,' Matt said, slipping his hand into his pocket. 'The tooth fairy returned this.' He placed next to my half-eaten plate of food, a cylindrical piece of plastic, about the size of my finger. 'Apparently,' he went on, with a mock seriousness to his voice, 'only teeth go under your pillow.'

I picked up the traitorous blood pressure monitor off the table and looked at Matt in surprise. 'How did you find that?'

He winked, and for a second, I thought he was going to lean in and kiss me on the cheek, but he pulled himself back. Instead, he said without as much humour, 'Not my first day as your husband.'

Hearing him call himself my husband was so reassuring, and just as I was bravely lifting my hand to touch his cheek, the little traitor made something so obvious come to me.

He hadn't been there when I woke up.

When he had come, did seeing me in the hospital make him reconsider leaving? Had it all just been him trying to see if he could make it work?

He'd lasted less than twenty-four hours at home with me before he knew he wanted out. I squeezed the traitor tightly. He wasn't telling me straight away, because the rise in my blood pressure would probably kill me. I choked slightly on a sob and played it off as coffee. What had I done so wrong in such a short time?

'What's that?' Isabella asked, eyeing the traitor. I focused on her with all I had and the hollowness threatening to consume me at the kitchen table, filled enough around the edges to stop me from throwing up.

'It beeps when you all drive your mother crazy.'

Isabella nodded as if she understood, and Jack asked, 'When's Charlotte coming home?'

Both Matt and I started laughing. I may not know personally how bad Charlotte was, but it felt good to be part of a private family joke.

'Tomorrow,' Matt answered. 'She's staying with Auntie Dawn again tonight.'

Jack nodded, satisfied with that answer, and went back to his eggs.

'Speaking of Dawn,' Matt said to me. 'Your mum was going to come over with them tomorrow. She hasn't seen you since the... revelation and wants to check you're okay, but I managed to buy you a few days.'

All I did was nod, scared my frazzled emotions would expose themselves if I said anything. All I wanted was my mum to wrap me in a hug while I sobbed into her shoulder, and told her that my husband was planning on telling me before the week was out that he was having an affair.

'What day is it?' I asked quietly, hoping my croaky voice didn't betray me.

'It's Sunday,' Matt answered, but Jack and Isabella were assessing me and my 'jumbledness'. All I could do was watch them. There was clearly intelligence in both of them, which made me proud.

'Dylan, get that out of your nose,' Matt chastised. To my left, Dylan had egg hanging out of his mouth and a green piece of Lego up his nose. I had to smile. It was nice to see his goofy side. Matt leant around me and plucked the Lego from his nose. His body resting against my left side filled me with a warmth, I wasn't sure I could live without. I tensed defensively and moved back, ceasing contact. Matt glanced at me without turning his head, and I lowered my eyes.

I focused on Dylan and how he was happily chomping on his food. I knew I was living a lie, but it was built on a foundation of self-preservation. There was only so much one person could take.

'Finished?' Matt asked, gathering up the plates. I nodded and looked into my mug.

'Good morning,' a loud male voice boomed from the dining room. I jumped and with wide eyes, looked towards the door.

'Alexxxxxx,' Jack bellowed in return. Both he and Isabella darted out from the other side of the table to greet a broad, dark-haired man in his late twenties. He towered well over six foot, as he appeared in the doorway. I was just taking in this new person, who could rival Matt in size, when pained sounds coming from Dylan to my left made me look to him instead. He was struggling against the harness in the chair.

I reached over, and he stopped fidgeting. It took me a few seconds to figure out the clasp, but when it was undone, and Dylan

94

lifted his arms to me, I felt love like nothing I had ever felt before. I picked him up, and he wrapped his arms around my neck, slapping an eggy kiss on my cheek.

'Alexxx,' he said, copying his brother and stretched out away from me towards him. Isabella and Jack were already clambering for Alex's attention with stories from Granny's, so I put Dylan down and watched him totter over to join the fray.

Isabella put her arm around Dylan, and the three of them followed Alex towards the kitchen island.

'Hi,' I said, not knowing what else to say.

'Mummy, this is Alex, our nanny. Do you remember him?' Isabella asked, looking between us.

'Of course I do,' I lied.

Alex smiled at me knowingly, and Matt passed him a mug of coffee. He took a sip and then declared, 'Right, you eggy bunch, upstairs. Let's get you cleaned up.' Looking between Matt and me, he asked, 'What are you guys up to today?'

Matt answered, 'Outside day.'

Alex nodded and then ushered the kids out through the dining room. For the first time that morning, Matt and I were alone. I hovered by the island while Matt filled the dishwasher.

'Who owns the house?' I blurted out, and Matt stopped what he was doing to look at me with confusion and possibly a little hurt. I let my eyes roam casually around the room. I still couldn't look him in the eye.

'Uhh, we both do.'

I nodded, hoping it looked nonchalant. Turning away from him, I stared out of the window behind the table at the pretty little flowerbeds and grass lawn. I sighed as quietly as I could. It looked like I would be moving out soon.

To the left, the library door caught my eye, but I wasn't ready yet. Before considering the 'work' part, I needed to get my head around my personal life.

'I'm going to go and get dressed,' I announced, and without waiting for a reply, I followed the kids' path out of the room so I wouldn't have to walk past him.

Chapter Eleven

With every step I climbed, I felt a little more pressure push onto my shoulders. Everything had changed so much, and here it was, all about to change again. I walked into the bedroom and was about to fall onto the bed and bury myself under the duvet, when Isabella came barrelling through the door towards me.

'I finished my book,' she said proudly, holding out a tattered copy of *Alice in Wonderland*.

I knew it was giving the game away a little, but I couldn't help asking, 'You read that? The whole thing?'

She nodded enthusiastically and held out her hand, palm up.

'And now you want money?'

'Yes,' she declared proudly. It stood to reason that I would bribe my children to read.

'Did you like it?' I took the book from her, turning it over in my hands. There was no other character out there who I could associate with more than Alice at that moment.

'Yeah.' She tilted her head from side to side as if contemplating what to say next. 'She could have had more fun, though.'

I sat down on the edge of the bed and gestured for Isabella to join me. With a smile, she bounced over, but instead of sitting next to me, she climbed into my lap and buried her head into my hair. 'What would you have done, if you were Alice?' I asked, holding her to me.

She looked up through her lashes, and with a playful glint in her eye that I recognised as my own, she said, 'Go with the flow.' The way she said it, I got the feeling there was a private joke between us that I was missing.

The love I felt for that little girl swarmed me, and to disguise the tears that were building behind my eyes, I said, 'Absolutely.' Then started tickling her. She had a wicked little laugh, and as she squirmed around in my arms, I decided I was going to be okay. I was going to go with the flow. Matt might be able to take himself and the house out of my life, but no one could take her away from me. She was mine!

I let Isabella run back to her siblings, telling her to ask her dad for the money as I wasn't sure where my purse was, which was true, and went into the bathroom to get ready. I stood under a showerhead as wide as I was tall and thought about the little things like my purse, handbag, small personal items. My phone.

Yesterday, I had thought only of Matt and the kids. I wanted to get used to the family life, but as that was about to come crashing down around me, my mind was skimming around, trying to find something else to hang onto.

Up until then, there was one thing I had barely considered; friends. Mum had told me Laura was living in the States and that we were still in contact. I thought about speaking to her, but I could hear the first question I knew she would ask, *'Are you okay?'* Honestly, I had no idea how to answer that question. I wouldn't even know where to start. She would want me to explain, lay it all out for her, but I couldn't even do that for myself yet.

I stepped into the wardrobe, still thinking about Laura and the simple life we led before, and caught sight of row upon row of material happiness. It was like therapy on hangers.

'Well, hello,' I said as I ran my hand over the different materials. I considered trying them all on, hoping they would return to me, the memory of the last time I wore them.

My eye caught on something green, and when I pulled it out a little, I saw it was the organza dress from the picture in the dining room of Matt and me attending the *Doomed* premiere. I caressed the little tapestry of flowers, but nothing came to me. Although, it did make me think of the black suit Matt had worn. I turned around, unable to stop myself from looking for it. I wanted to put my dress next to it, to put them back together, but lined up on Matt's side were ten black suits, and I couldn't find the right one.

'Looks like I had it right to begin with.' I stroked my hand down the length of a pinstriped jacket. 'He ain't yours, sweetheart.'

At the end of the room, in front of my shoe collection, was a flat dark blue sofa. I let the jacket go and went to sit on it. My head fell into my hands. I didn't know if I wanted to cry, scream, laugh, or even jump for joy.

The utter contradiction of emotions was almost paralysing. My breath quickened, and I was thankful that the little traitor was still on the kitchen table.

The problem was; every emotion was too high. On one side of the scale, the joy for the children was the most wonderful, exciting feeling I had ever experienced. Below them was my career. I was a successful, published author. The house was a dream come true, and apparently, money wasn't in short supply.

Then there was the other side of the scale. Sat upon the gold plate, suspended from a chain, were only two things. One of them was so heavy that it could almost hold its own against the other side of the scale with ease.

My husband was having an affair, and what seemed to make it worse, was he was ready to tell me about it. Which meant he was ready to leave me. He didn't love me. I had so little certainty in my life, but sickeningly that was one I did have.

My arms wrapped around my waist, and I bent over, trying to steady my breathing. So many realisations about what life would become came at me. I would not give up my children for anything, but because of them, Matt would always be in my life. I would have a front-row seat to him and the woman he loved, walking off with my children every other weekend. I had only yesterday placed myself in the 'mother' slot of the family picture, and I was already being replaced by someone else.

I half laughed and half sobbed. My head throbbed, and I wanted it to explode. Everything needed to stop. I couldn't take any more.

My knees slipped forward. Even sitting, my legs were unable to hold my weight. Through my rasped breathing, ringing out loudly from another room, I heard, 'Muuummmm.'

Enough warmth filled me, that I was able to pull myself away from my descent towards the floor. I wiped my eyes, took a deep breath, and stood up.

With the sound of that word, something obliterated my scales. I was losing my husband, but *my* children were about to lose their dad. I didn't remember family life, but they did. I needed to be strong for them. I was not alone; this loss was not only mine.

Opening the first drawer my hand found, I saw underwear. I did the same again and found jeans.

'Muuuummmm!' It came again closer and a little more urgent this time.

'In here,' I called out. Slipping on a pair of casual brown ankle boots, I stood up and looked at myself in the mirror. I wished I hadn't. Pulling my hair into an untidy ponytail, unfortunately, only highlighted the red dominating my eyes. After locating and applying a little concealer, I pinched my cheeks, trying to draw out a bit of colour, but I still looked awful. I wondered when the time would come when I didn't want to cry.

'Mum?' Jack said, bursting into the room. I couldn't help smiling. His cheerful enthusiasm was contagious.

'Yes.'

'Where's my blue jumper?' he asked, running over to the sofa and throwing himself across it to kick his legs in the air like a turtle.

'I have absolutely no idea,' I said honestly. 'Go ask your father.'

'Okay.' Leaping from the sofa, he darted from the room.

'Jack?' I called out after him. He reappeared in the doorway. 'I love you.'

He lifted his palms upwards and, with a shrug, said, 'Obviously.' Then ran off again. The smile that spread over my face practically closed my eyes. That little boy was all the medicine I needed.

Without looking back at the mirror, I left the room and headed downstairs. Silence greeted me in the kitchen and living room. Even Wisp was nowhere to be seen. In search of the little voices I needed to hear, I went back through the dining room, ignoring the array of family photos.

At the other end of the room was an open set of double doors that displayed a dimly lit corridor. The only light was coming from a room to my right, and when I stepped inside, I was presented with another living room.

This one was slightly smaller, cosier, and more informal than the other. Plump, slate grey L-shaped sofas encircled the room. Toys littered the floor and cheap holiday souvenirs sat next to homemade picture frames on the mantlepiece. The fireplace rivalled the one in the other living room in size, but whereas that one's pristine white tiles had never seen a flame, this one had blackened bricks giving off wafts of burnt charcoal. Wood piled high at its edges, ready for the colder nights, and close by, in front of an ornate fireguard, were little beanbags. I pictured the kids tucked up in them on a winter's night, watching TV, while Matt and I were snuggled into the corner of one of the sofas.

In my bleakest of moments, I'd found the bloody 'family' room.

My palms pressed into my chest, willing my heart to stay where it was. Reminding myself that it would only be Matt that was removed from that image, I kept the agony at bay. Watching him slip out of the perfect family image was painful, but I had to focus on the kids.

I was about to leave, but the TV in the corner caught my attention. I needed a break from overthinking, and I was intrigued about what had happened over the last seven years that had nothing to do with me.

I found the remote control on the oak coffee table, littered with colouring books and half-empty glasses of water. Sitting down on the edge of the sofa, I pressed the 'on' button. The TV guide came up, and I selected a News channel.

First, I got to hear about a war that threatened world war III, that people were dying due to a severe drought in one part of the world, and others were dying from flooding in another. The British government was a shambles, and then right at the end, the good news story was that I had left the hospital. The video showed me walking out and Matt passing me the pink roses.

Reality settled in a little further. Seeing myself on the TV with Matt seemed to solidify me further into his world, in the world as a whole, and everything hurt just a little more.

Next, I pressed the search button and typed in Freya Lord. I was taking Isabella's advice and heading down the rabbit hole. A longer list than I expected appeared, which was a little unsettling. I clicked on the top listing, dated 2016. A light-hearted, 'make fun of your guests' talk show. I prayed to every God I could think of not to see myself do something embarrassing.

I fast-forwarded through the credits and introductions, and then on a black sofa, I had seen many celebrities sitting upon, there was me. I shook my head in utter disbelief and pressed play.

'Now Freya, you weren't even meant to be in the show, is that right?' the host, a short, stumpy man wearing brightly coloured glasses asked. I thought his name was Michael, but I couldn't remember his last name.

'I was contracted for five minutes, but no, I was essentially just meant to be the ghostwriter travelling with Craig to document it for the book.'

Hearing my voice through the TV was so eerie. I was wearing a triangular-shaped black dress held up with a thick golden metal ring around my neck. There was a lightly tanned glow to my skin, and my hair was still blonde and tied back in a tight bun.

'I think you're actually in it more than me.'

My mouth fell open. I'd been so narcissistically focused on myself that I hadn't noticed the Scottish actor, Craig Mack, sitting next to me. He had light brown hair with tones of gold and a face that made teenagers to OAPs swoon. One of his shows was massive; It was about a Scottish man who moved to Australia. Even I had watched it.

'I think everyone could agree,' the host said, spreading his arms out to us while slightly chuckling, 'you two are hilarious together.'

The screen changed to the sound of the audience laughing, to show Craig and me standing somewhere high. I could see mountain peaks in the background, and we were on some kind of manmade enclosed ledge. I was wearing a harness and leaning back against a barrier, just in the shadows.

Craig was standing close to the edge, with a bungee rope connected to him, talking to the operator. He was rattling out question after question, and after each was answered, he would move closer to the edge, but every time he looked over, another question came to him, and he would turn and pick up the conversation.

The screen went black, and the words, 'FIVE MINUTES LATER' came up in white writing.

The image shifted back, and Craig was still ploughing through the questions, but he was standing full-on, looking out with the operator leaning against the railing at the end.

With what appeared to be absolutely no hesitation, I walked forward, and as my palm lightly pushed into Craig's back, I sighed out of exasperation. 'Oh, for the love of God, jump.'

Craig tumbled over the edge with a jerk and screamed. I turned back to the camera with a look of mischievous happiness on my face. While giggling, I said to the cameraman. 'We need to get out of here, now.'

The studio and the black sofa came back into view, and I was sheepishly trying not to laugh. Craig was looking at me with a mixture of hate and admiration. The host was wiping laughter tears from his eyes.

'So, I'm guessing that's when production moved to include you more,' The host squeezed out through more laughter.

I nodded solemnly, and in what appeared to be an attempt at justification, I said, 'I was so jealous that I couldn't jump.'

The host nodded knowingly. 'As fun as it was, it wasn't all plain sailing for you, with you being pregnant and all, was it?'

Both Craig and I agreed, and the screen changed again, showing a city centre. It was raining and grey, and by the looks of all the people wrapped in scarves and hats, it was bitterly cold.

Craig was standing next to a female fan, posing for a picture. I recognised something about the back of the person holding the camera. Even though I had never seen myself from behind before, I knew it was me.

After I took the photo, the woman hugged playfully into Craig and then came to me, arms outstretched, like I was a marvel she couldn't quite fathom. 'You are seriously the luckiest woman in the world,' she said with her hands moving in to clasp over her chest.

I said something I couldn't hear and then turned to walk back toward the camera.

'Do you think you're the luckiest woman in the world?' the cameraman asked, humour lacing his voice.

I looked deadpan at him. My scarf was wrapped tightly around my neck, and I was wearing a puffed up waterproof jacket that made me look like a ginormous, burnt marshmallow. 'I'm about to go throw up in a public toilet in the centre of Glasgow. What do you think?' I walked away to him chuckling.

The studio reappeared to a roar of laughter from the audience, and me saying, 'That was not a good day.'

The host tilted his head towards me sympathetically, then asked, 'Had you two met before you went running off around the Highlands together?'

'No,' Craig said. 'I got a call one day to say everything was up and running. They gave me all the dates and stuff, and then at the end of the call, they said, oh, and by the way, the ghostwriter is Freya Patrick, Matt Lord's girlfriend. Matt Lord's pregnant girlfriend. Just thought you should know.'

The audience chuckled, and I joined in to be polite.

'That had to be a bit daunting. Was it?'

I answered for Craig before he could say anything. 'No, it wasn't, was it?' It was all light-hearted, but I did seem genuinely curious.

Craig smiled and cocked his head from side to side before admitting, 'Yeah, well, yeah, it was, a bit.'

I didn't seem convinced. 'Really? Why?'

Craig scrunched his face up to me. He was intimidating to look at, but there was something friendly in our interaction. Comfortable. 'Well, to start, one badly timed photo, and I was never working again.' He answered while laughing, but there was a slight hint of seriousness there.

'And secondly, Matt looking like this,' the host said, jumping in. The screen before me filled with an image of Matt. It had been taken from a film he was in that I remembered. It was a story about some heavyweight boxer. There was a deep cut above his right eye, and he was standing, fists raised, wearing royal blue shorts in the middle of a ring that he was making look small.

'Yeah, and there's that,' Craig jokingly agreed when the screen returned to us.

'How did Matt react when you told him you were heading off around the Highlands with this one?' the host teased, and both Craig and I laughed.

'Quite comically,' I started, then rested my hands across my massive belly. It was then I noticed it. I couldn't believe I hadn't seen it before.

I felt the desperate pang to remember what that felt like. I recalled the date on the TV listing. It had to be Isabella and Jack.

'When I got the call asking if I'd be interested, Matt was in LA filming *Placid*.' I stopped and smiled with a raised eyebrow towards the audience.

Everyone laughed.

It was so weird to be on the outside of a joke that I had made. 'We were on a video call when I was telling him all about it, and when I finished, he just sat there, and I knew he could see what was behind him on the split-screen. He didn't have a leg to stand on. I started to smile wickedly, and Matt just sighed and said, "Yes, I can see them." Behind him, there were like twenty women scattered around a pool on the set, and only half of them were wearing the full bikini.'

More laughter, and then the host said in jest, 'Craig, did you get a little warning before you left?'

'No.' Craig laughed. 'But, I did get a call off Matt the night before we left.'

The host gasped with a little chuckle, and I sat back, looking surprised.

'He called you?' My voice was slightly higher than it had been, but I was still smiling.

Craig nodded and laughed at my ignorance, but then his expression turned a little more serious. 'No. It was all good. He just wanted to point out that I was literally taking his entire world off into the wilderness, and wanted to kindly ask me to look after you all.'

Everyone, including me, said, 'Ahhhh.'

'He ended the call by saying, "Whatever you do, don't let her near a bookshop."'

Everyone erupted into laughter, and I sat there looking smug.

'That was advice you did not heed,' the host mocked. 'I have to say, that is one of my favourite parts, when you, Freya, come across that carpark with a young lad trailing behind you, wheeling that cart full of books. You looked so happy.'

'Seven hours we lost her for in that book warehouse,' Craig interjected, looking pained.

I shook my head and tutted. 'Craig, you were warned.'

'On that call, I also told him that if he touched you, I'd beat the shit out of him,' Matt included from behind me.

Tears were running down my face, and I didn't want to turn around and let him see my pain. I was once something he had cherished, and I just got to see first-hand, exactly how happy that had made me. I wanted to ask him where it all went wrong, but like a junkie, I wasn't prepared to voice that I knew there was a problem.

I stood up and tried to discreetly wipe my eyes while turning off the TV. 'Where are the kids?' I asked, coming around the other side of the sofa, away from him, to get to the door.

'In the garden, waiting for you,' he said with a sullen edge to his voice. I reached the door, but that junkie in me wanted more. The clear argument made in my head was that if there was no problem, why should I not indulge?

Before reason and self-preservation could voice their opinion, I turned around, lightly pushed my body against his, and kissed him. My hands instantly found their way into his hair as our lips moved gently together. It all felt so familiar.

Relief washed over me when he returned the kiss, but his body was tense, and his hands remained at his side. When I deepened the kiss, needing more, he lifted his hands and gently placed them on my waist. I pulled away slightly, but remained within millimetres of him, just to see if he would move away from me.

The desire was so strong it pulled the breath out of my chest, and just when I thought he was going to back away, a pained look crossed his face, and he raised his hands into my hair, pulling me back into the kiss. He relaxed and fell into a motion I knew felt natural to him.

'Uwwwww,' I heard from behind me. Matt broke away with a wistful sigh before looking over my shoulder at the little girl and her disgust in us.

'May I help you?' he asked in a dramatically polite tone. His hands fell away from me, but I tried to hold onto the feel of the kiss.

'Dylan's eating worms,' she announced, and that got my attention.

'What? That's disgusting.' I scooped her up and placed her on my hip, and she curved into me, resting her head against my shoulder. I kissed the top of her head and then looked back at Matt because I had no idea where I was going.

The elation I was feeling vanished when I saw the look on his face. He looked sad. There was no other word for it. His shoulders were slumped, and tears filled his eyes.

'You coming?' I croaked out.

'Yes,' he said, plastering on a fake smile while catching up to us. I let him lead the way and made no comment. I just held Isabella tighter.

Chapter Twelve

After four hours of Matt trying not to make eye contact with me, pulling weeds, mucking out stables, brushing reindeer, and rescuing worms out of Dylan's mouth, we all headed inside.

Shedding jackets and wellies as they went, all three kids and the dog, headed for the main stairs. I followed, and Matt headed off in the opposite direction. When the kids reached the top, they turned left and opened the first door on the right.

'Bloody hell,' I said under my breath. Like the kids' playroom, the bathroom before me was decorated in fantasy worlds from the seas. Finding Nemo was on one wall, the Little Mermaid on another, and Moby Dick was sailing over the top of the washbasins. Even the bath that held centre stage was shaped like a shell.

Isabella ran over to the other side of the room and turned a wheel about the same size as her head. Tiles slid down on the wall to my right, and a cascade of water fell into the shell. The bath was full before the kids had undressed. Jack added the final touch by throwing in a green ball, and an eruption of bubbles covered the top of the water.

I was seriously impressed with myself.

Isabella and Jack scrambled in, but Dylan needed a little help, so I swept him up to the sound of his giggles and plopped him in next to his sister. I spent the next half hour fetching an array of bath toys and encouraging them to wash.

After the room was soaked as much as the children, I bundled them out and wrapped them up in massive white, fluffy towels. They pushed through another door, and we were in their bedroom.

I dressed Dylan in purple jeans and an orange jumper at his request, while Isabella and Jack put on matching cowboy outfits and declared war. By the time we were finished, Alex had walked in. He hesitated for a second, considering something, then said, 'Coming back at 8pm for storytime?'

I nodded, feeling that was the correct response.

Isabella must have picked up on my confusion because while jumping on her bed, she said, 'Alex cooks us dinner on Sundays, and you work.' She seemed utterly unfazed by the whole befuddling situation.

I nodded again and said, 'Okay, well then, off to work I go.' I kissed each of them on the head, smiled thankfully at Alex, and left the room with no intention of working. I wouldn't even know where to start.

Where I did want to start this evening was in the swimming pool. I was yet to even see it.

I walked past the TV room, but I couldn't hear anything. I kept going, hoping the smell of chlorine would lead the way. I passed a couple more doors and a large window seat with a reading nook that looked inviting. To the left, there was a blackened glass door. I pulled on it, but nothing happened. Instinctively, I looked up to the top of the door for a handle, and found a protruding green button. Even I had to go on my tiptoes to reach it.

The door opened, and I stepped into the smell of chlorine and a higher temperature than the rest of the house. The lights were on, which could have been automatic when I pressed the button, but I still called out, 'Matt?'

I kept walking, waiting for a reply, but none came.

At the end of the small passage, it opened up into the largest room I had been in yet. The entire fifty-foot wall to the left of me and in front was glass. To my right, closed sliding doors and what looked to be a changing room at the end. In the centre was a very inviting looking swimming pool.

In my twenties, I once stayed in a private villa with an old boyfriend while on holiday in Greece. I had been really excited that we had a private pool, which meant I could swim naked. When we got there, another villa overlooked ours, and I never had the guts to drop the bikini.

I started to undress where I stood. I was alone, in my own home. I stepped in, and even with everything else going on, it was hard not to be excited about dipping into my own pool for the first time. It was lovely and warm, the perfect temperature.

For a while, I just swam lengths, letting the motion relax me. Then while resting against the side, trying to think of anything other than Matt, he walked in through the sliding doors. By the looks of the sweat covering his t-shirt and his panting breath, I assumed that room was the gym he had told me about.

I was going to call out, but then I saw his earphones and could even hear the blaring music from the other side of the room. He stopped just outside the door, next to a bench. While removing his t-shirt and earphones, he flicked off his trainers and then dropped his shorts.

I couldn't have spoken even if I had wanted to. His body glistened with sweat, and my gaze followed the droplets that glided over his taut muscles. I was fairly sure that what swung happily between his legs was, at one point, my favourite toy. He was right. It did look... edible.

A little embarrassment kicked in at seeing him naked, but I stubbornly reminded myself, that I was actually, legally, the only woman allowed to see him naked.

He turned away from me, and the view continued to be an extremely pleasurable one. He dipped into an open shower by the door, and then, while running his hands through his hair, he walked towards the pool.

When his eyes found me in the water, he was slightly startled, but then a wicked smile lit his face, and the temperature in the pool rose.

'Hi,' I said a little breathlessly.

'Hi.' With his eyes locked on mine, he put his foot into the pool. Then something in his expression changed. The sadness I had seen there before returned. I nearly burst into tears when I realised that the look was probably because he thought he was cheating on his mistress.

I suddenly felt exposed. The nakedness of both him and me, that only moments ago had felt liberating, made me feel vulnerable.

He was waist-deep in the water when a phone rang over by the door. He ignored it and dipped under the water. I wanted to cover myself with my hands and cross my legs, but it was a gesture that would tell him I knew there was a problem, so I stayed where I was, inwardly cringing.

He rose out of the water, and the phone continued to ring. I couldn't resist saying, 'I think somebody really wants to speak to you.'

He looked between me and the phone, and my heart sank, waiting to see who he would choose. With a resigned sigh, he clambered out of the water, wrapping a towel around his waist as he walked to the phone. I silently cried, allowing the pool water to aid me as a disguise.

'Ello,' he casually said, answering the phone. He listened for a while and then looked back at me. There was a look of desperation there, like when he had found me on the roof terrace, ready to make my escape.

'I can't.'

The other person spoke, and I felt intrusive, just bobbing against the side of the pool, listening, but if I got out of the water, I would have to walk past him to get a towel.

'I don't really give a crap if it's in the contract or not. My wife came out of hospital yesterday, for fuck's sake.'

Whoever he was speaking to, it was probably safe to assume it wasn't his 'bit on the side', and where Matt was looking distressed, I was feeling utter relief.

'Oh, for fuck's sake. Let me speak with Frey, and I'll call you back.' He ended the call and looked back at me.

'You off somewhere?' I asked lightly.

He walked back over to the pool, and sitting down on the edge, he dangled his feet in before looking at me. 'I wrapped up with a film last month, but the director wants some re-shoots. It's in LA.' He did seem genuinely distressed about this, but I supposed that was because he didn't want to leave his kids with a woman who didn't know them.

'I've got Alex and the other nanny, Jane, is it? We'll be fine. How long will you be gone?' I tried to make it sound as light as I could, but I was sure there was a little hurt in his expression.

'You really don't mind me going?'

I shrugged. 'I haven't gotten too used to you being around that I'll miss you.' I hadn't meant it to sound so harsh and cutting, but once the words were out, it felt cathartic. He was leaving me after all.

When I saw the effect my words had on him though, I wanted to pull them back and drown them. He had blanched, and with a strained cough, he rose, dropping his eyes back to the water.

'It's uhh… three days.' With that, he left the room without another word. Whether I wanted to admit there was a problem or not, it was refusing to be ignored.

Chapter Thirteen

8pm arrived, and I had not seen Matt since the pool. That was the one thing about living in a mansion; it was easy to stay away from each other. I found the kids in their pyjamas gathered on the giant beanbag in the centre of their room. They were chattering about the horses and something to do with an event. I stood, leaning against the doorframe, watching them.

'What story do you want?' I asked when Dylan spotted me.

They all shouted, 'George,' and Jack jumped off and ran to the bookshelf. He returned with a very worn copy of *George's Marvellous Medicine*.

I climbed in with them, and in one fluid motion, they nestled around me. For a few seconds, I just pulled them in close, soaking in the moment.

'Read, mummy,' Dylan said, prodding at the book.

'Okay.' I kissed him on the top of his head and opened the book. 'You'll have to remind me what part we're at.'

'Grandma burst through the roof,' Jack said as a matter of fact.

They all helped me find the page, and I began. The familiar words tumbled out of me, and as sleep pushed each of them further into me, I felt a sense of peace that I had never felt before.

When I was sure they were all asleep, I slipped off the beanbag, and one by one, I picked them up and tucked them into bed. Dylan was the last, and after he was settled, I crawled onto the bed next to him. He moved in closer to tuck himself in against me, and I just lay there, stroking his hair and basking in the beauty of my youngest son, while he lightly snored. My eyes grew heavier, and I made no attempt to stop them from closing.

When I opened my eyes the next morning, I was greeted with one of the most beautiful sights I had ever seen. Dylan was lying inches from my face on his side, with his hands resting under his cheek, watching me. When he saw my eyes open, a huge smile covered his face. Very quietly, he said, 'Hello.'

'Hello, darling,' I said, kissing his forehead. He giggled, wiggling away.

'I'm hungry.'

'Why are you whispering?' I asked, also whispering.

He shook his head seriously. 'No wake Issy.'

Sitting up, I looked over to the other side of the room, where Isabella and Jack were still fast asleep.

I nodded as if I understood why Isabella shouldn't be woken and scooped him up. 'Let's go find you breakfast, little man.' He kissed my cheek, and the world could go be damned. All I wanted was in this room.

A bolt of excitement hit me. My entire world wasn't here, but today, I was going to get to meet my baby girl. At the same time, the words *'my entire world'* rang through my ears, and I wondered when Matt had stopped seeing us as his.

I left the nursery, thinking about the woman he was leaving us for. The masochist in me again reared her head, desperately wanting to know every excruciating detail about her and the life she was offering my husband that apparently, I couldn't.

'I want eggs,' Dylan said, putting a stop to my self-torturing.

'You, my little angel, can have whatever you want,' I said with a squeeze.

He pulled away, looking at me with wide eyes. 'Chocolate?'

Screw it. He was losing his dad in a few days. If he wanted chocolate for breakfast, then so be it. 'Yes.'

He threw his arms up in the air, and I nearly lost my grip on him. 'Yaayyyy.'

We entered the kitchen to find Matt sitting at the table. He was wearing a loose pair of jogging bottoms and a faded grey hoodie. His eyes were red, and his complexion pale. I'd put easy money on he hadn't slept.

'Morning,' I said as nicely as I could. Lifting his eyes from his mug, he smiled weakly.

'Mummy said I can have chocolate for breakfast,' Dylan announced.

Matt's smile flickered into his eyes, but there was a weariness there. He was clearly smothered in pain. There was still a part of me that wanted to cross the divide between us and do everything I could to try and soothe it away, but anger was starting to work its way in. I didn't want it to be that easy for him.

'Did I hear something about chocolate for breakfast?' Alex boomed, coming into the room. He was far too chipper for seven in the morning. I needed to sit down soon and have a chat/catch up with the man I entrusted with my children, but for now, it was just getting added to the list. I had decided that I needed to trust the decisions I had already made. With that thought, I passed my youngest son over to him.

'Yesss,' Dylan squealed, falling into Alex, who was broad enough to take the impact without flinching.

While they discussed various chocolate breakfast alternatives, I opened the first cupboard my hand found. I was so happy it was full of coffee mugs. I did the same with the drawers and found the spoons. I beamed with pride when I opened another cupboard and found the sugar.

While monitoring Dylan, who was going through the bottom shelf of the fridge, Alex reached over his head to pass me the milk, whispering, 'You don't take sugar.'

Taking the milk, I held the sugar pot out in front of me. This was the first time the past me and the present me had conflicted. I glanced at Matt. Well, maybe that statement wasn't entirely true.

I got the urge to launch the pot at him, but he looked so pathetic sitting there, staring into the garden.

I put the sugar back in the cupboard and picked up the bubbling coffee jug. Pouring myself a mug, I considered it as a weapon. It would have a lot more impact than the sugar bowl.

'Chocolate pancakes,' Dylan said decisively behind me, and I lost the urge to maim his father… in front of him.

I took my coffee over to the table, leaving Alex and Dylan to the pancakes. I was quickly getting used to having help.

'My flight's at one,' Matt said as I sat down a few seats away from him. 'You're going to need this.' He slid something over to me, and when his hand retreated, I saw a phone. I leant back in my seat, trying to get away from it.

'It won't bite.' Matt laughed. It was strained, but it was still nice to hear. Annoyingly, I couldn't help but care for him.

'It's just… It's all on there, isn't it?' I sipped my coffee, but my eyes remained on the phone.

'Everything is either a fingerprint scan or facial recognition. How everything works hasn't overly changed in the last seven years. You don't have access to your social media. You lost those passwords years ago.' He paused, lightly chuckling at something. 'You can get on social media, but it's a dummy account under the name Helena Winkleforth.'

'What do you mean, lost the passwords?'

'They took them off you.' He laughed again, but kept his head down.

'They?'

'Agent, publicist…The police.'

'Why?' My voice and eyebrows rose at the mention of police.

For the first time, he looked at me, and whatever pain had been coursing through him was masked by nostalgic bliss. 'You asked on Twitter what everyone thought about calling a book; she dies at the end.'

'And?' I was failing to see the connection there.

'This was just before the last book in the series came out. You were thinking of future books, but everyone else thought that was what you were going to call the last book in the series. They went absolutely mental, thinking you were going to kill off the main character after everything you had put her through. It was bloody crazy. Scotland Yard had to have meetings to discuss riot plans. We were put into lockdown. Everybody was running around fighting fires, and you were just in the middle of it all, finding the whole debacle hilarious.' He wiped away tears of laughter and, for reasons I couldn't fathom, a voice inside my head declared, '*I love you.*'

As pathetic as it would sound, I wanted to beg him not to leave me, to give me another chance. I wasn't the woman he wanted to leave anymore. I was the woman he had fallen in love with. I sipped my drink, swallowing my tears.

'After that, you were banned from social media. If you want to post something, you have to get it approved.'

He needed to give me more time. It wasn't fair. With every story he shared, I could see that he was remembering a time when he loved me. Was that what was causing him so much pain? Was he questioning his want to leave? Hope nestled into me.

'As scary as the phone is, please just switch it on so I can check in on you and the kids,' he said with a stern tone.

I agreed as Alex and Dylan left the kitchen to go and see if the others wanted pancakes. Apparently, they thought offering chocolate would soothe Isabella's temper at being woken.

'Look, there's something I need to tell you,' Matt blurted out with a sigh while fidgeting in his seat.

My entire body ran cold, and I nearly threw up. Instantly, I understood what was about to happen. He had till Wednesday to tell me, but he was going away for three days. He was out of time. I was out of time. I wasn't prepared for this.

'No more,' I stuttered out. 'I'm meeting Charlotte today. I can't.' My breathing hitched, and his arm slid across the table, but his hand stopped before reaching me.

'It's okay. It's okay,' he said soothingly.

I made direct eye contact while begging, 'Please.'

'It can wait. Everything can wait,' he said pacifyingly, but there was an edge to his words that told me, he wouldn't or even couldn't hold out for much longer.

We both nodded reassuringly at each other, and then with an eruption of garbled chatter, we weren't the only ones at the table.

'Who died?' Isabella asked grumpily from the bench opposite me.

Before I could answer, Jack slid in next to her and said sadly, 'Someone's died?'

'Yeah,' Isabella said through a yawn. 'The last time we got chocolate for breakfast, Misty the pony died.' I couldn't make out if Isabella was not bothered about Misty or anyone else dying or if she was just half asleep. Her hair was practically standing up on end as she slouched over the table, looking like she was about to go back to sleep.

'No one died, sweetheart. I was just feeling irresponsible.'

Jack jumped up and shouted, 'Yay.' He was the opposite of his sister. He was wide awake, fully dressed, and he had even brushed his hair. Isabella was only wearing one slipper.

I lifted my eyes, meeting Matt's contemplative gaze. 'If you want someone to talk to while I'm away, that knows, nearly, as much about you as I do. Go on WhatsApp and send a message to the group called the Witches of Eastwick.'

He rolled his eyes while I laughed. I couldn't really ask any more in front of the children, but I was a little intrigued about people who knew me as well as Matt. Perhaps it would be nice to get another perspective on things.

'What time is my sister bringing Charlotte over?'

'They'll be here in about an hour. I wanted to see her before I left,' he said casually.

A sob tried to erupt from my chest, but I caught it just in time. He was being so flippant about what he had intended to be a final goodbye. That in itself was enough to break my heart.

'Who wants pancakes?' Alex asked, placing a toppling pile in the centre of the table. The kids all shouted, 'Yes,' and Alex went back into the kitchen, returning with plates, cutlery, and a few bowls of fruit, which I was happy to see.

I didn't eat anything, and neither did Matt. We just politely sat there through the kids' dream breakfast while I tried desperately not to fall apart. It kept repeating in my head that he had made his decision. If I hadn't stopped him, he would have told me he was leaving me, right there and then.

The next hour passed in a blur of despair and, 'Mum, where's my....'

I was digging through a pile of clean washing, trying to find Dylan's jeans, when I heard my doorbell for the first time. Moving slowly, I left the kids' bedroom and stood on the balcony staring at the front door. Matt came into view below, and I held my breath.

I heard the same sucking sound as I had the night I first entered, and my sister walked in carrying a baby across her shoulder.

My mind was blank, but my legs moved of their own accord down the stairs. My sister stopped, watching me descend. Matt took the baby from her arms and scanned the room, smiling.

Before I reached the bottom, my sister rushed forwards and wrapped her arms around me. 'We've been so worried about you,' she cried into my shoulder. I hugged her back. I wanted to comfort her, but I needed to get to my baby.

I pulled her away from me with a reassuring smile and then moved with open arms toward Matt. He turned slightly so Charlotte's face was in view. When I was within touching distance, she took one look at me and screamed. I nearly backed away, but even while screaming, she reached for me.

I took her from Matt and held her against me. She started to calm down, and by the time we reached the dining room, she was fast asleep.

'Yeah, she sleeps now.' My sister tutted. Her dark curls were straightened, and wrinkles gathered next to the red circles around her eyes. Matt side-hugged her, which she tiredly fell into. 'Please tell me there's coffee,' she pleaded.

'Yeah, come on,' Matt said, leading the way. I moved slower, wanting a quiet moment to just look at Charlotte's sleeping face. Her cheeks were red and chubby, and her thin lips were blowing bubbles. She had long, dark eyelashes like Dylan and Isabella's nose. She was gorgeous, and she was mine.

I decided not to follow them into the noisy kitchen. Instead, I climbed the stairs and took her to the Hundred Acre Wood.

Chapter Fourteen

'There you are,' Matt whispered, coming into the little room to find me in the rocking armchair, staring lovingly at Charlotte.

'She's beautiful,' I said when he was in my eye-line. He crouched in front of me and rested his hands on my knees, looking at her. I desperately wanted to know what had happened to make him want to leave all this.

With the hand that wasn't cradling our baby, I took his, rubbing my thumb affectionately over his knuckles.

'Are you going to be okay?' he asked apprehensively.

I didn't know if he meant being without him for the next few days or the rest of my life, so I answered in a way that would cover it all. 'Fuck knows, but there's only one way to find out.'

He sighed and squeezed my hand. 'I have to go,' he said, but he didn't move.

'I will miss you,' I said.

His eyes filled with tears that he brushed off with his free arm. Standing up, with one more squeeze of my hand, he let it slip away. Without making eye contact, he leaned in and kissed my temple. I leant into it, savouring the moment. He paused a little longer than any of the other times he had kissed me there, and I couldn't help thinking it was a goodbye.

He kissed Charlotte on the forehead, and with another brush of his hand across his tearing eyes, he left. I watched him go, but then my gaze fell back to the small part of Matt I would always have.

A little while later, cramp and thirst made me place my sleeping baby in her cot. Quietly, I left the room and headed back into the kitchen, feeling a little dazed and extremely overwhelmed.

'Hi.'

Sat on the bench alone was my sister. My breath caught seeing her there. It was the knowing smile and glint in her eye that was disarming. She wasn't looking and speaking to the woman lavishing in the various photo frames around the house. My sister had stepped back in time, and at last, someone was speaking to 'me'. Another piece of the bridge between my lives clicked together, and I slipped into the seat in front of her, soaking up the relief and pleasure of finally being seen.

'Dawn, what the hell is going on?' I rolled back my shoulders, letting go of some of the tension.

'Your head must be fried to shit at the moment,' she said casually, then gulped down what looked and smelt like a mug of espresso.

'I mean, yeah. I... man, this is insane. I get how Matt and I met and how, this.' I waved my arms around the room, and she just watched me like I was a circus entertainer. 'I mean, how the...? What the...?' I gave up and dropped my forehead onto the table. Everything was still feeling so impossible, and I needed something from her that could ground me. The problem was, I didn't know what that was.

I heard her place her cup on the table before asking, 'What would you like first? The what? Or the how?'

I knew she was playing with me, but I lifted my head and answered, 'How, please.'

With a nod, she took a deep breath. I jealously watched her mentally scan the last seven years, looking for my answer. 'You rang me after your second date with Matt. That was the first I'd heard about you and him.'

'What was the second date?' I knew my sister, unless probed, I was going to get the CliffsNotes version.

She rolled her eyes and scoffed. 'He wasn't even there for the first part of it.'

My brow furrowed in confusion, and she laughed.

'A car picked you up and took you to a bookshop, one of the big ones. He had gotten the store to close, allowing only you in. Shop till you drop. You style. All on him. He dared you to try and shock him with the number on the bottom of the receipt. I believe you rose to the challenge.' She stopped to look over at me with pride and humour.

'Matt was pretty impressed with himself for that idea. You were in heaven. What he's not that happy about, is even after marrying him and having four children, you still consider it the best day of your life.'

I thought I was just winding Matt up a bit, but not being able to remember that shopping spree, was making me feel a little queasy.

'Anyway,' she continued with a lovingly gentle smile. 'While some poor shop assistant was shipping all your books home, Matt whisked you to Tuscany for a picnic on a hillside. Matt tells everyone it was your first date. Whereas we all know your first date was a tequila-fueled sex-fest that produced Isabella and Jack.' She scrunched her face and shoulders up in jest, and I returned the gesture. 'The next day, you were head over heels, but absolutely shitting yourself. A little like you are now. You kept saying nothing felt real.'

'Pfft. That I can relate to.'

'When you found out you were pregnant, you went into full-blown panic mode. You and Matt had only been together a couple of months, and you'd convinced yourself that it would all come crashing down, and you were never going to have to deal with the media frenzy that followed Matt. The realisation that you were tied to the celebrity life, well, for life; you didn't cope.'

I took a calming breath, trying not to think too much about it, but I was curious. 'And now? How do I deal with it?'

Her smile grew, and it made me want to hug myself.

'You take it all with a pinch of salt. It's kinda normal for all of us, now. Sometimes we all forget that you and Matt are who you are. Then, there are other times, like when I was known across the world as the prostitute Matt picked up.'

'What?' She wasn't amused, but I was.

'It was outside bloody Sainsbury's on a Sunday afternoon. I was on my way to Dad's sixty-fifth birthday barbeque, and Matt stopped to give me a lift up the road. For the love of God, how many prostitutes do you know who pick up men carrying bright orange plastic bags?'

'I can't say I know enough to make a fair assessment.'

'Very funny,' she quipped. Pushing that moment to a dark space in the back of her mind, she let the wheels of my life spin through her memory, looking for another to select.

'The kids ground you. Most of the time, you all live in your own little bubble, only stepping into the limelight when you have to.'

I ran my hands over my face. I still wasn't used to the fact that I had kids, let alone the fame bit. Also, hearing about dream dates with Matt made me want to throw things around the kitchen. Something about having my big sister there spurred on the child in me who wanted to have a full-blown tantrum.

'What should I know?' I was testing the waters a little. If I knew Matt was having an affair, so did my sister. We were never completely integrated into each other's lives, but we did use each other as a personal vault—Free therapy without judgement. There's something reassuring about a confidant that has to love you unconditionally, no matter what you do.

She stared at me with the big brown eyes I spent my childhood trying to find myself in. We looked nothing alike, and as a child, that had upset me, which probably had more to do with the fact she kept telling me I was adopted than anything else.

Her cogs spun again, and I watched. She'd actually done alright with the ageing. Either that or I was paying for Botox.

'There was a point, just after the TV show you wrote, *Brighter* aired, when something clicked for you. It was like you finally looked around and realised you deserved everything you had. Your books were selling and getting great reviews. Everyone was raving about *Brighter*. Your confidence rose. Not in a cocky way. It was like you dug your heels in, lifted your chin, and put yourself out there. Everything around you is not something someone gave you. You *own* everything because you worked your arse off, and you're good at it. Matt says everything you touch is gold. That's not strictly true. In everything you write, create, it's a representation of you. You are the gold.'

My mouth had to be hanging open.

'Oh yeah, you also walked into a door once, on camera. Absolutely hilarious. You should check that out online.'

'And I needed to know that?'

'Yes. People make a lot of door jokes when they're walking through one with you.'

'I'm glad I'll now know why they are laughing at me. Ta sis.'

She heard my sarcasm but ignored it. 'You are very welcome.'

There's nothing like a sister to build you up and then knock your arse back to the ground.

'What's it like?' she asked, resting her chin on her fist.

'I'm fucking Alice in Wonderland.'

'Trippy.'

'Tell me about it.'

'That reminds me.' She sat up straight and huffed. 'You're currently in the middle of planning your niece's gap year with her.'

'And why don't you look that happy about that?'

126

Her eyebrows raised, and I knew her tone was about to go up a couple of octaves. 'You are obviously going completely over the top, and well, it's a gap year. I wanted her to head off with a sat phone, pepper spray, and a rape whistle.'

I sat back and contently folded my arms. 'Ahh, Dawn, not everyone can have our travelling experiences.'

'We didn't have a sat-phone.'

'We didn't have shit,' I spluttered. The year I spent travelling with my sister was the most carefree and relaxed I had ever been. I was twenty, and her twenty-two, both still living at home with our parents, working office jobs we hated.

One lunchtime, she called me for her daily, 'I hate my job and want to quit rant', and I just said something off the cuff like, 'Go on then. I'll quit as well, and we'll jump on a plane and sod off for a bit.' She replied with a quip of, 'Yeah, okay. I'll stop by the house, grab the passports, and meet you at the airport.' It then went on with us semi-calling each other's bluff, until we found ourselves standing outside Stanstead airport, with nothing more than the suits on our backs. We did though, have a rape whistle and pepper spray, the only items my sister apparently saw fit to grab from home, along with our passports.

'You two have got every minute of the trip planned. There's no room for spontaneity.' She looked disappointed by this, which was a little confusing.

'Seriously? Spontaneity saw us in the middle of the jungle at night, with you off trying to find a guy who was selling a scooter, while I taught English to a little girl whose grandma kept an AK47 on the stove.'

She looked to the table. 'We got the scooter, and grandma shot no one.'

I shuddered. 'I don't remember. Fear has blacked it out. And…' I sat up straight, enthused with the ability to recall times in my life. 'It was spontaneity that put us in that boat… raft. No, let's give it credit. It had inflatable sides; I'll call it a boat. Either way, we nearly died.'

The shiver that ran over her paled her cheeks. 'That wasn't spontaneity; that was blind stupidity. We could clearly see the holes before we got in, but I really wanted to see the monkeys on the island.'

'They weren't the most welcoming of monkeys if I remember right.'

'Monkeys are on Lucy's itinerary. She will be working at a conservation centre with them for a couple of months,' she said with an affectionate smile.

'Yes. It sounds like I have planned a terrible time for her.'

'Yeah, yeah, okay. I suppose it has been nice for you two to re-bond with the planning.'

'What do you mean re-bond? Were Lucy and I not close?'

Dawn sighed, realising that she had let on to something she was hoping to leave hidden in my amnesia. 'Your fame, it had a pretty big impact on Lucy's life. She was thirteen when you essentially became a global superstar. To impress friends and boys, she obviously told people who her aunt was. She learnt the hard way that people will use you to get close to someone famous. She ended up moving schools, actually went to a boarding school, and never told a soul about her connection to you and Matt. Being a typical teenager, she wanted to spend all her time with her friends, and whatever boy was on the scene. She couldn't bring them home, so she distanced herself for a while.'

Tears welled, stinging the backs of my eyes. All I could picture was the little girl I knew, hurt because of me. 'I'm—'

'Don't say sorry.' Dawn leant over the table and took my hands. 'She is a great kid, who is turning into an amazing woman. She just needed time to find herself away from the limelight, and she did. She has a lovely set of friends. A boyfriend, who Lance actually likes, but Matt scares the crap out of him, so he doesn't push to be around you both.' She reached up and wiped away an escaped tear from my cheek. 'She wants to be an actress.'

'What? No. She was going to be a doctor.'

'Yeah, doctor is off the cards. Jack broke his arm a couple of years ago, and Lucy fainted. Matt keeps saying no every time she mentions it, so she's going to have a fight on her hands, don't worry.'

The pain subdued by the trip down memory lane washed back over me, and I didn't have the energy to tell her that Matt probably wouldn't be having a lot to do with my side of the family soon. I also couldn't bring myself to say it out loud. I couldn't make it real.

'You look exhausted,' I said, desperately needing to go and sit in the Hundred Acre Wood and watch my baby sleep. 'Thank you for having Charlotte. I'm okay if you want to go home and get to bed.'

She looked at me a little like a small child looks at Father Christmas. 'That would be lovely.' Before getting up, she hesitated. 'You've got to tell Mum I stayed with you though. I promised I would.'

'Promise.'

She hugged me from behind saying, 'You might not know what the hell is going on, but I promise you, you already know who you are.'

I squeezed her arms to me. 'Thank you. I'll be fine, I promise.' With that, she was gone before I could change my mind and ask her to stay.

Chapter Fifteen

'What do you want?' I pleaded to my nine-month-old baby at 4am the next morning. She had been screaming blue murder since midnight, and no matter how many times I read that bloody baby manual, fed her, changed her, and soothed her, she screamed. Occasionally, Jane, the nanny, who I learnt earlier in the day was there just for Charlotte, came in and took over so I could go scream into a pillow. She was a kind-looking woman in her fifties, who doted on Charlotte and was used to minimal sleep.

Apparently, there wasn't enough money on the planet for Alex to take on all four, and at that moment, I had to agree. I was besotted with my baby. After less than twenty-four hours, I would take a bullet for her, but I desperately wanted to take her back to my sister's.

In an attempt to get *some* rest, I cuddled Charlotte into bed next to me. She fell asleep for precisely ninety minutes. I gave up then and took her down to the kitchen. I needed coffee, and since I had no idea what Charlotte wanted, I felt one of us should have our needs met.

Popping her in the highchair, I set the coffee machine going. While it bubbled, I gave Charlotte a banana. That seemed to do the trick, and while she smushed it into her hair, pyjamas, and table, I drank my coffee in peace. When that one was gone, I gave her another that she seemed thrilled with. She even ate a little of that one.

I was sitting at the table watching her when I spotted the phone. With the whirlwind that was my youngest arriving, I had forgotten all about it. I picked it up and switched it on. It beeped like the little traitor that I had managed to elude for the last couple of days.

'Do you think we should have a look?' I asked Charlotte, and she threw a bit of banana at me. 'Okay then.'

I held it up to my face, and it unlocked. The screensaver was a picture of Matt and me with the kids on a beach. It had to be a recent one because Charlotte was in it, and she couldn't have been more than six months old. It beeped at me a few more times, and I saw it was coming from the little WhatsApp icon. The number was up to one-hundred and forty-two. I had no intention of reading them, that was a little too much for 6am, but I wanted to see if there was anything from Matt.

I clicked the icon and saw the last message in was from him. I opened it, and it said, *Arrived. Call tomorrow your time 8am x.*

I ran my thumb over the kiss. The last message from him, before that one, was from seven days ago. I did the math. It was the day of the accident. I was too tired to stop the tears. It just said, *I love you.*

Sobs raked my chest, which set Charlotte off. Dropping the phone on the table, I picked her up. 'Come on, baby. Mummy's okay. Let's get you in the bath and out of the banana.'

I took her into the bathroom by the wardrobe to avoid waking up the others, and even though my heart was breaking, the sound of her laughing at the bubbles had me crying out of happiness. I was starting to think that Valium wouldn't be a bad idea. Charlotte was too busy with the bubbles to notice my tears.

By the time I dried us off and dressed her, Jane was waiting in the Hundred Acre Wood, ready to take her off me. I handed her over with ease as there was a chorus of three other little voices bellowing 'Mum' from different spots around the house.

I found Jack in his room. Apparently, he was trying to make his bed, but the mattress had fallen on the floor, and he couldn't get it back up. I asked him how it got there, but he just repeated it fell off. I asked no more questions, just picked it up and left him to it.

Isabella was outside the door to the pool, looking a little bedraggled from sleep and demanding entrance. To start, I just stared at her. 'What? You're going swimming alone?'

'No, I have Wisp.'

There was, in fact, a large Mastiff sitting next to her.

'I also have my alarm on,' she said sleepily, holding out her wrist to show me a white band wrapped around it.

'And what does that do?' I wasn't convinced.

With a shrug, she said, 'If I drown, it tells you.'

I raised both eyebrows. My daughter had a very blasé attitude towards death.

'Mumm, please open the door.' She rolled her head around with dramatic exasperation.

'Hang on a minute.' I ran back down the hall, through the dining room, and into the kitchen, where I found Jane feeding Charlotte something orange. It smelt awful. 'Is Isabella allowed to go swimming alone?'

Jane looked up and nodded pleasantly.

'Okay then,' I said, walking back to the pool, regretting letting my sister leave.

When I got there, I pushed the button, and Isabella sighed loudly. 'Finally.' She pushed the door open and padded down the passageway. Wisp followed.

'Umm,' I said to the empty doorway, then forced myself back towards the kitchen. I passed Alex in the dining room. He was on his way to sort out Dylan, who had accidentally flicked a bowl of coco puffs over himself. Charlotte was still content, eating whatever slush Jane was feeding her, and Jack was nowhere to be seen. I assumed he was still trying to make his bed. Grabbing a fresh cup of coffee, I picked up the phone on the way past and headed back to the pool.

I plonked myself into one of the loungers, and Isabella looked excited to see me there. She performed a few perfect dives before swimming the entire length of the pool underwater. It didn't take long to understand why she was allowed in alone. There was also Wisp, sat in the corner on high alert, his eyes following her every move.

I settled into the cushioned lounger and picked up the phone. It rang as soon I looked at it, and I jumped, spilling my coffee, but I didn't care. On the screen was a selfie of Matt and me. He was kissing my cheek, and I was laughing while I tried to hold onto a brown sunhat and take the photo. We looked sun-kissed and happy.

I swiped the call and put it to my ear, holding my breath. It was heart-wrenching.

'Babe. It's a video call.'

I pulled it around in front of me, and there he was. I hated him for being so pretty. Like me, he was sitting on a lounger, but all around him, it was dark apart from the soft glow of the twinkle lights in a tree behind him.

'Hi,' I said weakly.

'Tired?' he asked with a knowing smile, and I laughed.

'Absolutely bloody knackered. There's no reason for it. None!' He joined in laughing. It felt so natural to just chat and joke with him.

'What time is it there?' I asked.

'Midnight. I'm just checking in before heading to bed.'

I nodded, wondering if he would be going to bed alone. The thought of another woman being there with him, made what could only be described as a concrete block seeping with acid, hit the bottom of my stomach. 'Where are you?' I said to disguise the air being pushed out of my body to make room for it.

He smiled warmly, and I shattered.

'Home point three. Want to have a look around?' It had never occurred to me that we owned more than one house. I also really liked that he was happy to show me around what I was hoping was an empty house.

'Yeah, go on then.' It came out scratchy. 'How many houses do we own?' I glanced over the phone to check on Isabella and saw her gliding through the water. 'And when were you going to tell me that our eldest daughter is a fish?'

He raised both eyebrows and shook his head. 'She is water mad, but if you need to get her out of the pool, she is easily bribed with food.'

Standing up, he turned the camera around, and I got a view of a lit outdoor pool surrounded by darkness. 'We have five. There's the one you're in; this one in LA, the vineyard in Tuscany, where we got married, and apartments in New York and Singapore.'

'Fuck,' I said quietly, and for the next twenty minutes, Matt gave me the guided tour of another mansion. It was a lot whiter and didn't have the same personal touches as this house. All I could do was shake my head in disbelief and wonder if I would ever get to go there, or would Matt get that house?

We spoke a bit more about the kids. He told me about his irritations with the re-shoots, and at the end of the call, he said, 'I wish you were here.'

I replied honestly. 'I wish I was there too,' but my nervous anxiety spat out a weird jerky laugh, making it sound like I was sorry I wasn't in LA sunning it up. Looking crestfallen, he ended the call, and the concrete block exploded, saturating me with acid. Any hope I had that he was thinking about staying with me, slipped away with that look.

Chapter Sixteen

The time had come. All the children were asleep, and I had to go in there at some point. So, with a large glass of wine in my hand, I turned the brass knob on the library door. Before it was fully open, the smell of old books and jasmine escaped. I stepped in, and the lights turned on automatically.

I just stood there smiling. I knew this room. I had no actual memories of being in there, but it was exactly how I always imagined this room would look.

The walls were covered in books. Next to me, a wooden encased spiral staircase led to the balconies that ran across the centre of the bookshelves. The balcony to my left, ended at the far end of the room, where the window interrupted the shelving. Past that point, access to the higher books was by a sliding ladder.

Moving further into the room, I took a large swig of my wine while peering up and around me. The second floor had been removed, but there was still a door at the top of the stairs. I thought it might come out down the corridor from the stairs to the kitchen. Above, doming over the room, was a blue glass roof that I knew, on a clear night, would give me a view of the Milky Way. It was incredible. Every inch of shelving was crammed with books. Scanning a few titles, I wondered which ones I had bought on my trip around the Highlands and which had been from my second date shopping spree.

Ahead of me, a massive, old-fashioned, dark wooden desk dominated the room. Behind it was a plush deep red sofa and a set of French doors. I shuffled over the parquet flooring in my fluffy slipper boots towards them.

The desk was beautiful, and even though the rest of the house had 'me' stamped all over it, I was yet to see anything so personal as what I saw upon that desk.

It was how the papers were arranged—my handwriting on them. The armchair-style desk chair angled as if someone had just gotten out of it.

There were two picture frames over on the right-hand side. One was of Matt and me attending an event. I was wearing a long glittering red dress with a slit up the one side, and Matt was wearing a navy suit that clung ever so slightly over his shoulders. We were looking at each other, laughing as if we were sharing a private joke. It must have been a good one for me to frame it. The second was of the kids. Charlotte was tiny, and from the way the others didn't seem to know how to hold her, I assumed it was the day we brought her home.

Running my hand over the surface of the desk, I brushed aside a silver pen to reveal a note underneath. In my handwriting, it said, 'Just think pathetic'.

'I'll bear that in mind.'

I was moving away from the desk, towards the only shelves that didn't hold books, when something on the edge of the desk caught my attention. Two highly polished gold plaques shone up at me.

The first read, *C.S. Lewis. The Chronicles of Narnia.*

'You're shitting me,' I said, running my hand over the plaque. 'Fuck.'

The second one read, *Freya Lord. The Occurrences Series.* I stood back and looked upon the desk in awe. This was the first time I became acutely aware that I was invading this woman's life. Neither of us felt like a ghost anymore. I wanted to apologise to her. I hadn't meant to wipe away everything she was.

If the desk wasn't spellbinding enough, what I saw when I turned back to the shelves was. I had won a fair few awards. Two Emmys and the Booker prize were amongst the little gathering.

'Fuck!'

Though they were not front and centre, that position belonged to a humanitarian award from an equality charity, made of glass with silver writing. The sudden rush of emotion drew my hand to my mouth. My chest tightened with so much joy that it was painful. My other arm wrapped around my waist, trying to hold me together.

'I did it,' I whispered through a convulsing sob that forced so much air out of my chest that I had to bend over and put my head between my knees. It also felt incredible to search for a memory and find it.

I was sitting on a bus, one row from the back on the right. I didn't see when a woman and young boy got on the bus, and because they were in the seat at the bottom of the step, lower than I was, I couldn't see them. I could hear them though.

The time had arrived for the mother to shatter the rose-coloured glasses of an innocent childhood. For the next ten minutes, choking back throat tightening sobs, I listened as she told her son, that many people in this world would treat him like a lesser person. At the end of a practised explanation about how the police could not be trusted to protect him, the little boy made one last grasp at holding onto his innocence.

I could still hear that optimistic little voice. 'Don't worry, Mum. When I'm big, I'll move somewhere without racist.' I don't know if it was his innocence getting the word wrong or the sigh of agony I heard from his mum, but something in me snapped.

It was absurd, really. There I was, on my way home, to a smack in the mouth for getting some inconsequential aspect of my first husband's routine wrong, but for that little boy, I would have slashed my way through an army of arseholes just so he could keep those glasses on.

During later writing times, I realised that this anger and desire to rip the world apart was used to form Bastine into the destructive, formidable warrior he was.

Getting up for my stop, I heard the words I knew were coming. 'There is nowhere in the world without racism, darling.'

I couldn't look at them as I passed. She didn't need to see my tears. That wouldn't have been fair. Instead, as I reached the bottom of the bus and the driver nodded politely at me, I looked at him, with what had to be a look of pure derangement, and said, 'Fuck that!'

Getting off that bus, I decided to create a world where not only I could escape the abuse I was living with, but somewhere that existed in the real world, where that little boy could find a place without 'racist'. I also opened the door wide into the world of Rathrin, for anyone else to escape through, should they wish. Over the next five years, I created a race of beings with no concept of racism, discrimination, or sexism, where disabilities were never considered weaknesses.

While I stood sobbing in my library, one of my characters, Penz, came to mind. He had been my favourite character ever to write. He was one of those bubbly, enthusiastic people who you just couldn't help but like. He also only had one arm, which in my world, meant he could channel his power more directly than someone with two. When Penz entered the fight, people actually ran away. I made everyone who would feel vulnerable in the real, evil world, strong… and safe. I wrote it all away, and it had felt so liberating.

I put the award back in its place and wiped my eyes on my sleeve, trying to pull myself together.

The little bubble of escape I created sat in the form of four books on the shelf below, next to four others. I reached for the selection with pride washing through me, and placed my finger on the top of the first book from my series, *The Strangest of Occurrences*. A wave of devastation crashed over me. It was no longer my escape. I had let this cruel, foul world leak through the pages.

I badly needed Bastine and the strength to get through all this, but as his image flickered before me, Bastine brought me only pain. I took my hand away, and my eye caught on two small white plates encased in a glass-fronted box on the shelf below. On the plates, in beautiful blue calligraphy, it said, *From Rome x*

There was something about those plates that I remembered. I downed my wine, hoping I could relax enough for it to come to me.

A song began playing in my mind.

Everyone has that one song that defines love as they see it. Mine was *Italian Plastic* by a band from the 90s called Crowded House. The song was basically about a woman who was won over, not by 'rocks' and flowers, but by sticking up for her, standing by her side, and of course, giving her plates from Rome. To me, it was love on a plate.

There was another inscription on the box that read, *Just in case there were any doubts about how I feel about you. Matt x*

I spun around angrily. 'What did you do?' I demanded of the woman who owned that desk.

I left the room without looking at anything else, heading for bed and oblivion. Thankfully, it was Jane's night with Charlotte. I was still on doctor's orders to rest, and I wasn't arguing this evening. I was exhausted, mentally and physically.

Falling into bed, I pulled Matt's pillow into me and cried. Sleep came and went, and I tossed and turned for most of the night.

Just before lunch, I finally ventured out of the bedroom after getting a series of apology messages from Dawn. Matt knew she hadn't stayed with me. While shuffling sleepily down the hallway, I sent a text to Matt saying the kids were fine and I was smashing the whole solo parenting thing. He didn't need to know I was only just getting out of bed.

Once I was caffeinated, I took Charlotte from Jane, who looked as rested as I did. For the remainder of the day, I ran from child to child to either provide nourishment or pull them out of whatever mess they got themselves into. When I was tucking them into bed, Jack still looked genuinely perplexed when I asked him how the pot of blue paint ended up all over the wall.

While I uncorked a bottle of wine, I glanced at the phone still on the kitchen side and bravely picked it up. There were messages from people I didn't know, but Matt hadn't replied to my earlier text.

I swallowed the hurt with half a glass of wine and then remembered I'd dropped in that I was cracking it as a solo parent and felt a little smug.

Scanning over a few of the other messages, intrigue about the rest of my life found a place in my crowded head. I answered the ones from my family and Laura with quick, *I'm fine. I promise. Talk soon*, messages.

Above the last one from Matt was a message from someone called Con. I didn't want to open it and let them know I had read it, but I could see in the preview, *We're going to get you through this*. Above that one, and the last one in, was from the group chat called the Witches of Eastwick. It said, *Pick me up en route*.

'Okay,' I said to the phone. 'That's tomorrow's conundrum.'

Below Matt's, I saw Amanda's name, and her preview just read, *Call me*.

'Not a chance,' I huffed out and looked to the next. There was one solo message from someone called Billy, which just said, *I will always be here for you x*.

Tears clogged up my throat at the sentiment, and an awful thought came to me. Was Matt not the only one having an affair?

While pouring another glass of wine, which I intended to take outside with my Billy puzzle, the doorbell rang. I moved quickly through the house and stared across the foyer at the door. What was I meant to do? Scampering over to it, I peered through the spyhole, expecting to see an angry looking mistress. As soon as I saw who it was, I pulled back, mouthing to myself, 'What the fuck?' I needed a second look.

Through the spyhole, I could clearly see the singer, Connie. No last name, she was that famous she didn't need one. At over six foot, she was as curvy as a river, with burnt orange wavy hair and eyes to rival Dylan's—with or without the fame, you remembered her.

Next to her—I shook my head in utter disbelief—was Princess Victoria. Cousin to the future king of England, and she was cupping her hands, trying to see through the glass panels running down the side of the door. Even as a peeping Tom, she looked regal with her sleek bobbed blonde hair, and a posture that could have only come out of a finishing school somewhere in the Alps.

'Freya,' Connie called out, then pressed the doorbell again. I couldn't move. I was in utter shock. 'Freya, open the bloody door.'

'Shhh.' The princess shoved Connie. 'You'll wake the children.'

'Hang on.' Connie stepped away from the door and started rummaging through her handbag. 'I've got a key in here somewhere.'

'How have you got a key?' she asked, sounding a little indignant.

'Haha, did you not get given one? Ah, got it.'

'You can't use that,' the princess said, stepping in front of her.

'Yes, I bloody can. She's my best friend, and I've had enough of being shut out. I'm going in. Now get out of my way, woman.' Connie pushed past her, and I was left with no choice other than to open the door.

'Hello,' Connie said softly when I just stood there staring at them.

The princess nudged Connie and said, 'She's not wearing the blood pressure contraption.' Then she smiled. It was a smile I had seen a hundred times on TV. She followed it with, 'You have to breathe, darling,' while swishing her hand back and forth over her chest, as if to show me which way the air should go.

I breathed in. I hadn't realised I'd stopped.

Finally, I said, 'Come in?'

They both walked in graciously but didn't stop in the foyer; they just kept going. Closing the door, I watched them walk into the dining room and turn left towards the kitchen.

I was just standing there, completely dumbstruck, when Connie returned. She walked over to me, bringing with her a cloud of Chanel, and linking her arm through mine, she guided me forwards. When we got to the kitchen, the princess had already set out three glasses and opened a bottle of wine.

I stood like a stranger in my own kitchen, not knowing what the hell to do.

'Pop this on, darling,' the princess said, holding out the little traitor. I took it from her and slipped it on. It beeped, but it didn't go off like the car alarm I knew it could be.

'Have a glass of vino,' Connie suggested. 'See if that shuts it up.'

Doing as I was told, I sat down at my kitchen table and looked up at them. 'So, I'm guessing I know you both.' I didn't know what else to say.

For a couple of seconds, they did nothing. Then the princess burst into tears and bawled into her hands.

'Oh, for fuck's sake.' Connie handed her a hanky.

'I'm sorry. I'm sorry.' She sat down in the seat next to me and poured herself a glass of wine. Connie sat on the edge of the bench on my other side and reached out to take my hand.

'Yes. You know us.'

I don't know what made it come to me, but I recalled the name of the WhatsApp group. 'Are you the Witches of Eastwick?' I couldn't help but laugh.

'Yes! Yes!' The princess seemed a little prouder of that than she should be.

'That git. He told you that, but didn't tell you who we were,' Connie said reproachfully.

'It's all been a bit overwhelming,' I replied in Matt's defence.

The princess patted my forearm gently. 'We are going to give you a minute, okay? Drink your wine.' She gently pushed the glass in my hand towards my mouth. 'And then we can have a chat and catch you up.' She made it sound like they were going to fill me in on last weekend, not the last seven years, but I was thankful for a moment to try and pull myself together.

Gulping down the wine, my eyes darted back and forth between them. Yes, they were both insanely rich and famous, but they were as different as you could get. Connie was from Scotland, a massively successful singer who came from a working-class family. Whereas Princess Victoria was not only cousin to the future king but had married a Swedish prince. When he died, she returned to the UK with a large chunk of the crown jewels. She'd then married an upper-class billionaire. He had also died. Neither of the deaths were suspicious, but the princess was more familiar with procedures around inheritance tax than most.

They were both immaculately but casually dressed. Princess Victoria was wearing a light coloured pair of cotton trousers with a grey cashmere jumper. Connie wore a long floral dress and enough diamonds to account for half of the Tiffany's counter.

I poured myself another glass, and with one more large swig, the beeping stopped.

'Ready?' Connie asked, pouring herself another as well.

'Hit me,' I said, leaning back into the chair, resigned to go with whatever the hell was going on.

It was the princess who began. 'We met first—'

Connie huffed, and the princess stuck her tongue out at her playfully. I shook my head, not bothering to hide my disbelief.

'We met at a gallery opening in London. You were about seven months pregnant with the twins. Matt was stuck in the States due to bad weather, and you came alone. They were serving sushi as canapes, and obviously, you couldn't eat any of it. We bonded over your anger and the hell that comes with pregnancy. Is none of this familiar?' she asked, tucking her hair behind her ear to reveal a ruby earring that wouldn't look out of place among the crown jewels.

'I'm sorry, no.' I shrugged. 'I've got nothing.' I stretched my arms out to show I included the whole house within that statement.

'Alright, then I shall continue. Indignantly, you decided you were going to leave and head to the closest restaurant that served cooked food, and you asked so casually if I would like to join you. From the start, you were very easy to be around. You have a very calming presence. We went to dinner and had some lovely, cooked, food. During the conversation, I accidentally revealed some royal stories, that, should they have hit the papers, there would have been a lot of embarrassed royals hanging their heads for a long time. As I said, you are very easy to converse with. I spent days in a panic, waiting, but nothing came from it. When I called to thank you, I could tell it had not even occurred to you to tell anyone. You hadn't even thought to tell Matt you had dinner with me. You've been a confidante, ally, and dearest friend ever since.'

I smiled warmly at the woman looking at me with so much affection on her face, but my eyebrows were raised so high that my forehead was hurting. I was both befuddled and bemused.

'What do I call you?' I asked, a little rattled.

'Vic in private.' She rubbed my hand soothingly, then downed her glass of wine.

'My turn,' Connie announced and then took a big gulp of wine. I followed suit. 'We're a meme,' she said with a shudder. 'We've won bloody awards.'

'What?' It was the last thing I expected her to say.

'Oh, please show her the video. Please. Please,' Vic begged next to me. I looked expectantly between them both, but Connie shook her head.

'Hang on a minute, let's give her a bit of context.'

Vic lightly grabbed my arm, swinging my attention back to her. 'It's hilarious,' she sniggered.

'Alright, alright.' Connie did not look impressed, and I couldn't help joining in with Vic. It was lovely to laugh and joke with friends, even if they were two of the most intimidating people I had ever met.

'We met on your honeymoon. Well, sort of. You did it all backwards. Matt proposed in Tuscany, and then you had him straight down the aisle at the villa three weeks later. So, you counted that as your honeymoon.'

I inwardly sighed. I really had tried grabbing on tightly to Matt, hadn't I?

'But,' she continued, 'you spent three days in Cannes after the wedding.' She waggled her eyebrows over the rim of her glass. 'Without the twins.

'I knew Matt, a little, and I was already a massive fan of yours. I loved *Brighter*, best TV show ever, and of course, *Occurrences*.'

'Ha!' It slipped out. Connie was a fan of mine. This was ridiculous.

'So, when I saw you both in a bar, I said, hi.' She was smiling so broadly at the memory. I desperately wished I could see what she could.

'You and I clicked in seconds. Totally got the same sense of humour.'

Vic agreed with an 'Umm' next to me.

'Anyway, I learnt that you hadn't had a hen night and decided that needed correcting. You needed very little encouragement. We lost Matt somewhere along the way, but man, can you drink.' She shook her head, and I got the impression she was remembering more than one night. She paled slightly. 'I was not used to it. I'm from Glasgow. We can hold our drink. Anyway, what we should have done at the end of the night, was find a kebab van. What we did, was saunter into a fancy restaurant—It was your fault. You saw scallops on the menu as we were staggering past and dragged me in.'

'I'm going to interject here,' Vic said. 'You tell that part a little differently. What actually happened was you spotted scallops on the menu but were cautious about going in because of how utterly plastered the pair of you were, and it was Connie who said, "I'm Connie, I'll go wherever the hell I want," and then you both skipped in together.'

'Yeah, yeah, ok. Arrogance bit me up the arse about three minutes later.' Connie winced and poured another glass of wine. 'So, we go in, and they are busy as hell. Instantly, some prat gets his phone out, and I can see him videoing us. A photo's one thing, but come on.'

I could feel and hear Vic laughing next to me.

'We're standing there waiting for the waiter to spot us, and I leant on this railing thing, trying to look all composed. You're lightly swaying next to me. Then, the door next to me opened, and just in time, you swung me around, out of the way of a waiter coming out of the kitchen carrying a tray of food.' She stopped for a couple of sips, and then she was ready to go again.

'So, I'm standing there, and I can still see that sodding phone pointing at me, so…' She stopped, and I watched a shiver run up over her.

Vic coughed laughter into her wine glass, making it bubble, and Connie gave her a dirty look before continuing. 'Have you ever seen an old TV show called *Only Fools and Horses*?'

'Yeah,' I said, confused by the sudden shift in the story.

'You ever see the one where Del Boy falls through the bar, and Trigger does that 360 and can't find him?'

Wine erupted from my mouth and nose, and while I choked on wine and laughter, Vic fell to pieces next to me.

'We played it out to a bloody tee, and that prick got it all on camera. Before you—' She stopped to point accusingly at me. 'Moved me, there was a railing behind me that was perfect for leaning on. As I was going down, the waiter came over to show us to a table, and you turned to check I was following and did the 360 when you couldn't find me.'

Even Connie was laughing now. Vic and I were a mess. I couldn't breathe. My stomach physically hurt, and I was close to wetting myself, yet that little traitor on my finger stayed silent.

'You even did the whole jumping bit when I reappeared next to you. When you clicked to what had happened, well.' She waved her hand at me. 'You did that.'

'I'm sorry, I'm sorry,' I croaked out but I couldn't stop.

'I overtook you, following the waiter, trying to hold my head high, but you were doubled over in hysterics. Then, you left me.'

'What?' I asked, still laughing.

'You tried to walk forwards a few times, but then just laughed out, "I can't, I can't," and headed back for the door with me running/staggering behind you.'

'Oh, let me see. Let me see,' I said, reaching my hands out, trying to find a phone. Vic passed me hers. She'd already gotten it ready to watch.

Vic made us rewatch it twice and then me twice more. Connie sat back and sipped her wine. She wanted to be disgruntled, but mine and Vic's amusement was too contagious, and every time we said 'again,' she shook her head with a smile.

For the next hour, the wine flowed, and so did the retellings of the life belonging to the woman who owned the desk. It was hard not to revel in their company. Though I still had moments when I couldn't see past their celebrity, they were speaking to me with such fondness, and I desperately needed that.

We were giggling over Connie telling me that her nickname for Vic was Magpie, because apparently, Vic was on husband number five—another one had died in there as well—and every time she either left or lost one, she always walked away with shiny things. Then Connie looked over to Vic, and what she said next froze the blood in my veins.

'You know I love you though, right?'

My memory was thrown back to standing on the stairs, the first morning home. I stopped breathing, and the traitor beeped manically.

'Frey, hun, what's going on? Calm down,' Connie said cautiously.

'Breathe darling, breathe.'

'It was you.' It was all I could push out. I was staring right at Connie, but I couldn't fit it all together. 'On the phone.'

'Okay,' she said, not catching on to what I was trying to say. What I was trying to say was; you're having an affair with my husband!

I took a deep breath. I needed to get it out. 'You told Matt on the phone the other day that he had to tell me about you.' She looked genuinely confused. I stood up and rubbed my hands over my face. I desperately needed people to stop being so weird.

Connie looked from Vic to me a couple of times and then said, 'Huh?'

Through rasped breaths, I pushed out, 'You said, "You have to tell her about us," and if he didn't do it by Wednesday, you were coming over to tell me yourself. Then you said you loved him.'

Her confusion only lessened a fraction. 'Yeah.' Then something clicked, and her eyebrows lowered back to normal. 'The 'us' I was referring to was not Matt and me. I was talking about Vic and me. He was being all protective and thought you couldn't handle the who we are bit, and yeah.' She shrugged one shoulder. 'He's a pain in the ass, but I guess I love him. It's hard not to when you see how much he loves you.'

And just like that, I went back to not knowing what the hell was going on. Vic stood up and placed her hands on the tops of my arms, her face full of concern.

'Have you been thinking Matt is having an affair?'

'Yes,' I half-shouted, and then it hit me. He wasn't having an affair. He wasn't leaving me. The beeping became just one long, incessant noise.

Connie stood up and spun me around. 'Calm the fuck down,' she demanded. 'If you don't, I'm going to slap you back to normal.'

All the emotion I had been feeling over the last few days crashed over me, and I fell into her arms, sobbing. I felt Vic fold her arms around me from behind, and they both held me while I fell apart.

When there were no more tears or wine left, Connie said, 'Call him. Tell him what you've been thinking. That is one of the annoying things about you two. You mastered that whole communication crap. Talk to him.'

I agreed and walked them to the door with promises to make friends with my phone and keep in touch.

Chapter Seventeen

The clock on the kitchen wall said it was 11pm. A drunken calculation told me it was mid-afternoon in LA. I picked up the phone, and as I had gulped down at least two bottles of wine, I said 'Hi' to it. I pressed call next to Matt's name. It went straight to voicemail.

Everything was swaying a bit too much for me to go to bed. So, I poured a large glass of water, taking it and my phone into the TV room, giggling on the way at the enormity of my home. Curling up on one of the L-shaped sofas in the corner, I felt brave enough to see what Google thought about everything. I was too self-conscious to search for myself, so I typed in Matt's name.

A list appeared, but right at the top was a picture of Matt in jeans and a green jumper, carrying a brown leather holdall out of an airport. Underneath the picture, the caption read, *Matt Lord returns to London.* Below that was the date; today's date.

I clicked on the article, and there were about two hundred words on how he was seen at Heathrow just before lunch. It was speculated that he had been forced to the States for reshoots but was leaving early, to get back to me.

'Don't believe everything you read,' I said, chastising the phone.

I was too drunk to work out the time zones, but he must have gotten on a plane early to get back to London by lunch.

I came out of Google and tried calling again. Straight to voicemail. I was going to leave a message, but the only thing I could think of to say was, 'you prick,' and I didn't think that would get my point across. I also wasn't entirely sure what my point was. I didn't know if I was angry at him, at me, or just about the fact that I never seemed to know what the hell was going on.

He might not be having an affair with Connie, but something was happening. He had been pulling away from me since my first morning home.

'Ah fuck it.' I downed my water and took myself off to bed. I fell into it and was fast asleep in seconds.

I woke up to crashing. Stunned, I sat up quickly, listening. There was another bang. Scrambling out of bed, I was about to run to the kids when I heard laughter. In particular, Matt's laugh. The little traitor was still on my finger, and it was going bat-shit crazy. I pulled it off and threw it on the bed.

I made it down the stairs before Matt was halfway through the foyer. Even with the help of his driver, his sheer size made it hard to steer him down any other path than the one he wanted.

'Ayyy, there she is.' He spread his arms above his head, and the driver needed to grab him around the waist to keep him upright. Matt looked down at the fifty-year-old, never stepped in a gym in his life driver, and said, 'That's my wife, she's cracking it as a solo parent, but shhh, she hasn't got the foggiest idea who I am.' There was so much sadness in his slur.

'Oh, I can assure you sweetheart, I am very aware you are my husband, because I'm the one about to tuck you into bed, then clean up the vomit, that I am fairly positive is coming.'

He chuckled at my answer, and I couldn't help smiling. In what I assumed was an affectionate move, he fell towards me, arms outstretched. He crashed into me, and if it hadn't been for the driver, I would have crumpled. With him, he brought a haze of whiskey fumes that, when added to my earlier wine consumption, made my head spin.

'Okay. Okay,' I said, adjusting him, so he was draped over my shoulder. 'Let's get you to bed.'

He giggled and tried tickling me but missed. I only just caught him. Even though I was being used as scaffolding, it was still a welcome reprieve from the vulnerable cold I'd been living with. His hands were also lacking inhabitation. Slipping around me, they squeezed and ran tenderly down my side. With a soft moan, his head fell into the crook of my neck, and he lazily ran his nose up to my ear, breathing me in. I quivered and nearly dropped him.

'I've got it from here,' I called back to the driver. 'Thank you.'

'Night, Mrs Lord,' he said breathlessly as he left.

I got Matt up the first three steps, and then he slipped, taking me down with him. Apparently, that was hilarious. All the anger I felt earlier was gone. I had no idea where he had been all day, but what I did know, was he had come home to me when it was time to go to bed.

It took about ten minutes to get him up the stairs and at least another five to the bedroom. I dropped him onto the bed, thankful I had put some time in at the gym over the last seven years.

'You're beautiful.' He was perched on his elbows, watching me while I pulled off his boots. 'I rushed back, my wife was alone, but… she's gone. She's off smashing it as a single parent.' He fell back onto the bed. 'My wife doesn't love me anymore.' I could hear him sniff away the tears, and I stood up.

'How do you know she doesn't love you anymore?'

'I *had loved* you. Loved. Past, gone.'

I sighed.

As I drifted to sleep on the first night, that was the last thing I said to him.

It was a relief to understand why he had been so distant, but it hurt to realise I had reinforced his thinking every day since. I remembered how I had pulled away when he was retrieving Lego from Dylan's nose. The sadness I watched smother him when I told him in the pool that I wouldn't miss him, and this afternoon, I told him I was fine as a single parent. My heart broke for him.

He pulled himself further up the bed on his side. As if he was in physical pain, he brought his legs up to his chest and fell asleep, repeating the word, 'loved'.

I sank down next to him, but it wasn't close enough. Crawling across the bed, I folded myself around him. When I pushed my hand under his arm, he lifted it and took my hand, drawing my arm around him. Edging backwards, he shuffled into me, so I firmly pressed against him. Every muscle and brain cell relaxed, and I was asleep before fully registering that I was finally warm.

I woke up the next morning in a cloud of pungent stale alcohol fumes, and Matt, sound asleep exactly where he should be. Even though my husband had gone to sleep tortured, I felt better than I had in days. There were a couple of things I intended to put straight today, and I would need that phone to do so.

Leaving Matt where he was, I found the phone on the living room floor and got to work. In the recent messages, I found some from a woman called Nicola, who in my phone was called 'Nicola Assistant'. I hit call.

She sounded a little jittery when she answered. 'Freya. Mrs Lord. I'm sorry, is everything alright?'

'If I wanted to book a private flight to Italy for this afternoon, would you be the person I would need to speak to? And please, call me Freya.'

'Yes, Freya, I would be,' she said confidently, more relaxed. 'I am the one you call for everything. Anything. Apart from to help you bury a body. For that, you would call Connie.' There was humour there, but I also detected a serious tone.

'Got ya.'

'So am I right in thinking you want to head to the villa?'

I looked up at the massive oil painting covering half of the foyer. I had come up with the idea last night while spread-eagled on the stairs, taking a break from carrying Matt's heavy arse up to bed.

'Yes, you are.'

'And would you like a car with a driver at the airport, or just the car?'

Matt was going to be over the limit for the next week, and I wasn't driving in Italy. I was meant to be keeping my blood pressure down. 'With a driver, please.'

'No problem. Is there anything else I can do?'

'I know there is a lot that I should know, but with this being my first time out of the house, is there anything 101 that I should know.'

She thought about it for a couple of seconds, then said, 'Don't let anyone take any photos when you're with the kids, but autographs are fine. Try not to stay in one place for too long, unless a car can easily get to you and get you out. For example, slumming it with food is all great fun, but with your more upmarket establishments, they are likely to have an exit plan if you get swamped.' I was enjoying her almost flippant attitude. There was an inclination to panic at the craziness of my new reality, but it was actually nice to hear some solid facts, after all the turmoil.

'Big sunglasses and hats are your friends, and no more running around town in scruffy, baggy clothes with no make-up. If you're in public, always assume there is a camera pointing at you. And lastly, for now, ignore any questions thrown at you by the public, press, or paps. Answer with the occasional, 'yes, I'm fine, thank you', but try and keep a low profile.'

I took a long deep breath. 'Okay, got it.'

'Right, I will get everything sorted. Lucy and Kyle will be there shortly to pack. Is there a particular time you would like to fly?'

'About one would be great. Who are Lucy and Kyle?'

'General dogsbodies.'

I laughed out loud. I liked Nicola. 'I don't think you are allowed to use that term anymore,' I playfully chastised.

'No, you can't say it. I can. I'm not the one who pays them.'

'Okay, well, thank you. Can you arrange a dog sitter?'

'Don't you want to take him with you?'

'Umm, yeah, that would be nice.'

'Okay. The car will be there at eleven thirty.'

Ending the call, I went to wake the kids up and tell them they were going on holiday. Jack was thrilled. He was up like a jackrabbit, already packing before Isabella had gotten both eyes open. Dylan, the little sweetie, came tottering over, shouting, 'Ice cream.'

Alex and Jane even seemed happy about it.

I left the kids, telling them to let Daddy sleep, and went downstairs to make a caffeinated breakfast.

Before taking the first sip, two people wandered into the kitchen. I was a little startled, but I assumed they were Lucy and Kyle.

'Ello, Ello,' Lucy said, air kissing me from a few metres away. She was wearing knee-high blue socks and green pumps that matched her baby doll dress. Her hair was in a tight ponytail on top of her head; it looked a little painful.

Kyle bowed like a Japanese fighter but stayed silent. He was shorter than Lucy, with shiny slick-backed hair and a look of the Mediterranean on his skin.

'Hey. Thank you for coming so quickly. Honestly, I wouldn't even know where to start.'

Kyle waved his arm through the air as if saying it was no trouble, then said, 'Qualcuno dorme ancora?'

'Solo Matt. I bambini sono svegli.' I sipped my coffee, then realised what had just happened. Neither Kyle nor Lucy seemed phased that when asked in Italian if anyone was still asleep, I

156

answered that only Matt was. I didn't speak Italian!—Well, I could order a drink.

Nerves and excitement coursed through me, but when I considered saying something else to them in Italian, nothing came to me.

Lucy held out a holdall to me. It matched the one I had seen Matt carrying out of the airport in the picture. 'We will get you all sorted, but if Matt's asleep, can you gather anything you want from your room? You keep a wardrobe at the villa, so usually, only a few things go over with you.' I took the bag from her, and she asked, 'Is there anything in particular that you want to make sure comes with you?'

'No, nothing in particular. Better take the kids.'

'How about Matt?' she joked.

'Yeah, go on then, better had.' Speaking of Matt, it was time to wake him up and tell him what was happening. There were also a few things I wanted to say before we left.

I left them in the kitchen. Lucy was packing up Charlotte's milk, and Kyle was telling her in Italian, to take the sterilising liquid. Jane didn't like the one we could get over there. Climbing the stairs, I thought about Arthur Dent in the *Hitchhiker's Guide to the Galaxy*. A babel fish had been put in his ear so he would automatically understand all languages. When reading the book in my teens, I wondered what that would feel like. The word that came to mind was discombobulated. This whole other person was living inside of me, but I couldn't find her. I did, though, feel like I had just found a breadcrumb.

Matt was still asleep when I entered the bedroom. At some point in the night, he had freed himself from his clothes and was lying on his stomach, with his arms triangled above his head. The duvet was resting in the curve of his back. All coherent thought evaporated.

Needing a second to realign myself, I sat in the armchair in the corner. With the view of the fields and driveway to my right, and Matt asleep in front of me, I quietly blew over my cold coffee. I had awoken with so much conviction, but it was wavering. Finding out he wasn't having an affair had given me hope, but that hope had blinded me from all the other things that had happened.

I was pitting my first-night declaration of 'loved' as the reason he had been pulling away from me. He had felt rejected, and I had responded by being distant and bitchy. It was a relief to feel like I was grasping onto some understanding, but his words from the night before would not get out of my head. *'She's gone.'*

When I thought he was having an affair, I found it hard to miss 'his wife'. As far as I was concerned, she was the one who had messed everything up. The woman I remembered being was the one he fell in love with. I had wanted him to embrace that, but once again, everything had changed.

It was so clear. He had adored the woman I became. He married her, created a family with her, and built a life with her, but he thought she was gone, perhaps never to return.

I looked at the sleeping form of Matt and thought about that bloody cat in the box. I had found everything I ever wanted in that box, but until I woke Matt, I wouldn't know if my marriage was alive or dead.

Being an utter coward, I put the mug on the side and quietly walked around the room, picking up a few bits I wanted to take with me. Just the book a marker told me I was halfway through, my slippers, and a little brown teddy that seemed to soothe Charlotte—occasionally.

I was putting the teddy in the bag, my back to Matt, when I heard him stir. At the sound of him stretching, my heart thumped painfully against my chest. I reached up and placed my hand over it as if I could stop it from jumping out.

'You're leaving.' I couldn't tell if it was a statement or a question, but the misery I heard in his words spun my stomach, and my heart hammered faster.

I turned and saw agonising vulnerability. He was leaning on his arm with his other hand raking through his hair. With a shattering realisation, I knew I wasn't the only one living with the possibility of a dead cat in a box.

'Yes,' I said. I knew I should immediately finish the sentence, but I needed to see his pain. If only for a moment, I needed to see what the thought of me leaving would do to him.

All the air rushed from his lungs, forcing him to sit up. Resting his elbows on his knees, he grasped his hair with both hands and stared down. My chest pulled towards him, and I rushed to say, 'We're all going.'

He looked back at me through red, watery eyes, and I saw the same confusion I had been feeling for the last week. Again, I felt myself being pulled forwards, but I stayed where I was by the cabinet, holding the bag. I had something to say.

'I just spoke Italian,' I announced. Matt raised his eyebrows, his confusion growing. That was probably the last thing he thought I was going to say. 'Kyle spoke to me in Italian, and not only did I understand him, but automatically responded. For the last four days, every time I walked up the back stairs, I stepped to the right on the fourth step. I hadn't even noticed I was doing it. Then last night, when I was slightly intoxicated, I went straight up, and the fourth step creaked. I'd been avoiding it until then and hadn't even realised why.'

He sat up further. Keeping his elbows on his knees, he lowered his hands, and the duvet slipped down a little more. I wanted to pass him a t-shirt, so I could think straight, but I just couldn't bring myself to do it. I shook my shoulders and continued.

'Everything smells familiar. I noticed that when I walked through the front door. Correction, I noticed that in the hospital.

159

That very first night in the family room, you leant over me to adjust my pillows, and I felt my body pull towards you. Whenever I was scared, or the doctor was talking to me, my hand reached out. I thought it was trying to touch something solid, to ground me, but instead, it made me feel alone. I couldn't understand that the desperate loneliness I was feeling was my hands' way of trying to tell my mind something was missing.'

Tear after tear fell from his eyes, and he let them, absorbed in what I was saying. I took a deep breath. I needed to hold it together long enough to make him understand.

'I've thought a lot about when I woke up and found you asleep in the little cot next to my hospital bed. Yes. I will admit,' I said with a small laugh. 'There was this incredible excitement. Of course, there was. Matt fucking Lord was sleeping next to me, and I had a wedding ring that declared him my husband. The teenage girl in me wanted to jump on the bed screaming.' He lightly laughed with me, brushing the tears from his cheeks.

'I wanted desperately to crawl onto that little bed and wrap your arms, your smell around me. I felt so cold and tensed up, and I didn't know a lot, but I knew with absolute certainty that if I got close enough to you, every muscle and even my mind would have relaxed.

'Since then, I have kept wondering about why I felt that. Was it just because, as I said, you were Matt fucking Lord? And well, you're….' I waved my hand up and down in front of him. 'You.' That got me a wink. 'Yesterday, I wondered if I would have felt the same, should a different, hot as hell movie star be lying there.'

'No need to name anyone,' he said quickly. Every inch of my body tingled at the sight of his jealousy.

'I won't,' I laughed. 'It doesn't matter anyway. When I did, there was no excitement. If anything, there was fear because I was picturing a stranger lying in the bed next to me. That's when something so basic occurred to me. Something I had known seconds into meeting you in that family room. You weren't a stranger. I knew you. I know you.' That was the first time I had said it out loud, and no matter what other confusion surrounded me, that was as clear as the window behind me.

I put the bag on the floor and walked to the end of the bed. He went to move, but I put my hand out, stopping him. His expression was expectant, waiting for me to continue.

'I know you are going roll over and get out of bed on my side, instead of taking the easy route on your side. I have no memory of you actually doing it, but I know you are going to.'

Walking around, I sat on my side of the bed, and in an action that felt so natural, I reached out and ran my hand down the side of his face. He closed his eyes and leant in.

The cat was alive, and he was almost purring into my hand.

'I might not remember loving you, but every part of me knows I do.'

His eyes opened, and I saw a lightness I had never seen before.

'I never stopped loving you,' I said slightly louder than a whisper.

All hesitation and restraint left him. His hands found my arms, and he pulled me towards him. Placing his forehead against mine, his breath was coming in short pants.

'I love you,' he exhaled, and his lips found mine. There was no caution or resistance. His hands moved down to my waist, holding me flat against him. Every muscle in my body sighed with relief, filling me with an overwhelming sense of familiarity. The feel of his hands running over every inch of me mirrored the need I had for him, and when his lips moved to my neck, I tilted my head backwards, letting go of all my anxiety and stress.

'Iceeeee creeammmmmmm.'

Lust and passion were throbbing through me, but the sound of my youngest son bellowing those words as he ran excitedly through the bedroom made us both laugh. 'Iceeee

161

creammmmmm,' he shouted again and bounded off towards Charlotte's room. Matt was only minimally impacted by the intrusion. He had stopped kissing me, and his hands had slowed to brush down my arms and back, but he had placed his forehead back against mine, needing to keep the contact as much as I did.

For those ten seconds, nothing needed to be said. Together, we let go of the insecurities that had been crippling us for days, and for the first time in my life, I didn't feel so alone.

Keeping his arms tightly wrapped around my waist, he drew back. His piercing gaze made my skin tingle, and I knew he was searching for her. With a sigh of what sounded like pure relief, he asked, 'So we're going somewhere?'

The smile on my face expanded. 'Italy.'

In the background, Charlotte bellowed, and Alex shouted, 'Dylan, do not do that.'

'You know, for a short time. It was just you and me in this house. It was very quiet.' He didn't look that unhappy about all the noise, but I did wish I could remember when it was just us.

Chapter Eighteen

Leaving the house was a little daunting, and when we passed through the gate, it was very apparent that Matt and I were a long way from being, just the two of us. A swarm of press and paparazzi covered the car, and it suddenly struck me that while I had been in the house feeling like the rest of the world was a distant place, it was actually gathered at my front gate. There were even little tents on the side of the road and News vans covering every available spot down the country lane.

I squeezed Matt's hand, and he rubbed my arm tenderly. Isabella and Jack were sat opposite me, utterly unfazed. Even when photographers banged on the windows, they didn't look up from the multi-coloured tablets they were playing on. Dylan, Charlotte, and Wisp were in a car behind ours with Alex and Jane.

'There's a decoy heading to a place we've stayed at a couple of times in Spain.'

'What?'

Matt laughed at my naivety. 'When we get to the airport, we will get on a flight to Italy as two people who look a lot like us, will go to Spain. The press have been tipped off about Spain. They'll go for a walk occasionally, be seen from a distance, that kind of thing. Then we get peace and quiet for a bit if we decide to head out of the village.'

'Huh.' That was literally all I could think of to say.

'Just relax,' he said, kissing me on the cheek.

We turned onto the motorway, and I didn't need to look back to know we were being followed. The little traitor that Matt had reapplied to my finger beeped, and I tucked my hand into the bag

163

Lucy had given me on the way out of the door. Apparently, it was full of everything that would keep the kids entertained.

I pulled out two pairs of headphones, handing them to Jack and Isabella. Whatever they were playing had a seriously annoying tune, so there was more than one reason I wanted the headphones on them.

'So, some friends popped over last night.'

Matt choked on fresh air. 'Bloody hell Connie.' Once he could breathe again, he said. 'I told her before I left, you said you didn't want to know any more for a while.'

I inwardly wanted to both slap and hug myself. He hadn't been trying to tell me he was leaving me before going to LA. He was trying to tell me my best friends were a princess and a pop star.

'How badly did that thing beep?' he said, nodding towards my hand.

'Oh, when it gets really high, it stops beeping and sounds like a siren.' Remembering the sight of the pair of them trying to get into the house had my chest fluttering again, and I laughed it out. 'There was a bloody princess and, well, Connie, on the doorstep, and she had a bloody key.'

Matt's face softened as he began to see the humour in it, and thankfully, the traitor had gone quiet. All the 'my life' things seemed easier to deal with; I'd found my anchor.

'They're a right bloody pair.' He shook his head in dismay, but there was an affectionate smile on his face. 'They've been on at me since the day of the accident. Neither of them are women used to hearing the word 'no', and I'm telling you now, with regards to Vic, I'm not entirely convinced number four went peacefully in his sleep.'

I recalled my conversation with Nicola and comically wondered if Connie and I had helped Vic move the body. Thinking about Connie reminded me of what she had said about

164

communication. Glancing over at Isabella and Jack, I found them engrossed and paying us no attention.

'I thought you were having an affair.'

'What?' He spun in his seat to fully take me in.

'I heard you on the phone with Connie, that first morning at home.' I didn't need to say anything else. I saw understanding cover his face.

'Sweetheart.' His hands reached into my hair, pulling my forehead to his. I felt his own realisations about my behaviour relax his shoulders. 'I never have, or would I ever.' He stopped to chuckle but kept my head pressed against his. 'You would never, for a moment, ever believe anything different.' He pulled back so I could see in his eyes how serious he was. It was a little chilling to see the certainty in his expression.

'When those two,' he said, nodding towards the kids, 'were about two weeks old, and we were still under the misguided impression that we could do it without a nanny, I had to go over to France. I hated being away, and when I wasn't working, I was sulking in the hotel.' He stopped to lean back in and graze his lips over mine.

'You, my darling, even in a completely sleep-deprived state, left alone with two screaming babies, encouraged me to go have fun. You would have happily swapped with me at that moment, so I think you were trying to live vicariously through me.' I was lapping up every word. He'd fallen into the story like he had on the rooftop of the hospital, and I suddenly didn't feel so desolate about my missing memories. They weren't lost. I had everything backed-up on Matt.

'Reluctantly, I went to a pool party a friend was hosting the next day.' He stopped for another chuckle. 'I even called you from the car on my way, moaning about not wanting to go, and you just said, "Oh, shut up and go get drunk. It might make me hate you a little less."' I got another kiss for that.

'I was a bit tense to start with, but there was a nice crowd, only about thirty people. The whiskey was good, and the sun was out. Just as I sat back in a lounger, this topless woman jumped into my lap, and snap, a camera went off next to me. I immediately got her off me, but by the time I got up, the photographer was gone.' He took a shaky breath. There was something about this story that was making him shiver.

'The woman also disappeared, but I couldn't relax. There was this sickening feeling in the pit of my stomach. I stayed a little longer and then left. I was on the way back to the hotel when my publicist called, and basically, as soon as I answered, he said, "You're fucked." My phone pinged, and I looked at what he had sent me. It was the picture with the caption, *Lord has fun in the sun with topless beauty.* The photo looked awful.

'I hung up on him and called you. Straight to voicemail. I kept calling. For hours, all I got was your answerphone. Only one scenario played out in my head. You'd seen the picture and left me.' He glanced over at the kids before looking back at me and continuing.

'I was on a flight a couple of hours later. It took four hours to get from the hotel to home, and until last week, they were the worst of my life. I was a bloody mess by the time I pulled up. When I saw the house in darkness, I thought that was it, you'd gone. I felt like I was walking through quicksand.' He smiled so affectionately at me that I had to reach out to him. He leaned into the touch before he started talking again. 'I walked into our bedroom, and you were lying star-shaped across the bed with the moon spotlighting you. Hair everywhere and wearing the same clothes I'd left you in four days before.'

'Umm sexy,' I teased.

The look of irrational desire he gave me loosened and then constricted every muscle from my stomach down, and I exhaled loudly.

'Before that moment, I knew you were the love of my life, but seeing you there, I knew I didn't even have a life without you. I stumbled over to the bed, and you stirred. I looked at you with absolute devotion, and you looked back at me with this dazed expression, and in a pained voice, you said, "I want a nanny. Seriously, this is ridiculous; they scream in tandem."' Apparently, he found that absolutely hilarious, but his laugh was intoxicating, and I reluctantly joined in, revelling in seeing a lighter side to Matt.

'I told you about what had happened. You had no idea where your phone even was, and you looked utterly uninterested. Although, you did point out that if I was having an affair, I got those two. Eventually, you looked at the photo, and—' He paused when he saw me dig into my bag and pull out my phone.

I tapped into Google, 'Lord, pool, beauty'. It was the first picture to pop up.

I raised an eyebrow. The photo on its own was pretty damning. Matt was, as he said, on a lounger with a topless blonde straddling him. There was a glass of whiskey in one hand, and he had the other hand on her waist. He was sitting forward towards her with a slightly scrunched up look on his face.

Matt rested his chin on my shoulder and whispered, 'Tell me what you see?'

I looked at it for a second more through eyes that weren't tainted with jealousy. It was there, the real picture. As cruel as it was, I had to laugh, but I told him exactly what I saw. 'You got a smack in the balls, and you're crunching up in pain, trying to move her off you.' I turned my head, so our noses were touching.

'I adore you,' he said, and if the kids hadn't been in the car, I would have stripped and straddled him to a different outcome than the woman in the photo got.

'Mum, I need a wee.'

Chapter Nineteen

We arrived at the airport, but I couldn't have said which one, because we didn't pass through the airport itself. Instead, we drove through barbed wire-topped metal gates and only stopped when we were parked about twenty feet from the steps up to the private plane.

Isabella and Jack were like little rockets heading for the toilet. I got out slower and was greeted by a smart looking woman in a tailored green suit and dark hair tied back in a bun. She smiled, extending her hand. 'Nicola.'

I took her hand and shook it. 'Thank you for arranging this all last minute.'

She knocked the thanks away with her hand and said, 'A couple of weeks ago, I was holding your hair after a messy night out with Connie.'

'Oh god. I'm sorry.' I was a little shocked, but I supposed this was something I needed to get used to.

'It was all good. You held mine a little later, returning the favour.'

I laughed, but she only lightly smiled. She was a quirky character, and I thought she was great. She made me excited about meeting the people I knew were scattered around the edges of my life.

'Right, unless you want me to, I won't be coming with you. Patricia's got everyone running around like blue arse flies trying to monopolise the press attention before the premiere.'

'Who's Patricia?'

'Your agent. There is a reason Matt has been keeping her away from you. She's a Pitbull with a wasp wedged up her arse most of the time.'

'I take it there are more than a few people Matt is keeping away from me.'

She snorted at that. 'The whole fucking world, darling.'

'Huh.' It was slowly turning into my go-to response.

She reached out, placing her hand on my arm. 'Just to give you a bit of perspective. You know about Victoria and Connie, right?'

I nodded.

'Out of the three of you, you are the most famous. Even my nan knows who you are, and she doesn't even know who I am.' With that, she tapped me on the arm and left.

I glided over to the plane, trying to let that sink in. I couldn't decide if the action of climbing the steps onto a private jet helped or hindered me in getting my head around that.

I stepped inside the cream-coloured luxury, and a smartly dressed hostess with dazzling white teeth, passed me a glass of Champagne, which I happily took.

Something about how comfortable the kids looked, sprawled out in this environment, helped me move forwards and take the seat next to Matt, who was already looking more relaxed than I had ever seen.

Just as the plane was taking off, something Nicola said came back to me. I didn't know how else to ask about it other than just say, 'What premiere?'

Matt scanned my hand, and upon seeing the little traitor, he said, 'Have you been delving into Google and your career at all?'

I shook my head. I hadn't liked what I found the last time I visited Google, but then I remembered Matt's statement about my career in the hospital. There was something said about movies, but there had been so much else happening that I had pushed it into a 'to be sorted out later' box and tucked it into the back of my mind.

'The *Occurrences* series, as I'm sure you have gathered, was a massive success.'

I turned to fully face him. 'What kind of success are we talking about here?'

He thought about it for a second. 'Do you remember anything about our conversation before leaving the hospital?'

'Carrots.'

'What?'

'Never mind.' I thought about the hospital, but before I could pull the memory from the fog, Matt gave me a quick recap.

'The last *Occurrences* book came out over three years ago, and it is still the number one bestselling book in most countries. No one has even come close to knocking you from that top spot. The whole series is creeping up to the three-hundred million copies sold mark.'

'What the fuck?!'

Luckily the kids had their headphones on, and Dylan and Charlotte were at the back of the plane with Alex and Jane.

Matt was laughing quite hysterically. 'And that is literally the tip of the iceberg. The two TV series' you wrote could have made your career.'

'Hang on a minute.' Something else came back to me. 'That night in the family room, you said your wife worked in the gaming industry.'

That got me another laugh, but this one came with a playful smirk. 'She does. The *Occurrences* series was adapted into an online game.'

'And that did well?'

'Highest selling online game for the last two years.'

'And the premiere?' My voice was trembling by this point. All over, my body vibrated with emotion that it didn't know how to even start comprehending.

'The second *Occurrences film*. Let's just say the first one went down well.' He stopped to chuckle at what appeared to be an absurd understatement. 'You'd be a billionaire, but—'

I interrupted. 'But then I would have failed.'

He nodded with such a proud glint in his eye. 'You'd have to go some to find a charity that doesn't benefit from your career. I'm a sucker as well, but if you put our wealth together, we're well over the billionaire line.'

'Huh.' I gulped down my anxiety with some Champagne.

'Jack, if you get your head stuck in there, you're screwed till we land.' Internally, I was running around in a blind panic, but I heard Matt speak, and out of instinct, my eyes sought out Jack. He removed his head quickly from the small space between the seats with a cheeky smile and rejoined his sister. I considered crawling in there and having a full-blown panic attack.

Instead, I watched the clouds roll past and applied a bit of grounding and objective distancing. I came from a working-class family. We were never breadline poor, but that was only because of how hard both my mum and dad had worked. They had hated the idea of me being a writer. The uncertainty had scared them. I must admit, I felt a little smug and was gutted I couldn't remember their reactions when the first big cheque came in. I stopped the thought train there and let the hostess fill my glass.

An hour later, a chef in an actual kitchen produced an inflight meal that was better than anything I had ever had in a restaurant. I couldn't wait to stop feeling like a stranger in my own life, but for now, it was exciting experiencing all this luxury for the first time.

The plane landed, and two cars were parked, waiting for us on the tarmac. There was something unnatural in how we all exited the plane and got into them. There was no disorganisation. No one was flustered, and the whole process just felt elegant and practised.

'How far to the villa?' I asked when we turned out of the airport.

'About 40 minutes,' Matt replied while retying Jack's shoelace. 'I was thinking, how about tomorrow night, you and I have a date night?' Over his shoulder, the seductive look in his eyes had me giggling, which seemed to intensify his desire.

'What did you have in mind?' I asked when he sat back and wrapped his hand around my thigh.

He looked past me out of the window, and with a knowing smile, he said, 'I was thinking a candlelit, poolside meal cooked by your favourite chef. Lots of red wine and then maybe a little swim.' He finished by drawing his eyes down to mine, and I could practically see the date play out behind his eyes. My chest fluttered. It sounded perfect, and I was certain I had enjoyed it the other times as well.

'You've basically got a cheat sheet to me, haven't you?' I joked, thinking about the perfect cups of tea and coffee and all the other little things that had shown how well he knew me.

'That I do.' The enticing edge to those words drew my eyes to his. 'Umm, you haven't thought about that cheat sheet, have you?'

I couldn't respond. I was numb all over.

'Imagine all the things I have gathered onto that cheat sheet over seven years.' His eyes held the most intense look of lust I had ever seen, and my mind turned to mush.

I obviously knew we'd had sex and even thought about it. Especially when I saw him in all his naked glory by the pool, but the full extent of what he was pointing out, was a revelation that had me pulsating with anticipation.

Gently kissing the side of my neck, his hand caressed my thigh. Sitting back, he looked rather proud of himself. I couldn't wait to find out why.

I was inwardly jumping around with joy when a thought burst my bubble.

I had lost my cheat sheet on him. This would be the first time with him for me, and I suddenly felt at a disadvantage and completely terrified again.

To calm my nerves, I sank into the seat and gazed out of the window. To my surprise, I knew where we were. When I was twenty-seven, I worked in Florence as an English teacher. I spent most of my time with the other teachers, so my Italian then was limited to 'essential for shopping/drinking'. So that wouldn't have explained my little outburst, but I had gotten to know the city well.

On my days and evenings off, I hopped from bus to bus. Walking around, I ate, took notes for stories, and just enjoyed the atmosphere. There was something about Florence that made me feel at home. Safe.

We turned onto a non-descript road that I couldn't have named, but I knew where it led and what was all around us. I'd been in the little shops and sat at most of the cafés in the sunshine, watching the traffic pass by.

I peeked around Matt to see the Ponte Vecchio flash between the buildings. Then we drove past Amici, the little bar with its big blue sign, where I got my heart broken by Simon Lancaster, a fellow teacher I was dating, before he left to take a job in Thailand.

Crossing the river, memories washed over me. It was an incredible feeling to finally see something I could connect with. We wound up towards Piazza Michelangelo, and I knew to turn again to the right to see Florence sprawled out before me through the lush greenery climbing with us.

'I love seeing how much this place means to you.'

'I love being here with you,' I said, kissing his cheek, then tucked myself under his arm and stared out of the window at the familiarity of the Florentine day-to-day life.

Thirty minutes later, small stone houses and olive groves took over the sprawling Tuscan countryside, and for the first time, I felt only excitement for the unknown ahead of me instead of the consuming fear I had been living with. I couldn't wait to see the house Matt and I had married in.

When the houses became less sporadic, we drove past an idyllic looking piazza adorned with pink flowers and blankets of ivy. In the centre a small fountain decorated with Neptune and a couple of dolphins, played host to a gabble of small children. Even the adults were dipping a toe in to cool off. Scattering the edges were market stalls towering with colour, and the residents gathered under the awnings of the cafes and bars to share a meal and snippets of gossip. It was a place I would be happy to make new memories in.

'This is Torencha,' Matt said. 'Nobody cares about who we are here. We get to be normal.' There was such a relaxed tone in his voice. Sighing with contentment, I placed my head against his chest, listening to the steady beat of his heart while relaxing into his warmth.

'The press don't come here.' He said it with such certainty that I looked up at him, confused. 'The town does not give them a warm welcome. When we bought the house, it came with the vineyard. We only wanted the view and house we got married in.' He chuckled. 'You tried. It was hilarious. Straight into research. How to run a vineyard. Your enthusiasm even got a couple of the locals to offer a bit of advice. Then one day, you walked into the villa looking so chuffed with yourself, declaring, "All sorted." We didn't have to worry about the vineyard anymore. You'd given it away.' He shook his head, lovingly mocking me.

'One of the locals told you his family had always worked at the winery. Most of the town had, but the last owner had brought in cheap labour from Poland that scattered when he sold up. Which gave you the idea to essentially give the vineyard to the people of Torencha. We own the land, but the town works it and takes the revenue. We don't make a penny, but we obviously promote the living hell out of it. I was on board straight away.

174

Personally, I didn't think it was a good idea, you having god-like powers over a place that makes wine.' He blanched a little, reminding me of Connie.

'You're all just a bunch of lightweights,' I huffed.

'The only one that stands a chance of keeping up with you is Princess Perfect.' He stopped for a few seconds but then continued, looking like he had remembered something a little disturbing. 'If Vic ever comes towards you with a bottle of gin, it means she's either getting divorced or planning a funeral. Either way, she's pissed off, and then no one is keeping up with her.'

'Noted,' I giggled.

'Anyway, the vineyard. You were on the phone with our business manager. She wasn't impressed you'd given away a massive asset and was talking to you like you were a bit of an idiot, but you had this ever so slight smirk on your face, and at the end of the call, you just said, "Some of the things you need for a good life can't be bought with money." You ended the call and walked off, calling over your shoulder, "You'll see."'

I had a rough idea of where this was going. I could see my thinking, and Matt had such a look of admiration for me that I actually wanted to swoon.

'Ever since, the people of this town have fiercely protected us. Early on, it was not uncommon to hear that a group of locals had gathered up a bunch of paps and bundled them off, leaving them in the middle of nowhere. They can't stay or eat here. They get stuff thrown at them. It's not a tourist town, so they stick out like a sore thumb.' He brushed the tips of his fingers across my jawline, and my entire body broke out in goosebumps, while I pleasantly shivered.

'You, my darling, with that gesture to the town, bought our family a place where we get to roam around the market on the weekend. The kids can run around the square with the other children without bodyguards. We can eat in the small, family run restaurants, lazily drinking wine with the locals, without a single person giving a crap about who we are.' He laughed fondly at a memory. I was so jealous.

'We get a lift home on the back of a tractor that runs like a bus dropping people off at the end of the night. The driver is the last person at the table to touch their nose. And none, absolutely none of it shows up in the papers. You gave our family a haven, and the town is thriving because of it. Ninety percent of the people are involved with the winery, in some way, whether it be making it or selling it.'

'I can't wait to see it.' There had always been something about the atmospheric Italian charm and culture that I loved. I was glad we had found an island there.

We left the little town behind and descended back into the countryside. The sun was dipping in the sky, and when we turned onto a dirt track, I was presented with an orange and pink sun peeking over the top of a square villa, that was as big as the mansion we had just left behind. The massive oil painting looming over my stairs did not do it justice.

'Wow.' That was all I had. Sprawling out as far as I could see to the left was the vineyard. To the right, meadows of wildflowers and olive trees nestled around the house that stood in front of a lush green landscape of rolling hills. It was everything paradise should be.

Matt perched his head on my shoulder. 'Charlotte was born here.' I beamed and tilted my head into his. 'We took a year out. Both of us. We came out here when you were about four months pregnant and left when she was a couple of months old.' He laughed a little and kissed my temple. 'You cried all the way back to the UK. This is where you and I are going to grow old.'

I was too full of emotion to say anything, so I pulled his arm around me and held him while we drove towards tranquillity.

Chapter Twenty

The entire house had an Italian farmhouse charm. The décor wasn't as whimsically personal as the house in the UK, but other personal touches made it feel like home. The kids' rooms had a familiar layout and style, but instead of the fantasy worlds of the books I loved adorning the playroom walls, they were painted to perfectly replicate the Tuscan countryside beyond the window. Vineyard included.

A large kitchen full of stone and terracotta opened onto a patioed terrace that I recognised from the wedding picture in the dining room. To the right, surrounded by low-cut green grass and flowerbeds, was an inviting pool with an unobstructed view of the mountains. Tucked into the side sat an outdoor kitchen housing a massive clay pizza oven, and a covered outside dining area that I knew would have hosted many wine and food-fuelled evenings.

Before the bags had even been brought in, Isabella, Jack, and Wisp were in the pool, and Dylan was summoning me from the terrace because he couldn't get his shoe off. I took Charlotte from Jane and went out to help him. Bathed in warm Italian air, the last of the tension I had been carrying melted away. It was impossible to feel anything other than peace.

I removed the persistent shoe as Matt appeared next to us, wearing a pair of blue shorts and holding out a bikini for me. The sight of Matt half-naked had me swallowing hard. I cocked my head to the side with what I hoped was an affectionately appreciative smirk and not the look of a deranged sycophant. He just smiled knowingly, seemingly delighted that I was gawking at him, almost daring me to reach out and take what I obviously wanted. My body pulled towards him, and I had to correct my stance to stop myself from stumbling.

Matt wiggled the bikini as if to say it was his turn to do some gawking, and Dylan ran off, shedding his trousers. It looked like I was the only one who hadn't left the UK with a swimming costume on under my clothes.

Passing Charlotte to Matt, I took the bikini. He leant into me, kissing my neck before whispering, 'Don't resist what you feel.' There was a slight desperation to his nervousness. 'I'm not saying jump all over me, unless you want to.' He nipped the base of my throat. 'You are an affectionate person, and when we're together, you're usually touching me. I see you go to reach for me, but you're hesitant. I'm your husband. I am literally the only person you are allowed to touch.'

I rose up and lightly kissed him while reaching around to stroke his perfectly rounded bum. It suddenly seemed ludicrous that my hands hadn't touched every part of him yet. I let my fingers drift over his stomach and then up to his toned chest, feeling goosebumps break out.

'There's a baby in my arms. Go away,' he said in a low, deep whisper.

When I glanced up with a wicked smile of my own, I found a look of excruciating desire. 'You told me to.'

'I underestimated your willingness.' His chest rose and fell quickly, and beneath my still roaming touch, I felt every muscle tense. The effect I was having on him was intoxicating. The babble behind me was snuffed out by wanton lust, and I no longer cared about cheat sheets.

'Yes, you did.'

He physically shook himself all over and made to walk away, but for just a few seconds, he looked back at me, then over my head to where the bedrooms were. Running out of patience,

Charlotte wriggled around, desperate to get to her siblings playing in the pool.

Matt sighed, running his free hand through his hair. 'Go put the bloody bikini on.'

With a little giggle, I bounced around, heading for the kitchen to the sound of Matt saying to Charlotte, 'I deserve a medal for saying that.'

Surrounded by rustic Italian splendour, I held out the skimpy pieces of material. It was ridiculous how scared I was. Matt had made me feel brazen on the patio, but alone, with a bit of clothing that might as well not be there, I was feeling exposed.

I knew this was nothing new to him. He already knew every inch and curve of my body, but for me, there was no comfort through familiarity. Producing a frustrated, almost silent scream, I slapped my hand on my forehead.

'I thought you might need a hand.' Matt walked over, not taking his eyes from mine. 'Alex is out there with them.'

I nodded, my mouth suddenly becoming very dry as he reached me. I didn't know what to do with my hands or even how I should stand.

His fingers brushed over the buttons on my shirt, and his gaze followed.

My heart hammered in my chest, and everything south of my hips was pulsing. I was having less and less of these moments, the more time we spent together, but right then, I was distinctly aware that Matt, fucking, Lord was undressing me, and it was taking everything I had not to giggle.

I was utterly at his mercy. One by one, the buttons were undone, and with each, my breath deepened to match his. Across his shoulders and down his arms, every muscle tensed with restraint as his eyes swept over my exposed cleavage. It didn't matter whether or not I considered myself desirable. Whatever I was, the lust and anticipation radiating through Matt made it extremely clear that I was what he wanted.

He pushed my shirt off my shoulders, pressing himself against me. When I felt the effect I had upon him against my stomach, I tingled all over and inwardly squealed with unrestrained excitement. Stepping back, his eyes darkened with yearning, and my whole body ached to connect with him. His thumbs hooked over the top of my cotton trousers, and his hands spread so they wrapped around my bum. I practically fell towards him, but he held me steady.

Pulling down, he followed my trousers, lightly brushing his lips between my breasts. I shuddered under his touch, feeling him smile against my stomach.

I still had no idea how on earth I had managed to pull together this incredible life, but if I ever did meet the mysterious woman living inside me, she deserved a bow.

Matt sank further, and my trousers fell to the floor. Slowly, his hands moved back up my legs while his lips kissed their way up to my panty line. Gripping around the sides of my pants, which, thanks to my extensive bank account, were black-laced Victoria's Secret, he slipped them down to join the trousers in a heap around my feet.

His breath sped faster, and all thoughts of exposure were gone. I wanted to be sprawled out and devoured. Every part of me was pulsing and pushing, trying to claim him.

Moving his head to the right to lightly kiss down the inside of my other thigh, he stopped to blow lightly between my legs. Jolting so hard, I had to reach behind me and grab the counter to keep myself upright.

He rose, retracing the kisses, and I became very aware of every nerve ending I had. When his eyes were level with mine, the longing I saw was impossible to resist. My core tightened, and my chest surged.

I was about to crash into him when he leant in, clasped his hands around the back of my thighs, and lifted me. The cold shock of the counter beneath me doused my wanton lust. He moved in closer, wrapping my legs around him. A low sound resonated from his chest, and I quivered all over, wanton lust restored.

I needed more. Drawing back, I wet my lips with the tip of my tongue. His eyes followed, his breath hitched, and his pulsing erection drummed against the inside of my thigh. Beneath my hands, he flexed, rolling my touch over his shoulders and down his back, needing to increase the contact between us.

Leaning in, his eyes stayed on my lips until they were skimming over his throat. He tilted his head with a light moan, giving me all the access I wanted. Closing my mouth around the warm, exposed skin, I gently brushed my tongue over the bristled goosebumps. He tasted of the banana Charlotte had been eating on the plane, and a wave of love smothered in lust shook me. I grazed my teeth upwards with a panting moan, so he could hear as well as feel the effect he had on me.

'Fuck,' he said breathlessly. Kissing my shoulder, he slipped a finger under each strap of my bra and flicked, letting it fall between us.

Cocking his head to the side, he said, 'God, I've missed you.'

I laughed. 'You're not talking to me, are you?'

He beamed. 'No.'

I squeezed my thighs around his waist playfully, and I was no longer the only one trembling.

'Do that again, and we won't be making it out to the pool,' he almost growled in my ear.

Fixing my eyes to his, I lightly bit down on my bottom lip.

'Fuck. I shouldn't have started this.' Consumed by arousal, he considered his options, then, with a full body shudder, picked up the bikini top, jiggling it in front of me.

'Tease,' I said breathlessly.

He leant in to tie the bikini behind my neck while kissing over my beating pulse. His fingers skimmed over my breasts, lingering indulgently as he adjusted the material. 'I'm the tease?' He chuckled to himself. 'I've spent the last eight days having you right there, unable to touch you how I wanted. At the hospital, on the roof, when you got all stubborn and determined, it was the hottest thing I had ever seen. I have no idea how I managed to keep my hands off you.' He kissed the base of my neck while pulling me flat against him. 'I'm starving.'

Lightly, he bit and kissed, moving down my body, and in the only action so far that I wasn't too happy with, he slipped the bikini bottoms up my legs. With his hands gripping the counter on either side of me, his voice deepened. 'Tonight, the teasing stops. I need my wife.' There was a definite order in there, and only a fool would disobey.

'Is that me?' I didn't mean it sarcastically or to be hurtful. It was just the massive weight hanging around my shoulders.

His expression softened. 'You look like her.' Burying his head into my neck, he lazily sniffed. 'You smell like her.' His hands ran through my hair, and he bought my lips up to his. It was deep and full of passion, but he pulled away far too soon. 'You taste like her.' He turned slightly more serious before continuing. 'You have the same look of desire for me as she does. Your body pulls towards me like hers.' His hands ran down my waist. 'You have that same look of love for your family as she does and the same almost flippant attitude towards your career and fame. I see her in every part of you. It's you that can't see her, yet.'

'What if I don't? What if I don't remember?'

His answer came quickly. 'Then you will grow into her, or become a version of her, exactly the same as you did before. Over the last seven years, your lifestyle and number of dependants have changed, but you haven't, not really. You are still in all sense of our craziness, the same woman I fell in love with the day I met her.'

I raised an eyebrow. 'You ran out on me the next morning. That doesn't sound like love.'

He stepped back, laughing darkly, and I jumped off the counter, pulling the bottoms up. Opening the fridge, he passed me a bottle of water and took one for himself.

'I did not run out on you. I ran out of the room to go and throw up.' He opened his own bottle and took a long swig. While I waited, I couldn't resist mentally replacing the water bottle with a can of diet Coke.

'As you know, we had cleared the hotel out of tequila the night before, and when I woke up, I needed to throw up, a lot. Actually, at one point, I wasn't sure which end it was going to come out of.' He shrugged. 'But you were asleep right next to the bathroom door. We were in your complimentary room. So, I ran for mine, and somewhere where the woman of my dreams couldn't hear me shit myself.'

I spat the water across the room, laughing.

'I'm glad that factoid pleases you,' he said sarcastically. 'So. I was ill. Really bad. It was horrific. I haven't touched tequila since, and never will.' He paled at the memory. 'Yes. What you saw when you woke up was me belting it from the room half-naked. By the time I came back, which could have feasibly been the next day, you were long gone. I didn't have your number, and I couldn't, for the life of me, remember your last name.'

I was giggling, and he was trying to ignore me.

'I went over to LA and was sat in a meeting with an array of suits when one of them said, "Patrick Hera will head over to New York," and it clicked. Phone came straight out, meeting be dammed, and an hour later, I'd found you on social media. You were pissed. I had to send you plates from Rome to appease you.'

He finished with a wink, knowing I would remember why that meant something to me.

'I found them,' I said softly, picturing them in the Library.

'Oh, so you finally went in there?'

'I did. Only briefly.' He didn't need to know I had a little bitch fit in there, then left without really looking around.

'Like what I did with it?' He leant against the counter opposite me, looking more than a little pleased with himself.

'You? I thought I decorated the house.' I was genuinely shocked. If one room in that house represented me to a tee, it was the library.

'You did. Everywhere other than the library. After we found out you were pregnant, you wanted to take it slow, be all grown up, and mature about the situation. You wanted us to live apart, to begin with, to get to know each other more first. We both wanted a big family home, and I saw no point in wasting any time. We both knew the other wasn't going anywhere. So, I lured you into my lair with a library.' He waggled his eyes playfully while swigging his water.

'It's perfect.'

'Did you like the desk?'

'It's incredible.'

'Most dads give the mother of their children jewellery when the kids are born, but knowing how pathetic you find rocks and flowers, I got you the desk. Look after it, it's the most expensive thing in the house.'

I threw my arms around him. 'Thank you.'

'Ice cream.'

'That kid's timing is incredible,' I said, watching as Dylan tumbled into the house, heading for the freezer. I should have told him no. I paid dearly for that rookie mistake a few hours later.

Just as I was tucking the kids into bed while Matt was downstairs opening a bottle of wine, Dylan threw up all over his covers and me. Isabella and Jack fled, dry heaving at the smell as they went.

Two hours later, Dylan was bathed, all sick removed, and Isabella and Jack had finally agreed to re-enter the room. Unfortunately, Dylan was asleep, spread-eagled in the centre of mine and Matt's bed.

Matt tried lifting him, but he threw up, and the process started all over again. I laughed more than once at the juxtaposition of the situation. The four-poster, cotton draped bed sat before a set of towering French doors, which led onto a balcony looking out over the Tuscan countryside for miles. It was the most romantic room I had ever been in, and it was splattered with vomit.

By morning, Dylan had been bathed three times, our bedding changed twice, and I was exhausted but also hornier than I could ever remember being before.

Charlotte had seemed pleased with the extra company in the middle of the night, but over-tired, she was living up to her reputation as the demon child and just sat bellowing at breakfast, while Isabella, who did not take kindly to having her sleep being disturbed, tried to beat her twin brother to death with a box of cereal.

Dylan thankfully managed to keep his food down throughout the day, and after several thwarted attempts to get back in the freezer, he contented himself with a film in the TV room while Isabella and Alex slept next to him. Jack, who seemed to need very little sleep to be enthusiastic about life, entertained Charlotte in the pool while Matt, Jane, and I took turns napping on the loungers.

The sun dipped, and it took every morsel of energy I had to get dressed up. I was so excited for what was to be my first date with Matt, but I was also bloody knackered.

Chapter Twenty-One

'I've altered the plan a little,' Matt said, walking into the bedroom in a tailored blue suit with an open-collared white shirt.

'Shit, you scrub up well.'

'Cheers, sweetheart.' He beamed. 'We're not staying here.'

'Where we going?'

'Florence. There's a hotel there with a restaurant overlooking the Duomo. It's one of your favourites. I want you all to myself, just for one night.' He inched forwards, passion burning in his eyes. My chest fluttered, and my body ached to feel him against me. It took everything I had to shake my head with a playful smile. If he touched me, we wouldn't make it out of the room.

He bit his lip and folded his arms across his chest. 'Is that okay?' he asked provocatively.

I knew there was a stupid grin on my face, but I didn't care. 'Fine by me.'

His eyes bore into mine, and liquid fire raged through me. 'Go get ready.' I was sure I heard the growl that time.

Reluctantly, I went back into the wardrobe that was almost as big as the one in the UK and ran my hands over the evening wear section on the far right. I'd already picked out a gorgeous, long-sleeved navy dress covered in tiny rhinestones that winked at me. I took it off the hanger and noticed the label said Gucci. Slipping into it with a smile, it clung to my chest and arms before fanning out slightly, stopping just above my knees.

Below where the dress had hung sat a pair of dark blue Jimmy Choo's that matched the dress perfectly. I marvelled at them for a few seconds before putting them on and going to stand in front of the mirror. I was generally a modest person, but Matt wasn't the only one who scrubbed up well.

'They all said before I married you that I was punching above my weight. Fuck, they were right.' Matt appeared in the doorway, and I gave him a little curtsy in acceptance of the compliment and bullshit. 'Right, come on,' he said, ushering me out of the door, picking up our overnight bag as I passed. 'Let's get out of here before someone throws up.'

Matt drove us into Florence while giving me a bit of knowledge that I would need for the evening.

'It's a private table. We're incognito, remember, but the owner, Giovanni, is going to come over and greet us enthusiastically. I'll squeeze your arm to let you know when he's coming. His wife is Maria. She will come over at the end of the meal and give us shots of limoncello. I hate the stuff, so you drink mine when she's not looking.'

I sat with the air whistling past the open window, taking in everything. I watched the way his hands moved over the wheel. How he wiggled his shoulders when he spoke about the little things that made us a couple, and how at this moment, I was the only person in the world to him.

Before me, Matt almost seemed to solidify. He no longer had the air of this out of reach celebrity. He was even starting to look different than I remembered from the occasional photo I fell upon online. Without the flash of a camera, his eyes were a darker blue. There was a scar on the left side of his chin and one above his right eye, just below the eyebrow. Close up, the stubble on his chin had flecks of white, and below his jawline, the same mousey brown as Charlotte.

'We should get left alone apart from that, but there is always a chance that someone will spot us and want either an autograph or a selfie. I have, at times, had someone ask for one at a urinal. You might want to Google what your autograph looks like.'

I took out my phone, wincing at what I was doing. My signature should be the most personal thing in the world, but I had to Google it.

'Have you actually seen or read any of your books yet?'

I didn't want to get into the emotional turmoil I had gone through in the library, but it was ridiculous to think I hadn't even seen the covers yet. I remembered then that I had also been dealing with a new home, royal friends, my own fame, four children, and what I thought was a cheating husband.

I shook my head, and he laughed.

After I Googled my autograph, which just looked like an 'F' and a squiggle, I went online to at least see what they looked like. All eight were five stars. I knew there had to be a bit of negative in there if I went looking, but I was proud to see that the good far outweighed the bad. Listed downwards, with tiny pictures of the covers on the left and the titles next to them, was my life's work, and not just the last seven years.

Five of the eight titles were familiar to me. The series was there. I only remembered writing three, but I had the fourth laid out. Then there was *Pursuit*, the book I won the Booker prize for. It was a literary fiction novel I wrote in my sister's box room over the year I lived with her and Lance because my publisher and boyfriend had dropped me. It looked like my abysmal agony and emotional hell came through.

Below was *Madness, Death, and Biscuits*. I clicked on that one and scrolled down to the reviews. It was a comedy I had written alongside the *Occurrences* series. When things had gotten hard, and the story wouldn't move, I would open up *Madness, Death, and Biscuits* and just enjoy writing freely without the restrictions I had created for myself in the fantasy world of Rathrin.

The first review was five stars. *Absolutely worth the read. Lord has a way of making the most mundane aspects hilarious.*

I had to laugh at the one below it. It had four stars. *I read the whole thing waiting for Bastine to turn up. This is NOT part of the Occurrences series. Still good, though. Took a star because anything that hasn't got Bastine in it shouldn't have 5*s.*

I came out, and below *Madness, Death, and Biscuits* were the book formats of the two TV shows I had written. The top one, *On a Ledge*, which I had no recollection of writing, was listed as Emmy award-winning. I was about to click on it when a stupidly obvious thought occurred to me, and I screamed with excitement. Matt jumped, and the car swerved.

'Sorry.' I laughed. 'You're Bastine. Aren't you?'

Matt beamed, turning away from the road for a second to nod triumphantly. 'Who else was it ever going to be?' he said cockily. 'It was my role before the book was even finished.' His smile told me he knew exactly what part he and Bastine had played in my life before meeting him.

I was too excited to think too much about that dark period in my life. 'And there's already the first film? With you as Bastine?' I was a giggling mess.

He nodded, laughing at my enthusiasm. 'Yes, there is.'

I squealed. I couldn't keep it in. How the hell none of this had occurred to me before was incredulous, but as I had already pointed out to myself, there was a lot going on.

'Oh, screw the restaurant. We're room servicing it and watching you as Bastine,' I declared, clapping my hands.

'Ahh, my wife's porn choices are still the same. That's nice to see.' There was a very proud look on his face.

I nestled into the seat for the rest of the trip, watching Florence engulf me, thinking about Bastine.

After pulling into an underground car park, the car had barely stopped when a man in a tuxedo opened my door. I stepped out. 'Buona sera,' I said.

'Buona sera,' he replied with an excited squeak.

'Can you please cancel our dinner reservation? We'll be going straight to our room,' Matt said to the porter who opened his door.

'Of course, sir. We'll have your bags sent straight up. If you would like to follow me?' The porter walked away from the entrance and further into the car park. He stopped by what looked like a service door and swiped a card across a little black panel box next to it. The door clicked, and he pulled it open to reveal a red-carpeted staircase.

'I told you. I want you all to myself this evening.' Matt hooked his arm around my waist and guided me forwards. The porter stepped ahead, leading the way up the stairs and into an old-fashioned lift. He pulled the doors closed to the sound of scraping metal, sealing us in Italian authenticity.

Ascending in silence, Matt's hand found the curve of my back above my bum just after we passed the first floor. By the fourth floor, he was roaming from cheek to cheek, cupping each one appreciatively. Nerves were trying to overwhelm me, but the love and desire Matt exuded for me was like a weighted blanket, holding me to a reality I wanted to be encased within.

Exiting onto a long, wide corridor, completely absent of any colour other than cream, the porter guided us to one of the two doors on the floor.

We were welcomed by a foyer holding an elegant, round, dark wood table. The porter who had opened the car door for me appeared, carrying our bag, and when he moved through the foyer, I followed.

It opened up into a huge living space with four sofas, a dining table, and room for at least thirty. It was extremely gold, elaborate, and Italian, but as magnificent as it was, it was nothing compared to the view. Like the whole window was a perfectly angled photograph, the Duomo and Giotto's bell tower sat against the Florentine skyline, with the sun dropping into a river of yellow and blue.

I was in awe. All I could do was stand there staring. A glass of Champagne appeared before me, and Matt wrapped his free arm around my waist. I took the glass and rested against him while sipping.

'It's beautiful.'

'Cheat sheet, remember. I've brought you here to seduce you many times before,' he said with a wicked edge to his voice.

I swallowed hard, and after downing the rest of the Champagne, I placed the empty glass on the table in front of me, making sure my bum was still pressed against him.

He groaned, and it was all the encouragement I needed. Turning around, I looked up at him, trailing my fingers over the exposed skin of his open collar. When I reached buttons, I undid each one without taking my eyes off his. Vulnerable love stared back at me, and I realised that with or without a cheat sheet, I wasn't the only one who was nervous. My hands needed no direction. My mind didn't know him, but as my palms slid under the material of his shirt, pushing it from his shoulders, it was clear they did.

Heat pooled around us, and even with him shirtless in front of me, my eyes remained on his. I let my hands feel their way over his body, and he trembled under my touch, soft moans escaping with each breath. When I reached his belt, I dropped my eyes. A desperate longing pulsed through me, I needed to feel him against me, inside me, but I couldn't resist the urge to savour him.

The belt came off, and with a pull against his trouser buttons, they fell to the floor. In all his almost intimidating glory, he bounced free, standing tall like a good soldier.

'Commando,' I said in approval.

He shrugged. 'I foresaw this moment.'

'Cocky,' I said in jest.

He kissed across my cheek, then whispered into my ear, 'You can't resist jumping me in this room. Something about that view

191

gets you all riled up.' Seductively, he lowered his eyes to my dress. 'My turn.'

His fingertips caressed my side while he slowly turned me back towards the other majestic view. His one hand curled around my stomach while the other swept my hair over my shoulder. Kissing over my exposed skin in a soft, seductive voice that made my core tighten expectantly, he said, 'The last time you wore this dress, we were at a charity function in Prague. Halfway through the night, you pulled me into a storage room at the back of the kitchen. You sat on top of a counter and opened your legs while, oh so slowly, and oh so seductively, lifting the skirt. It was seeing your choice of attire for this evening that made me think to go commando.' The zip lowered at the back, and so did his lips.

'What did you do?' I asked breathlessly.

Instead of pushing the dress off my shoulders, he turned me back around, lust and passion emanating from him. Pulling me to him, he clutched around my thighs and picked me up. I wrapped my legs around his waist, and he dusted my neck with warm, soft kisses while walking me over to a dresser against the back wall. Placing me on top of it, he stepped back with a wild, hungry look in his eyes. I felt like I was drowning, and every fibre of my being was calling to him, to the air my depleted body needed.

It was the most agonisingly pleasurable feeling I had ever known. Leaning back slightly, I slowly opened my legs, and his erection bobbed around excitedly. An immense feeling of power and arousal exploded within me. Before me was a living god, and he was enslaved to my mercy.

My hands came around to the hem of my dress, and as slowly as I could, I lifted. When the material reached the top of my thighs, I said silkily, 'This was as far as you got in the story.'

A deep moan vibrated in his throat, and he placed his hands over mine. Moving them upwards, he exposed another pair of lace knickers. 'Well, to start, these weren't there.' Before I could shuffle out of them, with one little bump, he swiped them away, and I watched them float out across the room.

'That was impressive,' I chuckled.

'They were in my way,' he said, brushing his lips over mine. His hands drifted back to my bum. Gathering the material in his fists, he pulled, and I slipped back, displaying myself before him. The arousal clouding in his eyes made every part of my body throb.

'I lowered myself to the floor,' he said temptingly, dropping to his knees in front of me. 'You then draped your legs across my shoulders,' he continued, lingering over slow, soft kisses up my calf.

I did as I was told. 'What happened then?' It came out huskier than intended.

'Let me show you,' he said provocatively, and I quietly gasped in anticipation. His mouth moved higher up my leg, kissing the inside of my thigh.

I was preparing myself for the slow torturous display I had gotten the day before when his mouth, hot and wet, covered me. He licked slowly but roughly upwards onto the ridge of my clit, and I came apart. My body convulsed, and I had to grip the back of the dresser to keep myself upright.

He didn't lessen the intensity for a second. The sheer breadth of his shoulders meant that he could keep my legs open while his tongue found every nerve ending he wanted to play with.

The building sexual frustration I had been living with, already had me tottering over the edge of an orgasm, when in a calculated move, he released me to blow over my wetness. Lost to the sensation, I was ready to freefall and take him with me.

In one fluid motion, he rose up, drew my legs around his waist, and plunged into me.

'Matt. Fuck!'

The dress found its way over my head and his hands pressed into my back, pulling my trembling body against his. I tightened my legs around him, tinkering between pleasure and pain at the sudden fullness.

'Oh God, I've missed you,' he groaned through lavish kisses across my shoulder. Reaching down between our bodies, he found the most sensitive spot I had with impeccable precision. My core constricted, kneading at him as he pumped harder into me.

The pressure inside me increased with every thrust, but I needed more. Rocking my hips, I held him to me and eased into the rhythmic motion. Tremors of sensual bliss pulsed through me, sparking every cell in my body to life. I was utterly oblivious to everything around me that wasn't him. I had never before felt so consumed by someone, knowing that no matter how close he got, it would never be close enough.

My lips moved between his neck and mouth, unable to decide where they wanted to be more. Our hands covered each other, caressing and gripping, trying to reconnect with what had been lost.

He drew back, and with one more hard thrust, bursts of euphoria consumed me, and I cried out in ecstasy as he came hard into me.

'Freya. Fuck!' he exclaimed through ragged breaths. The sensation pushing me further into my orgasm.

His mouth found mine, and with insatiable passion, our lips moved together perfectly synchronised.

He lifted me, and while he walked me to the bedroom, his tongue teased over my nipples to the sound of our blissful moans. I ran my hands through his hair, ensuring he didn't break contact.

Lowering me down onto the cold sheets, he stood to admire what he had before him.

'Fuck, I love you.' The lustful sincerity in his eyes and voice was paralysing. Before I could respond, he crawled onto the bed over me. Keeping a small gap between us, he kissed every spot of skin he could find while I softly panted, relishing in every moment of him, savouring me.

My mind went blank.

When we were face to face, the passion and love in the intensity of his expression made my chest throb. He lowered onto me, the pressure and heat captivating me. Moving my leg to the side with his hip, he eased himself back inside me. My back arched as I stretched to accommodate him and my hands ran over every part of him I could reach, letting them fill in the blanked-out spaces in my memory.

Moving slowly back and forth, he kissed me softly before lifting himself onto his forearms to watch me. Every part of my body felt like it was being electrified.

'I will never get enough of you,' he whispered. 'You're so beautiful.' He kissed me sweetly. 'What are you?'

I stared into his eyes and replied with what felt like the most natural response. 'Yours.'

His face fell, and he gazed at me in loving awe; apparently, that was the right answer.

Nudging his waist with my thighs, I made my intent clear. I wanted to hold him at my mercy. The darkened look of desire returned, and he spun us around, so I was on top.

'Ummm,' he said, letting his eyes roam over me with a wicked smile on his face. Tucking his hands under his head, he cockily submitted to me.

I rocked slowly to the sound of his breathless moans.

Leaning back, I increased the pace.

His eyes rolled backwards, and he lifted his hips, pushing further into me.

I breathed in deeply, letting the sensual bliss consume me. Filling me as much as he was, it should have been painful, but my body had moulded to accommodate him long before now, and all I felt was pleasure.

I moved faster, increasing the friction against the top of my clit, and everything tightened. Our breathing accelerated, and his hands dove out from behind his head to grab my hips.

'Oh, god. Frey, that feels incredible.'

Dipping his head backwards, he slid me rapidly over him. Electrified waves of serenity inched me closer and closer to the mind-altering orgasm I knew awaited me, and I no longer knew who was at whose mercy. I felt him expand as he rose towards it with me, which only heightened the building pressure and my arousal at seeing how much I turned him on.

Taking his hands from my waist, I rested my palms against his and drew myself upwards. I may not have had a cheat sheet for Matt, but he was still a man.

I was about to tease his tip in and out of me when his eyes shot open. He tried to pull his hands free, but I held on.

'Frey. Frey, don't,' he breathlessly warned with wide but daring eyes. I couldn't resist. Clenching around him, I eased him in and out, making sure to rub him over my ridge.

'Fuck! Oh, fuck, Frey.' His hands tightened around mine, and he lifted himself up. I was about to plunge him deep within me when a low growl rippled through his chest, and I was spinning through the air.

My back fell against the bed, and Matt towered over me. The predatory look on his face made me pleasantly shiver. I was not prey that would run. Drawing back, he pushed hard and fast into me. I cried out, revelling in the delightful torture, and dug my nails into his back. He responded by driving into me harder. His lips found the nape of my neck, and he kissed upwards until he reached my mouth.

Folding my legs around his waist, I encouraged him to raise up. He moved to my will, and as he lifted himself to his knees, he drew my thighs up with him. I thought he couldn't reach any deeper into me, but I was so deliciously wrong. Running his palm over my blazing skin, he pumped into me, keeping his eyes locked onto mine. Every sensation was so heightened that it was almost unbearable. I fell back, succumbing to his will.

'Oh, God.' I reached out and grabbed the bedding into my fists as I tumbled into the orgasm.

'Frey. Babe. Yes. Fuck!' Feeling him cum inside me turned my entire body into a vibrating entanglement of nerve endings. Endorphins flooded my clouded mind, washing light into the darkened spaces that had walled me in. Sated contentment pulled against my chest, and for the first time in days, it didn't feel like a struggle to breathe.

Lowering himself on top of me, he lay his head against my breasts, and together we panted, enjoying the cathartic release. All coherent thought was a pipe dream.

When we had both gotten our breath back, he turned his head into my breasts and skimmed kisses over my damp skin. Resting his chin between them, he looked up at me with a slightly agonised look on his face.

'I've missed you so much.' He kissed my neck. 'I've missed the warmth.'

My heart thudded in my chest in response. That was precisely how I had felt from the first day I remembered meeting him.

'I'll never leave you cold again, I promise,' I said, stroking down the side of his face.

His eyes bore playfully into me. 'If you leave, I'm coming with you.'

It was a beautiful, loving moment, but a question popped into my head, and it just slipped out. 'What does our prenup look like?'

He sat up onto his knees. 'What the fuck? You can't ask your husband about divorce proceedings after he's just made love to you, for what was essentially our first time for you.'

I laughed while stroking his chest and enjoying his nakedness. There was a hint of humour in his voice, but there was also an apprehensive flicker in his eye.

'I'm sorry. Random things come into my head, and I'm too relaxed to stop them tumbling out.'

'I'm not sure that makes me feel any better, but….' He fell over me, encasing me in his arms. 'You haven't got one,' he teased. 'When I was the money bags in the relationship, you offered to sign a prenup if I wanted one.' He kissed me on the end of my nose. 'I said no.'

I sat up on my elbows, and he rested back on his knees, looking rather chuffed with himself. 'What, you really didn't want one?' I didn't remember a lot about the extent of Matt's wealth back then, but I was pretty sure it was well into the three-digit millions.

'Nope.'

'Why?' I was genuinely curious.

'A few reasons, really. For one, if it ever came down to revenge, you'd find far more creative ways to do me over. Being taken to the cleaners would be the least of my problems.' Just for the briefest of moments, his expression changed to show me there was one memory that we did share from long before I met him, but like me, he knew it was a memory for another time and continued. 'Also, you don't look out for yourself.' His fingers trailed down my cheek as he looked at me with so much love. 'You'll take on the world for a worthy stranger in need, but you wouldn't do that for yourself.' I shuddered internally at how well he knew me. 'Plus, when we met, you had sod all and didn't seem overly bothered about it.'

I nodded. That I remembered.

'You were living in that flat. Don't get me wrong, it was a cute place, we had a lot of fun in there, but it was in a rough ass area on the edge of Birmingham, and your car was running purely on your will; it had to be.'

'Oh, I'd forgotten about that car.' I looked around, a little confused. In my memory, I was driving that little rust-covered Fiesta less than a fortnight ago, but when he mentioned it, it felt like something from years ago. I wasn't sure if that was a good or bad thing.

'I tried everything to get you out of there. Honestly, three weeks in and I was trying to buy you a house and a new car. You were having none of it.'

I giggled. 'It's not really what you're meant to do after a few weeks.'

He shook his head at the recollection. 'It was bloody absurd. I got home one day, and I was switching on the burglar alarm, sticking myself in this protected bubble, and there you were, the only thing I actually gave a fuck about, in that flat, with a front door that only locked properly if the weather wasn't too hot.'

I reached up and kissed him. He looked so agonised by the memory. I also remembered using duct tape on that door where the wood had thinned into gaping holes.

'I nearly just moved you,' he said with a shrug. 'You know, distract you and then move all your stuff into a house with high-tech security. I thought that might be going a little too far, though, so I went down a different route.' He pulled the blanket over us and curled into my side.

'I'd say knock me up, but you'd already done that.'

'That is true,' he said proudly. 'We just didn't know that at the time, or all bets would have been off, and you would've been out of there. Instead, I dropped *Occurrences* in front of a publisher. Anonymously,' he added quickly on the end. 'Within a fortnight, you had a book deal, but it wasn't enough for me. To start with, you weren't planning on moving.' That got me a little bite to the shoulder, making me squirm and giggle.

'Our first argument, by the way.' He kissed almost apologetically up my neck. 'You dug your heels in and got all stubborn on me, and I was angry because I couldn't figure out if I was horny or pissed off. I got my way when I found a little cottage that had ducks.'

I loved how well he knew me.

'Then, a few weeks after we found out you were pregnant, my business manager asked me to come up with a figure. Basically, if the shit hit the fan, what would you walk away with to make sure you and the kids were looked after.'

He stroked lovingly down my side, absorbed in his story. 'I thought about those high gates, doors that would lock, security, comfort.' He stopped for a second and took a deep breath, and I felt him shudder. 'And reinforced cars to keep you all safe.' Leaning into the crook of my neck, he inhaled deeply and pulled me closer. 'The number I came to was more than I had, so what was the point of a prenup?'

His hold on me didn't relinquish, and it was obvious he wasn't thinking about prenups anymore. I turned, and the distant, forlorn expression I saw made my throat tighten.

'I'm okay,' I whispered. He brushed his cheek against mine, but his mind was no longer in the room with me.

'When I got the call.' His voice sounded strangled, and he wrapped his leg over me like he was trying to use his body as a shield against what was playing out across his memory. 'I have never felt paralysing fear like it. I was on set. We were about to get going, and I don't know what made me look at him, but Dan... my assistant, was just off-camera on the phone, listening intently. When he looked up, I saw his face.' Pulling himself up, he exhaled so loudly that I thought he was going to start hyperventilating.

'Hey, hey. I'm okay.'

He shook his head, but he wasn't looking at me. His hands raked through his hair, and with the same distant look, he fixed his eyes upon the wall opposite. 'But you weren't.'

All I could think to do was touch him, assure him that everything was okay. I brushed my hands roughly over his arms and let them join his own in his hair. I ran them down his back, pulling him towards me. He fell into me as all the strength he had been holding onto left him.

'Dan's face,' he said against my shoulder, 'was white. It was the look someone has when they're about to tell you your world has burnt to the ground.' He leant back, looking like he was in physical pain, but he was seeing me again in front of him. His eyes were searching all over my face as if trying to make sure I was real.

'I knew it was you.' He shook his head. 'I just knew. When Dan told me what had happened, I went numb. I have absolutely no memory of leaving set and getting in the car.'

'That I can sympathise with,' I said with a small chuckle trying to ease his pain.

His hand drew up to my face and cupped my cheek. For a few seconds, he just stared at me, fighting back the tears. I wanted to stop him, do anything I could to remove the look of agony on his face, but I realised he probably hadn't said any of this out loud before. Reaching for his other hand, I stroked my thumb over his knuckles, encouraging him to continue.

'When I got there, you were in surgery. You were only a few rooms away from me, but I couldn't get to you. I just kept repeating to myself that I couldn't lose you. It seemed completely unfathomable that there could ever be a world without you in it, but there was also this sick voice in my head that just kept telling me I'd had it too good. You and our life together wasn't just everything I ever wanted. I also had this mass of everything I thought was too ridiculous to even think of asking for, and you were the centre of it.'

He stared past me out of the window. His hands gripped mine so tightly that I knew he was using my touch as a lifeline to what was real and not what he thought his life would become.

'While you were in surgery, I sat in the Chapel, offering it all up. If someone was up there, trying to balance my scales, I begged for them to take the money. Every last penny. I didn't give a flying fuck if the world forgot my name. I would have taken you and the kids back to that bloody little flat in Birmingham, kebab smell, broken door, and all, but it still felt like I was asking for too much.' His voice was little more than a whisper.

'You came out of surgery after what felt like a bloody lifetime, but the doctors just kept telling me they wouldn't know anything till you woke up.'

'Where were you when I woke up?' I didn't mean it to sound so accusing, but he heard the abandonment I had been feeling.

'Right there.' He held my face, and I watched him try to pour all the love he felt for me into that one look. 'I never left.' He kissed me fervently and then leant back with the pained expression that I didn't like I was getting used to. 'I'd gotten pissed off waiting for the doctor to come round, plus your dad was doing my bloody head in with those knitting needles.' He stopped to laugh darkly. I couldn't help joining in as I thought about my dad proudly holding up his misshapen orange blanket.

His voice lowered further when he started talking again. 'When I heard the doctor outside, I went out to him, and I was just ushering him into your room when my phone beeped. A message from my mum. Something about Jack wanting to go to a friend's. I was typing the reply when the doctor walked in, and I heard your mum say, "She just asked what year is it."'

He gulped loudly. 'I couldn't move, but I could see you.' He looked at me, taking me in. I smiled reassuringly, not knowing what else to do.

With a deep, shaking breath, he continued. 'When the doctor told you what year it was and you started hyperventilating, I knew what was coming. It felt like a sick joke. All I wanted was a world you were in. I just forgot to ask for a world that you knew I was in.' Tears dropped onto the bedding between us. They could have been from either of us.

'You looked at me. Straight at me… Straight through me. When you said, "2015" my legs just went from under me, and as I hit the floor, I felt our life crumble down around me.'

His body trembled, and I broke out in cold, hard goosebumps. I had gotten a glimpse at what it would feel like to have Matt ripped away from me. My chest constricted. There had been so much else going on that a wall had been built, stopping me from feeling what it would truly be like. An abyss of despair reflected back at me, and I knew that, like him, I wouldn't have survived.

'All I could think while I sat on that floor was how the hell was I going to make you love me again? Because even after seven years and four kids, I still couldn't fathom how I had managed to get you to love me as much as you did the first time.'

To try and lift the blanket of pain smothering us, I wanted to say, *'Have you looked in the mirror recently?'* but the shallow joke slipped from my mind when he said, 'That's why when you said 'loved' that first night home, it felt like you were confirming everything I thought.'

'Is that why we're here?' I said, looking around the room I had apparently been seduced in many times before.

Arousal crossed his face, but there still so much pain lingering behind his eyes. 'All I have is a cheat sheet,' he whispered.

I lifted his face, resting his forehead against mine. There wasn't a lot that I did know, but there was one thing I had known with absolute certainty from the second I saw him in that family room. 'You have me.'

Relief poured from him, and I felt him release the tension gripping his shoulders as he lightly pushed me back into the bed. Tenderly, he kissed all over my face and down my throat while his hands moved through my hair. His body pressed me into the mattress, and his weight over me was a comfort I wanted to treasure for the rest of my life. With no thought for orgasms or even lust, he moved inside me in slow, tender strokes, needing to eradicate the distance he had felt between us.

Outside, the hue of the Florentine night descended all around us, but even in this city that I loved so much, all that existed was him.

For hours we used our bodies to re-find the familiarity that had once passed so easily between us. Only when every inch of the other was set firmly in each of our memories did I lie next to him, curled into his side.

'Just an FYI,' he chuckled quietly. I lifted my eyes to his. It was so lovely to see the lightness there that I had only caught moments of before. 'You're worth ten times what I am now. I dare you to leave me.' There was such a mischievous but proud look on his face that it made my chest ache.

I shrugged. 'What's the point? You'd only come with me.' I finished with a smile that I hoped told him I would be happy for him to follow me anywhere.

'Now you're getting it,' he said, lightly kissing me. 'Anyway, I'm not sure either of us would overly notice if the other cleaned them out. You've done a week in our day-to-day life. It's hardly caviar and cocktails. It's more fish sticks and apple juice.'

'You get you're saying that from the bed of a five-star Florentine hotel, and our means of getting here was by private jet?'

'I said day to day.' He poked me playfully in the side. 'This was a treat so I could have my wicked way with you.'

'Umm,' I said. Turning into him, I moved my leg over his, and he sighed with happiness. My lips skimmed over his throat, biting.

'I am nowhere near finished with you tonight, Mrs Lord, but I'm not in my twenties anymore. You're going to have to feed me first.'

My stomach grumbled in response. 'That's my girl.' He slapped my ass. 'Pass the menu over.'

I looked around and saw the menu on the dresser against the wall at the bottom of the bed. Equal distance between us. 'Why me?'

He clenched my bum in his hand. 'When you're naked, it's the only time I enjoy you walking away from me,' he purred into my ear.

After the body quaking orgasms, I wasn't sure if I could stand, but how could I refuse? As I rose onto shaking legs and the sound of a moan rippled out behind me, a question came to mind.

'How old are you?'

He leant back into the pillows, resting his hands behind his head, and with a proud glint in his eye, he answered, 'Thirty-nine. I'm your toyboy, baby.'

Chapter Twenty-Two

'What's it called?'

Matt laughed, dropping onto the bed wearing only a baggy pair of grey jogging bottoms. He removed the steak sandwich hanging from his mouth to answer. *'The Strangest of Occurrences.'*

'Cool, they kept the name,' I said, flicking the TV on to find the film adaptation of my book.

'It's practically word for word to the book. I think they did it mainly out of fear. Your fans, the hardcore ones, have a tendency towards rioting, remember?'

I tried to imagine that many people being fans of my books that the police had to consider riot plans, but I couldn't envisage my random words on paper inciting so much passion in others that they would take to the streets. I had ached over the story so many times and, on more than one occasion, considered abandoning it. I never felt it was good enough.

For the first time in days, I saw Bastine leaving the room while saying, *'You should have listened to me sooner, instead of fart-arsing around with all those pathetic idiots.'*

With a quiet huff at his arrogance, I watched him walk away from me through my mind, marvelling at his absolutely perfect bum. Silently, I said to every fan of Bastine's beyond my window, *'You're welcome.'*

Picking up my slice of pizza, I typed the name out on the remote. When I saw Matt, or I should say, when I saw Matt as Bastine, I squealed through my pizza. 'This is crazy.'

'Tell me about it. Though, it is great to see this excitement in you again through a rerun.'

My finger hovered over the 'Play' button.

'You okay?' Matt said, leaning over my shoulder.

I took a deep breath. I wasn't sure if I was. This was a far cry from seeing a little picture of the book cover on my phone. It wasn't just seeing the world I had created come to life, but Matt as a living and breathing Bastine.

My mind drifted back to only a few weeks to me, to the last time Bastine had been there for me.

The country was starting the slow descent into the Christmas festivities, and I had been dumped. My blood ran cold. I couldn't remember the boyfriend's name. I pulled hard at the memory of him standing at my front door. His hand was resting on the handle, ready to leave for the last time, but I couldn't make out his features. I knew his eyes were green, but I couldn't hold them in my mind. I couldn't have described his lips or hair or said what he was wearing.

The rest of the image around him was also fading. The more I pulled at the memory, the more it pushed away from me. I couldn't see what was next to the door, what furniture was there, or the colour of the carpet. Every time I got close to zoning in on a memory that would show me, it blurred, and my mind skipped over it to another, looking for the answers, but they weren't there.

Finally, a beige carpet and a cream wall next to a white door, with bits of duct tape over it, came into view. The boyfriend was gone, and next to me was Bastine. His gold armour, dulled by use, clung to the brown leather beneath. Intricate patterns covered the metal that, to view, looked almost flexible. His muscular, bare arms folded across his chest, and I heard him sigh. The familiar sensations of finding myself abandoned and alone flooded me. I did not acknowledge the manifestation of Bastine but took in his stance, the way he flexed his shoulders in irritation, looking almost bored.

'If you cry over that, I'm gonna fucking slap you.' Bastine and Matt may look the same, but they were two very different people.

The closed white door was ahead of me. The despair was still there, and I remembered drawing my arms around my chest, trying to hold myself together, mentally and physically.

'You can't stand here forever. You're moving at some point, so you might as well do it now.'

I didn't move, but I felt the almost medicinal sensation of drawing from the abundance of strength coursing through Bastine.

'Just so you know,' he said through a yawn. *'You look pathetic just stood there. You might be a bit weird, but you're not pathetic, so go finish the fucking book. You belong with me.'* It was not said lovingly but simply just as a matter of fact.

'Hey, you okay?' Matt wrapped his arms around me and pulled me into him. I rested against him and nodded my head so he could feel it against his chest.

I pressed 'Play', and the agony of abandonment and white doors disappeared, and excitement coursed through me. The scene opened with Sarah, my main character, walking through the woods. I squealed again and picked up another slice of pizza.

Lee, her eventual love interest, came into the scene. Bless them. I really did put those two through the wringer.

'Oh bloody hell, that's what's his name.' Lee was being played by what I remembered to be one of Hollywood's young heartthrobs.

'William Pace,' Matt said with a flat tone. 'Arrogant little shit, but even I had to admit, he's the living embodiment of Lee.'

'Oh fuck.' Other characters arrived, and it was like a line-up of the Oscars.

'You can't name one of them, can you?' Matt laughed against my neck and drew me in closer.

'Nope,' I said, taking a bite of pizza.

His forehead fell onto my shoulder. 'I'd forgotten how little you knew about 'this' world. We had to do you flashcards last time. They're still in the house somewhere.'

He was right. I watched my story play out on the screen, and although I knew I was seeing fame, I couldn't have named most of them with absolute certainty. Personally, I didn't think it was that strange. You don't usually wait around at the end of a film to watch the credits, and I'd never clicked with social media or even celebrity magazines. They cost nearly the same as a book, which I thought was absurd. I did, though, recognise them as other prolific, famous characters. It was a very humbling experience seeing them as the embodiment of characters that, up until ten minutes ago, had only ever existed in my head.

Then Bastine appeared, sword swinging through the opposing army. I was utterly engrossed. Bastine was solid and very much alive outside of my mind.

In awe, I watched, waiting.

Overall, the series was young adult, but some of the scenes had a few sexy suggestions, especially when it came to Bastine. Out of all the books I had written, one scene was my favourite, and it was coming up. There wasn't a chance in hell that I would have agreed for it not to be included, and from the reaction I'd seen about Bastine so far, it appeared it was well received.

I tensed against Matt. Lee and Sarah were in a dungeon cell for the night, being half-drowned, which meant—The scene changed, and there he was.

'Outside this door, you are my queen, and I, your devoted subject. Inside this room, you will not refuse me.' Bastine walked around the woman who I loved writing. Madeline was a calculating, slightly deranged character, who I used to wind-up Bastine, the warrior who would fight the devil himself to protect her.

Bastine slipped his fingers under the thin straps of her black silk gown and pushed them off her shoulders. I remembered how Matt had removed my bra in the kitchen the day before, and my body pulsed.

Madeline let the straps fall, but the material stretched across her breasts, holding the dress up, and her modesty remained intact. She raised an eyebrow at Bastine, then turned away from him.

I smiled at her as she glided. I didn't recognise the actress, but she was pulling off my idea of Madeline perfectly. She slowly sat in a green velvet high-backed chair and crossed her legs.

The camera focused on Bastine's expression, and I internally melted. It was a predatory stare seeped in passion that I was familiar with. A quiet 'Hum' escaped me.

Matt laughed lightly, pushing my hair away from my shoulder. Between kissing my neck, he whispered, 'You were stood next to the camera for that shot. Paul, the director, wasn't stupid.'

I couldn't speak. Before me, Bastine walked confidently over to Madeline. He lowered himself onto the little step in front of her and lazily ran his hand over her calf towards the inside of her thigh.

'I will still expect progress reports,' Madeline said through strained breaths.

'You may have whatever you want, my queen.' Bastine glared at her, lust pulsing from him. Seeing the man, I knew to be my husband staring at another woman like that should have sparked a flicker of jealousy. Instead, my heart swelled with love, and I was seconds from crying with joy.

To anyone else, the way he was looking at her was heart-stopping, but it didn't even come close to what I knew lust could look like from Matt.

'Three. Two. One,' Matt whispered with a smile against my shoulder. He knew, as I did, what was about to happen.

As he mouthed 'one', I was turning into him. My lips and body found him, and he did not deny me. We fell back against the mattress, and placing my hands around his wrists, I drew them up over his head, lightly draping myself over him.

Fixing my eyes to his, I said with devoted conviction, 'Mine.'

With a boyish grin, he clinked his wedding band against the wooden headboard. 'Legally.'

Chapter Twenty-Three

I awoke with the dawn the following day, feeling more contented and satisfied than I could recall ever feeling before. Matt was sound asleep, but I was too excited. I was in a five-star hotel in Florence that overlooked the Duomo. I wanted coffee, pastries, and a seat in front of the glorious view beyond my drawn curtains.

Slowly, I slithered from the bed and went in search of my overnight bag. It was a little disconcerting to find everything from my bag either hung up, in a drawer, or perfectly positioned on a dressing table. Matt hadn't done it. I'd spent the last week picking his clothes up off the floor.

I lifted a long pale pink cotton wrap-around dress off a hanger, and while pulling my hair into a high ponytail, I slipped into a pair of cream ankle boots. After a quick trip to the bathroom, I found my phone on the coffee table. There were no missed calls from the kids, so I slipped it into my bag and headed for the door.

When my hand touched the handle, static sent a shock up my arm, and with it, it delivered the memory of why I was there, standing in Florentine luxury. Cold shivers raked over me. From the moment I reached into the wardrobe, I had forgotten and just slipped into the simple routine of getting dressed. I even remembered walking into the bathroom, picturing where I was in Florence and the cafes that were close by, where I could sit peacefully with a little breakfast, while indulging in a bit of people watching. At no point had I remembered that I was no longer invisible.

I staggered back to the sofa, falling onto it, staring at the back of the door. I'd forgotten it all, even that Matt, my husband, was asleep in the next room. I focused on the kids. I had remembered them. While dressing, I wondered if they were up, and if so, what were they doing? Had Dylan been sick again?

The doctor had said there would be moments of confusion. I focused on that and ran my hands over the material of the sofa, determined to keep going. Less than half an hour before, everything had been so clear; I couldn't lose that. A lot had happened, and I had to expect confusion, but I didn't need to let it consume me.

'Right. Fuck this.' I picked up the hotel phone and pressed '0'.

A well-spoken woman with a strong Italian accent said, 'Good morning Mrs Lord. Would you like breakfast?'

'Si per favore.' As the words left my lips, it occurred to me that the woman had spoken to me in Italian. I sighed with a bit of relief and asked for coffee and pastries. The Italian continued to flow. I was also informed there was a terrace on the next floor with an open view of the Duomo.

Still remembering Matt was there, I found a pen and pad and left him a note. Grabbing my sunglasses, I quietly left.

It was both exhilarating and scary being out of a 'safe place' alone. Until I saw my characters depicted by Hollywood's finest, the level of my fame had felt abstract. It should have sunk in with who my husband and friends were, but that was personal. The film had shown me I was famous in my own right, and it made me feel extremely visible. I almost went back to wait till Matt woke, but the thought of coffee walked me into the lift.

The doors opened on the next floor into warm sunlight, and I was just basking in the moment of freedom when someone squealed. It didn't stop with just one. I blinked past the sunshine, and a young girl of around sixteen stepped in front of me with a slightly manic smile on her face.

'Oh my god! Oh my god!' She bounced up and down in front of me, clapping excitedly.

I thought I had prepared myself for this, but there was something about the nervous energy she was exuding that made me want to run away from her.

'I can't believe it. Oh my god! I am a massive, massive fan.' Her hands fell to her knees like she was trying to catch her breath. She reminded me of myself when I found the equality award in my library.

I pulled myself together enough to smile weakly and say, 'Thank you.'

'My favourite is the first one. *The Strangest of Occurrences*. Bastine is like, wow. Hot as fuck.'

I chuckled, relaxing slightly.

'Can I get a selfie? My mum's going to be so jeal'. You think I'm a fan. She's crazy.' Her eyes widened, and I believed her.

'Umm,' I was trying to remember if I had applied any make-up. There was a slight recollection of using mascara. 'Yeah, okay?' I hadn't meant it to come out as a question, but I felt like I was having my first alien encounter in this freaky new world, and I didn't know what the customs were.

She squealed and bounced again, then wrapped her arm around me and snapped the camera at least ten times, moving her head from left to right.

'Mrs Lord, your table is this way,' a woman in a smart dark blue suit said, appearing in front of us.

'Uhh, yes. Thank you,' I stuttered, stepping out of the girl's arm.

'You're amazing,' the girl cried out after me, and I smiled as warmly as I could muster.

All I could think to do was say, 'Thank you.'

I blinked heavily at the woman beckoning me, hoping she saw the thanks in there. Her smile told me she understood, and I followed her onto a large square terrace. She led me over to the far side. It was tucked a little out of the way of passing traffic, but the view was precisely what I was looking for. On the table was a pot of steaming coffee next to a tray of the most wickedly inviting pastries I had ever seen.

'Would you like me to pour?' she asked.

'Yes, please.' I sat down, and while she poured the coffee, I gazed back out over the skyline towards the impeccable design of Giotto's bell tower. With its mainly blue and white façade, it stood taller than all the terracotta buildings. It had always reminded me of one of the toy soldiers from the Nutcracker, standing guard over Florence.

The waitress left me with my breakfast, and I settled into the seat and sipped. Any anxiety I felt faded away, and I just enjoyed the simple pleasure of a beautiful view.

'Good shout,' a voice said to my side, snapping me out of my trance. Matt fell into the seat opposite and swiped the last croissant. He was wearing a loose pair of pale grey linen trousers and a white t-shirt that clung to all the right spots. His hair was damp and tousled from the shower, and stubble, shorter than I was used to seeing, dusted his jawline. For the first time, his eyes weren't red. He was almost as pretty as the view.

'Umm, yes, please, lots of coffee,' he said as the waitress returned. Once she had poured and left, he sat back and looked me over. 'So, what would you like to do today?'

Almost hypnotised by the Florentine atmosphere, I said the one thing I truly wanted to do. 'I want to walk around. I just want to… be.' I considered what I had said. 'Does that make sense?'

Matt nodded and picked up another pastry. 'Absolutely. I do have to go back to the villa, though. I made a bargain with Amanda. She stops pestering about you doing interviews, and in return, I'd do some video interviews. We should be on a press tour with the premiere so close, but….' He looked around at the view and then back at me. 'I'm going to call this a silver lining.'

'Thank you,' I said affectionately. I was learning more and more every day about the slack he was picking up with me being 'absent'. 'Am I ok to do that?' As great as Florence looked from up here and how relaxing it felt to remember just walking the streets, dipping in and out of shops and cafes, I felt more exposed than before.

Matt considered it for a few seconds, then said, 'Yes. With a couple of bodyguards in tow. Just keep your head down as much as possible. Sunglasses and a hat, and don't stay in the same place for too long. Everyone thinks we're in Spain, so that will buy you some time.'

I raised an eyebrow over my coffee cup. It sounded like a military operation. A bit of the shine smudged. It wasn't the idea of peace and tranquillity that I had been seeking. My thoughts then wandered back to the kids. I missed them. In itself, it was an incredible feeling. I had been so panicked about not immediately connecting with them, but that was precisely what I had done, and only a little over a week later, being away from them was causing me physical pain.

Another thought skimmed through my mind that showed promise of alleviating some of the pain, and I voiced it. 'Can Isabella come into town? Mummy/daughter day?'

That seemed to please Matt. 'She's yours. Really, as long as you stay within the constraints of the law, you can do what you want with her.' He looked at his watch. 'You might want to give it an hour before calling her, though.'

A little while later, we headed back to the room, and with so many warm, happy feelings coursing through me, I showered and then called my daughter. Although it was expressed through yawns, she was excited to have a day out with her mum. I hung up feeling like a teenager who had just gotten a date to a dance. Picking up the phone again, I called reception to ask about a stylist and make-up artist. If this did turn into my first public appearance, I was determined not to look like a sleep-deprived mess.

Chapter Twenty-Four

Within a cloud of hairspray and perfume, I was slipped into a slim-fitted pair of three-quarter length jeans and a soft cashmere jumper that purposely fell off one shoulder. Holding the cream Valentino sandals in front of me, I gazed at them lovingly before slipping my feet into them.

'No museums,' Isabella announced, gliding into the room. Her mousey hair was scooped back into a loose ponytail, and in her white floral dress and matching pumps, she also looked like a professional had gotten their hands on her.

I grabbed her and pulled her into my arms, kissing her. She squealed and squirmed, but when I went to put her down, she clung to my waist and neck. Fuck, I loved that kid.

'I was thinking shopping, food, and fizzy drinks.'

'Yayyyy,' she shouted, raising her arms in the air in glee, reminding me of Dylan when I said he could have chocolate for breakfast.

'Right, you two, have fun.' Matt came around the corner in a pair of loose jeans and a black t-shirt that read, *'There's only one Bastine'* on the front.

I burst out laughing. 'Are you seriously wearing that out?'

He held his t-shirt out at the hem to look at the front. 'What? You gave it to me, and…' he lifted his eyes temptingly towards me, 'it's true.'

Memories of the night before pulsed through me in hot waves, and I had to lower Isabella to the floor before I dropped her.

'Okay,' I said to Isabella, but Matt knew the goofy grin on my face was all his. 'Shall we?' She jumped around again and then threw her arms towards her dad. Matt scooped her up and kissed all over her face while she giggled.

I leant into them and kissed him on the cheek. 'I will see you later.'

'Umm, yes, you will.' The innuendo had my legs wobbling. I needed some fresh air. 'And Frey,' he said when we reached the living room. 'I dare you to try and make a dent.'

I had always been cautious with money. It was what came with being skint for most of your life, but I also did like to rise to a challenge. 'What would be considered a dent?'

Matt moved his head from side to side in contemplation. 'Something that comes out of a museum with its own security detail.' He roared with laughter when he saw my mouth fall open.

'This is fucking insane,' I said under my breath, so Isabella didn't hear.

We were all out of the door and heading towards the lift when another of those random thoughts fell out of my mouth. 'What's my pin number?'

'five, six, seven, two,' Isabella answered.

'Thank you,' I said laughing, but with that, other questions appeared. What were the kids' dates of birth? When was my wedding anniversary? When was Matt's birthday? How old was Matt?

The lift opened onto the red stairs I'd seen the night before, and we were greeted by the same two men who had escorted me out of the hospital. This time they were wearing dark chinos and cream polo shirts instead of suits. I was a little taken aback to see them. Had they flown over with us?

'Hi,' Isabella said, tumbling out of the lift towards the blond-haired mountain.

'Hey trouble,' he replied warmly. 'Where we off to today?'

'Shopping,' Isabella exclaimed, jumping about.

'Shopping it is then.' He swished his arm through the air, indicating the way. Isabella curtsied at the gesture and then bounded down the stairs. Matt guided me forward with his hand on my lower back, his other hand taken up with tapping on his phone.

'I don't know your names, I'm sorry,' I said to the blond one and then smiled apologetically at the dark-haired one. They both had a kind look about them, but there was something about the dark-haired one, whose face and arms were littered with scars, that made me want to keep a bit of distance, unlike the blond one, who came across more like a well-toned teddy bear.

'Mike,' the blond said, placing his palm on his chest. 'Paul,' he said, pointing across from him.

Paul smiled, and it didn't do a lot to make him look any more approachable.

'I've been with you for about six years, and Paul has been with us for about three.'

'We need two because our children have a tendency to try running off in different directions,' Matt said, only briefly looking up from his phone.

Both Mike and Paul nodded, then said, 'Umm,' to acknowledge how correct that statement was. I couldn't resist the smile that spread over my face at the thought of Paul running around after the kids, trying to catch the slippery little suckers.

'So, when we say shopping,' Mike began to ask as we walked down the stairs towards the car park. 'Are we talking food markets or clothes shops?'

'Clothes,' Isabella bellowed from the bottom of the stairs.

'I like her thinking,' I agreed.

'Right,' Matt sighed, putting his phone back in his pocket. I wanted to ask what was wrong, but it was obvious it was about the work world I was yet to be fully immersed into. 'You two have fun. Please stay with Mike and Paul. Shop till you drop, and remember, sunglasses and hats are your friends.' He kissed me, and while everyone else got in the car, I held Matt to me. I was so grateful, not only for him, and the world we had created with our little family, but for everything he was doing for me behind the scenes, without complaint.

'I love you,' I said, letting him go. His smile filled his eyes with tears, and he pulled me back to him, pouring all the passion he felt for me into a kiss. When he pulled back, I was only standing because he was holding me.

'I adore you. You are the love of my life.' With a light kiss on my forehead, he left me standing there, blazing with desire but cold with the sudden absence of him.

'Humph,' I said, pulling myself together, then climbed into the car next to my daughter, who was listing all the shops she would like to be taken to.

'At five, you shouldn't even be able to pronounce Moschino,' Paul remarked in what sounded like both jest and seriousness. My daughter had style.

'I'm five and three quarters, thank you,' Isabella declared indignantly.

'I stand corrected,' Paul said, folding his arms. He was a strange one who I couldn't quite get a read on, but if at any point I found myself in need of rescue, I was heading his way. If nothing else, he was so tall and broad that he could act as a wall.

'Okay, so this part of town,' Mike said when the car pulled over after only a couple of minutes, 'is pedestrianised. The car will loop, but Paul and I will be with you both at all times.' I tensed up at the sound of the serious edge to his voice. 'If, for some reason, you are separated from both of us, we are speed dial three on your phone, or Isabella's watch has a panic button.'

Isabella held her little white and pink flowered watch out for me to see. There was a digital clock face at the top, but underneath, there was a little plastic case that you could lift up.

221

'We can track your phone and Isabella's watch. Find somewhere away from the general public and wait for us. A locked bathroom is always the best idea, but most restaurants will hide you out in their kitchen until we can extract you.'

I swallowed loudly, suddenly petrified to get out of the car. Isabella just swung her legs around impatiently.

'I just wanted a walk and to do a bit of shopping with my daughter,' I said feebly. 'Maybe get a bit of lunch.'

'Uww, can we go to Zeb's for lunch?' Isabella shouted while jumping on her bum.

'Okay,' was all I could get out.

'You'll be fine,' Mike reassured. 'Just as Matt said, head down, hat and sunglasses on.'

I took a deep breath as he slipped a little pink sunhat onto the top of Isabella's head. I put my oversized sunglasses on. 'I forgot the hat,' I said, looking around for it.

'Come on, Mummy. I see Gucci. We'll buy you one.'

'She's not actually as spoilt as she sounds,' Mike said softly in Isabella's defence. I patted his arm and got out of the car. Mike was out straight after me, then Isabella with Paul behind her. The bouncy little girl in the car changed before my eyes, standing very still and looking down. I wasn't sure what was happening, but then I saw Mike and Paul scanning the area while she waited between them. When they considered everything was okay, Paul tapped Isabella on the shoulder, and my excited, bouncing little girl came out from between them and took my hand.

Isabella clearly knew where she was going. Being dragged forwards with Mike and Paul close behind, I just went with it. I couldn't stop repeating over and over what I had just seen. It had obviously occurred to me that there would be media attention around my children, but it felt like a sub-story to my own. That little display had shown me that I wasn't the only one who was famous. As mine and Matt's daughter, her face would be known

222

to the world. She had been famous from the minute she was born. I had already assumed there would be a decent price paid for photos of me, but it suddenly occurred to me that the price was probably higher for a picture of Isabella, or any of my other children.

I saw this little girl's life from a completely different angle. I knew her as the sleepy, generally bedraggled child who bossed her brothers around, but gliding towards Gucci, I saw she had a presence in the world, processes and restrictions that she had to adhere to. I thought about my childhood, which existed within a bubble of three streets and a car park. I made a mental note to sign the kids up for some charity work as we entered Gucci.

Isabella headed straight for the hats. Before I could catch up with her, a young woman, so stunningly beautiful that she made me want to run away, stepped in front of me with a stern look on her face. I suppose my small child was running through the store.

She opened her mouth, and I couldn't resist. I took off my sunglasses. It felt a little like producing a gun at a knife fight. Her mouth visibly dropped open, and her back straightened so quickly that she looked like she had been electrocuted.

'I'm so sorry,' I said sweetly. 'She knows where she's going.'

Her classic Italian features softened to reveal a welcoming countenance. 'No. Of course. Isabella is most welcome here. Is there anything in particular that you are looking for with us today, Mrs Lord?'

Hearing her name Isabella, made my thoughts about her fame come back, and I winced slightly.

'I believe we are looking for a hat.'

The woman nodded as if this was the wisest choice anyone had ever made. 'And the outfit?' she enquired.

'This one,' I said, parting my arms slightly to display myself.

She looked me over again, as if my clothing choice was perfect, then nodded. 'Please follow me.' She led the way over to Isabella.

'Miss Lord, is there anything you have seen that you think would suit your mother's outfit today?' she asked, sounding like she was genuinely interested in the little girl's opinion.

'That one,' Isabella said confidently, pointing to a cream sunhat with a black ribbon.

'Ah, perfect,' the woman praised and lifted the hat off the shelf, handing it to me.

I walked over to the closest mirror and placed it on my head. Isabella and the woman followed, and after a brief assessment, they folded their arms and smiled.

'Yes,' Isabella proclaimed.

The woman looked over at her with a nod. 'I agree. Perfect choice. You have style, Miss.'

'I do,' Isabella said with a display of confidence that saw us all laughing.

I spent what I considered to be four months rent on the hat and another two on a lightweight pink coat for Isabella. A few people glanced our way, then stared or did a double-take as they passed us, but overall, Isabella and I traversed the street full of designer brands with minimal interruption. I got the sense that Paul and Mike had a lot to do with that. If someone looked like they were heading towards us, one stepped in the way while the other corrected mine and Isabella's course away from them.

I had, though, been cornered coming out of the dressing room in Fendi. After trying on a dress, I knew Matt would get as much pleasure out of as I would, two Italian women in their thirties saw me, and one screamed while the other staggered back against the cubicle. Mike had run in, but I held my hand out to stop him and took a deep breath. Isabella was safe with Paul, and this was something I needed to get used to.

I smiled warmly at them and listened as humbly as was humanly possible while they gushed over me. They took a couple of photos, and I signed my first autograph with a black marker across a Fendi bag that still had the label on.

By the time we left, a small crowd had gathered, intrigued by the twenty or so paparazzi who had appeared. In a practised move, Isabella lowered her head and fell in between Paul and Mike while holding onto my hand. They all called out to Isabella, trying to get her to lift her head, but she didn't react in the slightest.

Mike turned us to the left, and Paul came around to the side. With the shopfronts on one side and the massive walls of muscle that made up our bodyguards on the other, they corralled us down the street. I stepped slightly in front of Isabella so the photographers running backwards in front of us couldn't get at her. People halted coming out of the shops, and to the sound of gasps and squeals, we finally made it to the car.

Within seconds it was moving. I spun around to see the photographers jump on scooters and into cars, then speed through traffic to catch up to us.

I let out a massive breath I had been holding since Fendi and panted. I expected to find everyone else in the same frazzled state. Instead, Isabella was swinging her legs, absentmindedly humming a tune, while she watched Mike trying to fish something out from under his fingernail.

I just watched them. I was a little in awe of them, especially Isabella. She was completely unfazed by it all. I was filled with pride seeing her resilience. Then a weight fell into my stomach. She knew no different. She didn't know a world where people didn't chase her down the street trying to take photos of her. That couldn't be healthy. What I had done with my life would define hers, whether she wanted it to or not. I hoped she wasn't in therapy, but perhaps it wasn't a bad idea.

'We're here,' Paul announced from the seat facing me. I blinked away from seeing the misfit my daughter stood a good chance of becoming, to find a grand Italian façade nestled behind tall gates. I was still a little rattled but didn't want Isabella to see, so I waited to follow everyone's lead.

'Here we go,' Mike said with a wink to Isabella. Like an eclipse, the light was blocked out by a mass of darkness gathering around the car. Before my eyes could fully adjust, Mike opened the door. Clicks and flashes flooded in, and Mike had to push past the invasion to get out. Without flinching or a modicum of fear, or even really interest, Isabella climbed out behind him. Her head was so low her chin was touching her chest.

Paul placed his hand on my shoulder. 'Now you,' he said, inclining his head towards the open door. I had stopped breathing, wanting to stay exactly where I was, but seeing my five-year-old daughter step into it pushed me forwards.

All I could hear was mine and Isabella's names, and all I could see were cameras and faceless people swarming me. Fresh, warm air hit me, and I fumbled around with my hat, trying to stop my hands from shaking. In a city that had always felt like it was wrapping me in a blanket, I was left bare and vulnerable.

I felt Paul's hand on my back, and he pushed me forwards, so Isabella was tucked in tightly between Mike and me. My attention caught on her hand wrapped around a white cord hanging from the back of Mike's jeans. It wasn't until Mike and Paul had ushered us through a set of elegant-looking black gates and Isabella reached up to remove the cord from her wrist that I realised it was actually attached to her.

My stomach dropped. She had tied herself to Mike to stop herself from being pulled away. With the gates closed, the calling out stopped, but my breathing was coming fast. I couldn't decide if I was more freaked out by the intensity of the attention or the measures put in place to stop someone from grabbing and running off with my daughter.

The edges of my vision darkened, and stumbling forwards, the scene before me changed. I could still hear Florentine life buzzing around me, but I was standing in a darkened corner on the side of a stage. The roar of the traffic past the gates swirled with the sound of a mass crowd laughing. Large spotlights spun out upon the stage but never touched me. I was holding something long and heavy in my hands. It was cold to the touch, but it grew warm where I was gripping it. My breath was catching, and my stomach rolled. I needed the toilet but couldn't move. I was trying to keep myself calm, trying to push all my anxiety into what I was holding. Someone moved something next to me, and I stepped to the right. The lights continued to roll across the stage, but now I could see out onto it. Shining black, all it held was a glass podium. Beyond it, row upon row of people sat.

There was a smartly dressed man at the podium, but what he was saying was muffled. All I could hear was traffic and people from the crowd laughing. That was until, as if he was standing next to me, he said, 'And to present the…'

'Mummy, are you coming?' I felt a warmth fill my hand, different from how it had been a moment before.

I blinked, and the darkness drew away from my vision, soaking me in sunshine. I blinked again, trying to force my eyes to adjust. In front of me, looking at me expectantly, was a little girl in a pink hat. She drew her arm back, and mine went with her. She was holding my hand.

'Mummy, I'm hungry,' she said impatiently. *'Isabella.'* The word sprang to mind just as I looked over her head, trying to find her mum.

She pulled me forwards, and I let her. I was scared to blink in case I forgot her again. Pushing all thoughts of standing on the

227

stage away, I followed Mike and Isabella through a glass door and into an all-white restaurant, with Paul coming in behind.

As soon as we were inside, Isabella did as she had in Gucci and skipped forward. Mike hung back to let me pass, and Isabella continued, going straight past the maître d', who was writing in a large leatherbound book with a jewel-encrusted fountain pen at a podium. A cold shiver raked over me seeing it.

His gaze swept outwards to follow Isabella as she passed, but he was a bit more clued in than the woman in Gucci had been, and before he reacted, he looked towards me. I was already removing my hat and glasses.

'Mrs Lord, welcome.' He stepped out from behind the podium. 'Please, right this way.'

I followed with a smile, but we didn't catch up with Isabella until she was already seated at a table with a reserved sign, on the veranda overlooking the Ponte Vecchio. The maître d' pulled out the seat next to Isabella's and, at the same time, removed the reserved sign.

'Thank you,' I said, taking the seat.

'And what can I get you to drink?' he asked, addressing Isabella.

'A Coke?' she said while looking at me. The maître d' lifted his eyebrow and cocked a smile towards me.

'Just this once,' I said, trying to sound responsible, but truth be told, I was so rattled that she could have asked for a Jack and Coke, and I would have agreed.

He dipped his head in agreement. 'And, Mrs Lord, what can I get you?'

'A glass of red wine of your choosing, please.'

'Certainly.' He bowed his head and left.

Another waiter immediately approached and filled our glasses with water. I thanked him but kept my gaze upon the view in front of me. I knew the scene before me. The way the streets led into

228

one another, leading away from the tourists into the suburban life of Florence. The little cafes I had sat at, drinking coffee, laughing with friends about the light-heartedness of life. I pictured myself there, trying to connect to the carefree woman who saw the world in perfect shades of black and white.

'One glass of Coke for the young lady, and a glass of Barolo for you, madam.' Like an elastic band had sprung, I was propelled back from the streets below. One moment I was twenty-seven and sipping coffee in a red and cream café, and the next, I was in an all-white restaurant with a little girl sitting next to me. Fear and shock were the only things that kept me seated. I had no memory of anything after that café.

My breath hitched, and I gripped the arms of the metal chair.

'Mummy, can I have the sea bass?'

I turned to see the little girl peering over a white menu at me, then looked around the restaurant for her mum.

'What are you having?' she asked.

I had no idea where she had come from, but there was something familiar about her. The way her eyes curved at the edge, the shape of her face. I gripped the chair tighter and felt something move on my finger. I looked down to see the sun catch on a diamond, dazzling me. The light cleared, and I was back standing on the side of a stage, but my feet were moving. The sharp light swung around to gather me within, and my eyes adjusted to take in a sea of people clapping. The light guided me forwards, and above the clapping, I could hear my heels clicking against the echoing stage. Approaching the podium, three more spotlights covered me. My eyes raised to the crowd, and they stopped clapping.

I opened my mouth.

'If you get the risotto and let me have some, I'll let you have some of my sea bass.'

229

I closed my eyes and rubbed my hand across my forehead. When I opened them, sunshine captured me, and that precious word fell into my head, *'Isabella.'*

'That sounds perfect, darling,' I said, picking up the glass and downing half the contents.

If Mike and Paul hadn't been there, I would have scampered back to the villa, letting Isabella play with my phone and credit card on the way as an apology, but I was determined not to let my discombobulated state ruin what was otherwise an amazing day with my daughter.

'What's your favourite memory?' I asked as Isabella swallowed the last of her lunch.

She jumped at that question, and I was humbled by the simplicity of her answer. A couple of years ago, when it had clicked to her that I wrote stories, like the ones I sent her to sleep with every night, she had asked me to write one just for her.

Apparently, I had not only written the story, which was about a boat trip full of colourful characters, but Matt had raided the costume and props departments of whatever film he was working on. Then between Matt, Mike, Alex, me, and reluctantly, Paul, we had re-enacted the story for her and Jack while they sprawled out across the beanbag in their room with bags of popcorn, watching the show.

Over the next hour, I realised I had spent the last week asking all the wrong people questions. What I should have done on day one was sit Isabella down and give her a bottle of Coke. She told me everything. I was amazed at what she knew. I got the lowdown on everyone.

My agent was scary and loud. I avoided my publicist as much as possible. I would get drunk once every six months or so with my publisher, then say yes to whatever the kids asked for. Auntie Connie and Auntie Vic were a big part of her life, and she spoke about them with such affection. Matt and my brother-in-law

Lance owned a company renovating country estates. Matt was apparently taking a course that had something to do with, as Isabella put it, 'arking'. I think she was going for architecture.

Matt had a brother and a sister. I got on really well with everyone apart from Matt's brother. Isabella had apparently heard me call him a 'male, showy pig', and Jack had heard him call me a 'gold digger'.

We had travelled a lot but were now making work come to us in the UK because Isabella and Jack were starting school in September. She was not impressed with that as we'd kept them out for the first year to homeschool. We had spent about six months in Asia when Dylan was a baby, and she and Jack had gone to stay for a bit with a nanny we had at the time at her family's home in Hunan Provence. They had loved it. Jack was basically fluent in Chinese and had a friend in Shaoyang, whom he spoke to over video call every couple of weeks. Both Isabella and Jack spoke Italian fluently.

She dropped mega stars' names like they were just 'Bob' down the road. She and Jack took lessons in sword fighting, which apparently had been my idea. Isabella was aiming for the Olympics. Swimming was everything to her. Jack had a yellow belt in Jujitsu, and the future king of England had come to her last birthday party. I choked on my wine when I realised who she was so casually talking about.

By the end of lunch and my second glass of wine, I had decided she didn't need therapy. She may live in a crazy world, but she had adapted to it, ignoring the bad parts and thriving in the good bits. I had also decided that me getting a bit of therapy wasn't a bad idea.

I politely signed a couple of autographs as we were getting up from the table, and when a middle-aged woman with white hair in a fur coat asked for a photo, Isabella automatically walked over and plucked a foil-wrapped sweet off the maître d's podium. She

231

came back to me when the white-haired woman left, and I just marvelled at my eldest daughter.

I collected my bag and her hand, and we crossed the restaurant, but when we were in the centre of the room, two of the largest men I had ever seen came into view, their eyes fixed on me. The dark-haired one had thin scars over his face and down his arms. I couldn't place where I knew them from. I felt my mind jump around again, but with absolute certainty, I knew there was something about them that made me nervous.

I pulled Isabella back to the table, pretending I had forgotten something, and thankfully they didn't follow. A waiter was clearing our table, and I breathed a sigh of relief.

'Is there a back door?' I asked quietly next to him. He looked over me once, then set down what he had been gathering up and gestured for me to go left across the veranda, away from the men. I followed him through a door and down a service staircase into the kitchens. Isabella didn't bat an eyelid, just chatted about the shops she wanted to visit next.

I told her she could have anything she wanted as I ushered her out of a fire escape and into a long alleyway. The high walls of the buildings looming over us made me feel protected, and I scurried down the street, pulling Isabella behind me.

'Freya! Isabella!' I heard someone call behind us. 'Freya! Freya!' they called again. I suddenly stopped, unsure why I was running.

'Mummy, we can't stay here.'

I looked down to see a little girl in a pink hat holding my hand. 'Where's your mummy?' I asked her.

She wasn't listening to me. She was looking down the alleyway with a wary expression on her face. I followed her gaze, and in shock, I stepped back. I tried to let go of the girl's hand, but she held on tightly. Coming towards us, running, was an endless stream of people. They all had cameras in front of their faces, snapping as they ran.

The scene before me went black, then blasted me with a strong white light. I felt excruciating pain coming from my abdomen.

'Freya, you're breach. We have to try and turn him.' A male doctor in green scrubs appeared before me. I heard myself scream, but it felt so far away. Matt came into view, his face contorted. I wanted to reach out and smooth the pain away, but my hand wouldn't move. It was covering my stomach. I looked down to scream and saw my heavily pregnant belly.

'Mummy! Mummy!'

My legs shook, and I blinked past the blinding light.

'We have to go,' the little girl holding my hand said.

'Isabella.'

I was panting heavily, and every thought in my head felt like it was raking against barbwire. My eyes stung, and I couldn't focus.

'Come on.' Isabella was pulling at my hand, and I let my body follow. The motion of running cleared my vision enough to look behind me when I heard my name being called. Cameras flashed, and I had no idea what the hell was going on. I only knew that I had to get this little girl away from the men running at us and that I was in Florence, a city I knew well.

I lifted her into my arms and accelerated forward. At the end of the alleyway, I turned left. We were only a few streets away from the Uffizi, and beyond there was a maze of small streets I could easily lose them in.

I turned right at a little café with empty seats and a broken sign, then immediately left. When we came out into the busy piazza, I kept going. Reaching the far end, I ducked us into a side street next to a florist and put Isabella down.

'Where did Mike and Paul go?' Isabella asked.

I closed my eyes in exasperation, remembering why the men in the restaurant were looking at me. I then became very aware that I was in a small, tucked away street with a child who I had forgotten was mine more than once.

I leant down to her, so we were face to face. It was agonising to see the fear in her eyes. 'Mummy's getting a little jumbled. I need you to do something for me, okay?' She nodded, but her bottom lip quivered. 'No matter what I say or do, you stay at my side.' She nodded again, but a single tear ran from her eye. I kissed it away. 'I need you to keep telling me that you're important to me. Okay?'

'Okay, Mummy.'

'You are.' I stroked her face, praying I would never forget her again. 'You are so very, very important to me.'

'I'm your little miracle,' she said brightly, trying to fight the tears.

I pulled her in and held her.

'Shall I push my panic button, Mummy?'

I had forgotten all about that. There was also something about my phone trying to push its way through. I pulled it from my bag while Isabella pressed the little red button under the casing of her watch. There were missed calls from names I didn't recognise. I skipped past them. There was only one name in my head, and I was repeating it, desperate for it to stay with me.

I hit call when I found it, and he answered on the first ring, saying brightly, 'Are we a happy shopper?'

'Help me,' I cried into the phone. 'I'm going to forget her. I know I am. Help me, please.'

'Freya? What's going on? Where are you?' His voice was fraught. 'Get Paul and Mike on the fucking phone,' he bellowed away from the speaker.

I forgot his name.

'Hello?' I asked. There was a phone next to my ear, and I had no idea why.

'Freya, I need you to listen to my voice, okay?'

'Okay,' I said, then took the phone from my ear and looked at it in puzzlement. The name 'Matt' was displayed. I had no idea who that was.

Something moved in my peripheral vision. Glancing towards it, I jumped back, startled. There was a little girl in front of me with tears running over her cheeks. Absentmindedly, I put the phone back in my bag and walked over to her.

'Are you okay?' I asked, leaning down to her. 'Where's your mummy and daddy?'

Her bottom lip shook, and her hands reached out to me. My gaze followed them, confused by the gesture. 'I'm important to you,' she stuttered.

It was the last thing I had expected her to say. I looked around her. We were in a street just off a busy piazza that I couldn't remember walking into. She took my hand, pulling my gaze back to her. 'I'm important to you,' she repeated. Then as more tears fell, she said, 'You're my mummy.' My stomach turned, and I retched.

'Isabella.'

I grabbed her into my arms and ran out of the street. I needed to get my daughter somewhere safe before I forgot who she was again. I repeated her name over and over in my head as I ran. I didn't care about anything else other than that name.

The piazza ended, and a busy road met us. The word was there, what I was looking into traffic for, but it felt as if I would have to forget her name to remember it.

'Isabella. Isabella. Isabella.'

I saw the word bathed in light upon one of the cars coming towards me, and I waved my arm towards it. The car pulled over next to us, and I bundled Isabella in, then climbed in after her.

'Hospital,' I said quickly, then went back to repeating her name. The taxi sped off, and I gripped Isabella's hand. 'No matter what, you don't leave my side. Okay?'

She nodded and wrapped her arms around me. I buried my face into the top of her head.

'Isabella.'

Chapter Twenty-Five

While Isabella gripped me tightly, my mind left the taxi and placed me back in front of the podium on the black stage, the crowd before me silent and expectant.

'When I got the call a couple of months ago, asking me to present an award at the Oscars, I answered, "That is very sweet, but no thank you."' The crowd erupted into laughter, and I felt myself shrug. Tight material pulled against me, and I shifted to adjust it.

'I politely hung up, but they called straight back and said, "Please hear me out. It's the lifetime achievement award for Billy Thomas."' I sighed loudly, which prompted the crowd to start laughing again.

'There is only one other person on this earth who could get me up on this stage.' I looked out into the crowd and immediately found Matt in the first row. My vision tilted, and I realised I had winked. Matt blushed slightly but smiled smugly with a proud shrug.

'I grew up with Billy featuring in the blockbusters that adorned my bedroom wall.' I stopped to chuckle. 'They wrote that. Matt, I promise there were no posters of Billy on my wall.' Matt burst out laughing, and my eyes scanned a few seats over to where Billy Thomas was sitting. He had a full head of salt and pepper hair and a set of dark brown eyes that looked back at me affectionately. I gave him a very obvious wink, and he, like everyone else, started laughing again.

Keeping my eyes fixed on Billy, I continued, 'You were the...'

'Mummy? Mummy?'

The crowd disappeared, and I found myself in the back of a car with a little girl next to me. She reached up and placed her hand on my cheek.

'I'm important to you.'

'Isabella.'

'We have to get out of the car.' She pushed something into a handbag, and I opened the car door with no idea where I was or why this teary-eyed little girl was important to me.

She followed me out, and taking my hand, she pulled me into a hospital. To the first nurse she saw, she said, 'My mummy's jumbled.'

I looked around for her mummy and found every other person in the hospital's reception area staring at us. A few of them took out phones and took photos of us.

'Come with me. Okay?' Someone touched my arm. I looked away from the snapping camera phones to see the nurse the little girl had spoken to trying to guide me away. I followed, looking back at the people still taking photos, thinking it was a bit rude.

We arrived at a little side room, and the nurse gestured for me to take a seat opposite a gurney.

'Can you tell me your name?' the nurse asked as I sat.

'Freya.'

She nodded approvingly. 'And do you know who this is?' she asked, and I realised the little girl had followed us into the room.

'Isabella.'

I burst into tears of relief and pulled Isabella towards me. 'You're safe, darling. You're safe.'

She gripped me tightly. 'I'm important to you,' she cried into my neck.

'You're my little miracle,' I corrected, and then to the nurse, I said, 'She's my daughter. I was in an accident. I have amnesia.'

The nurse reached over and stroked my hands reassuringly. 'You are both safe. Is there someone you would like me to call?'

'Matt!' I remembered speaking with him in the side street off the piazza. While still holding Isabella against me, I reached into my bag, pulled out my phone, and passed it to the nurse. 'Matt.' I didn't trust myself to make the call. I could only concentrate on one thing, and that needed to be my petrified daughter pressed against me.

The nurse took the phone, and I heard it ring once on speaker and then Matt's voice. 'Freya?' he half cried, half shouted it.

'This is Louisa. I'm a nurse at the Santa Maria Nuova hospital. Mrs Lord is here. She's okay.'

'Is Isabella with her?' he choked out.

'Yes. Yes,' the nurse reassured, and I heard Matt let out the emotion of knowing his daughter was safe.

'I'm twenty minutes away,' Matt said with a strained voice.

'You can move, or I can move you,' I heard from the other side of the door, and then it opened, and Mike was in the room with Paul close behind. With them in there as well, it felt very crowded.

'What the hell, Freya?' Mike demanded. He looked petrified.

'I'm sorry. I'm sorry,' I said to Mike, Paul, and even Isabella, as I buried my face into her neck.

'Aww, this is a cramped room,' I heard a new voice say.

'Yes, it is,' the nurse announced. 'You two out. She is well cared for. Out you go.'

'You run off again, and I handcuff you to me,' Mike said, leaving the room, and there was not a doubt in my mind that he meant it.

'Sweetheart, can I have a look at Mummy?'

I lifted my face from Isabella's neck to see a doctor in his late forties with ebony black hair perched on the edge of the gurney.

'How about you and I go and get a drink?' The nurse held out her hand to Isabella.

I shook my head.

'No. She doesn't leave my sight.' I did relinquish my grip on her, though, so she could sit on the seat next to me.

'Can you tell me what happened?' the doctor asked in a soothing tone. I relayed the afternoon to him, and he listened, nodding as I spoke. When I finished, he reached into his coat pocket and retrieved what looked like a thick white pen. It made a clicking sound, and when he swept a light into my eyes, I blinked and saw Billy Thomas crossing the black stage with arms open towards me.

'Freya?' The light dulled as the doctor leant over me. My mouth filled with saliva, and I swallowed to stop myself from throwing up. 'I understand it can be very scary,' he said when he saw my eyes refocus. 'As your memories come back, it can be very disorientating while your mind tries to sort through everything, trying to get all the right memories in the right places. We'll get you upstairs for a CAT scan and some rest just to be safe.'

Tears slipped from my eyes, and Isabella curled herself into me.

'Can someone call Matt?' I asked, and the nurse informed me that he was on his way. I desperately needed to hand Isabella to him. I was hanging over the edge of a cliff in my mind, holding on with the tips of my fingers, and I couldn't let go until my little miracle was with the only other person in this world I fully trusted. A deep cough seeped through my mind to remind me that wasn't technically true.

'We survived before Matt, Freya. I've always got you. You're safe. The sprog's safe. So, chill the fuck out before you have a bloody heart attack.'

'Unless I forget you as well.'

'No one forgets me.'

240

Chapter Twenty-Six

After a trip to the CAT scan, with Isabella in the next room where I could see her through a window, I was put in a room that looked more like a hotel room than a sideward of a hospital.

Isabella was flicking through the channels under the instruction that no matter what happened, she was not to leave the room.

I lay upon the bed watching her, and in a slightly calmer fashion than what I had been experiencing, memories came back to me. I was at home in the UK, sat up in bed. My belly was so far out that, while I was watching the TV, I could see it pushing against the covers. I was crying, only lightly, but I could feel the sadness.

'Hey, what are the tears for?' Matt placed a hand on my heavily pregnant belly and kissed one of the tears on my cheek.

'I'm scared,' I said softly, laying my hand over his. Matt looked younger than I was used to seeing. His hair was shorter, his face thinner, and he was clean-shaven.

'There is nothing to be scared of,' he cooed reassuringly.

'They're running out of room,' I cried.

'And that's why you're on bed rest. As long as you don't move too much, they have plenty of room.' He kissed away my tears, and I rested my forehead against his, drawing warmth and solace from the man I adored.

'Do you think zombies and mummies are the same thing?' I blinked past the memory and the tears it brought forth to see Isabella sitting in the chair with her feet resting on the edge of the bed. I turned to the TV to see *The Walking Dead* was on.

'That is not five-year-old little girl watching,' I said, reaching out, trying to get the remote control while she held it out of my reach.

'I'm nearly six. And, it's not real. They're just bad actors making funny noises.' She impersonated one of the zombies and then laughed at herself. I couldn't help joining in. She was a whimsically wonderful little weirdo.

'I suppose you've seen behind the scenes of a lot of movies.'

'Yeah, but Jack's scared of the pretend monsters. He is such a wuss.' She shook her head and tutted at her twin brother.

'Where? Just tell me where?' I heard Matt's voice outside the door, and I was about to call out when he burst in.

Isabella, who had looked relaxed only seconds ago, darted into her dad's arms and gently sobbed against his shoulder. She spoke in a whisper that I knew she didn't intend for me to hear. 'Mummy forgot me.'

He wrapped his arms around her while looking at me. His face was full of fear, sadness, and pity.

'Hey Tigger tiger, want to get some ice cream?' I recognised Alex's voice, but Matt was blocking him from my view. Isabella lifted her head and nodded but then turned to me.

I loved her so much and even more at that moment for not leaving the room until I told her she could. 'Go get some ice cream, sweetheart. You deserve it for being such a brave girl.'

She looked a little smug as she clambered out of Matt's arms to go with Alex.

As soon as Isabella was out of the room, I broke apart sobbing. Matt ran to me and pulled me against him. 'Shhh, shhh,' he soothed, but I could feel him shaking. 'She's safe. You're safe. I've got you.'

Through tears and chest convulsing sobs, I told him everything. When I finished, there was a hopeful look on his face. 'So, you remember?'

I laughed slightly manically. 'I basically remember anything that ever caused me stress.'

A dawning crossed his face. He, like I, knew exactly where my TV show *Brighter* came from, but that was a memory for another day. Some things were just too big to be thrown into conversation; they needed wine, and time. Silent agreement passed between us, and I watched his mind flicker over everything else I could have remembered before screwing his face up. 'I'm not sure I want to ask how much of me you remember.'

I rested my hand against his cheek, and he sighed. 'I remember what has to be every event we have attended where cameras flashed at me. I remember Dylan being breach. Being on bed rest with Jack and Isabella. Waiting to go into my first book signing and TV interviews. Presenting an Oscar to Billy fucking Thomas.'

Matt burst into laughter. His shoulders dropped, and he looked at me side-on, adoringly. He was finally speaking with more than an echo of his wife. I'd found her. She hadn't embraced me yet, but I could feel her at the edges, trying to come home.

Finally able to talk about something I had a point of reference to, he cocked his leg onto the bed and said, 'So it all started with a game of Twister.'

'What?' I laughed out. 'I played Twister with Billy Thomas?' It felt crazier than seeing Princess Victoria peering into my house. Billy Thomas was an actor I'd known of since I was about ten. He was the big name. Never overly typecast, he never faded, and everyone from ten to a hundred knew who Billy Thomas was. I really did have posters of Billy on my wall as a teenager. Everyone did. I decided to keep that fact to myself, just in case it hadn't come out yet.

Matt was shaking his head. 'No. I did.' A vague look of embarrassment washed over his face, and I settled back into the pillow to listen. 'Billy and I were in *Placid* together.'

'I remember that one,' I jumped in proudly and then remembered why I remembered it. Everything about it stressed me out. It was filmed in LA, and Matt was playing a sex addict billionaire. I was pregnant and had to stay in the UK because my first book was coming out.

'You were about eight months pregnant with Jack and Isabella, and Billy was in town to promote *Placid*. I came home one day to find Billy sat at the kitchen island eating cake.' Matt stopped to laugh. 'He looked so happy. You were sat next to him, sipping your tea, utterly unfazed that Billy Thomas was in your kitchen.' We both chuckled at the general absurdity that was me.

'He only slightly acknowledged my presence. Cake was life.' He laughed again, and I squeezed myself. I couldn't wait for a memory to come back that didn't make me want to throw up.

'Anyway, cutting a long story short, Billy and I started drinking while you were writing. Once we were absolutely plastered, we decided that even though you couldn't drink, you were being a party pooper. So, we bugged the crap out of you. To appease us, you produced Twister. I still have no idea where that game came from,' he said, shaking his head.

'It didn't do the trick. Billy hid your laptop while you made us bacon sandwiches.' He reached out to stroke my face. 'I love you so much.' He finished with a little giggle and got back to his story. 'We got to see a preview of the face you use on Isabella and Jack that makes them run. The problem was, Billy, for the life of him, couldn't remember where he'd put it. He'd sobered up slightly at this point, so he and I decided the best thing to do was get drunker and see if it came back.

'Did it?'

Matt shook his head. 'No. We found it the next day when you put the oven on. We didn't look there cause you were at the cooker leaning over a frying pan when he hid it. We still don't know how he slid it in there.' He gripped onto his sides, trying to hold himself up against the laughter. 'Not only did you get your own back, but you went batshit crazy at him. You had Billy Thomas in front of you, holding out a new laptop, looking like a little boy getting told off by the headmistress. It was absolutely brilliant to watch.'

I was dumbstruck by all of it, but I was also curious. 'How did I get my own back?'

Matt stopped laughing, looking more concerned. 'It went on for three years, back and forth between you both. My favourite…' Before he could even get it out, he was bent back over, crying with laughter. 'You drugged him!'

'What?' I sat upright, shocked.

'It's alright. It was one of Billy's tablets.' He wiped his eyes. Taking a long breath, testing if he could continue, he finally said, 'The one thing you need to know is that Billy helped you a lot with the fame thing. It came at you hard. *Occurrences* within the first couple of months was fucking massive. Add in you appearing in the *Highland Trip* with Craig Mack, and being my pregnant girlfriend, you were a household name before Isabella and Jack were even born.

'Connie came later, and Vic couldn't really help you. She's never known a normal life, and neither have I really, but Billy, well, he's Billy fucking Thomas. Who better to help you get your head around fame?'

I remembered the message I found on my phone before Vic and Connie turned up. It was reassuring to know he was just a friend.

'The problem is.' Matt took a deep breath. 'You're a pair of idiots when you get together. You and Connie together are… entertaining. You and Billy are mischievous. At one point, he put you on the wrong plane. It cost him thousands. You thought you were getting on a flight to LA. You ended up in Latvia.'

All I could do was stare at him. My life was insane.

'About a year later, you persuaded him to go to the theatre in Stratford-upon-Avon, and talked him into taking the train. Well, Billy occasionally takes sleeping tablets. On the train, you spiked his drink then left him,' Matt bellowed. I desperately wanted this memory. 'He ended up in Skegness. But,' Matt was waving his arms around, and I was crying with joy I never expected to feel, 'you took his phone and wallet.'

Matt got up and paced around, trying to compose himself. I got the impression this was a therapeutic release for both of us. Eventually, while trying to hold back the laughter, he sat back down on the bed and continued, 'It all ended with him throwing you off a building. It was getting majorly out of hand. You'd even sent tigers to his house.'

'Excuse me?' That was a lot of information to get in seven seconds.

'One day, we called in to see him when he was on location in London. They were doing this stunt scene on the top of a building, and there were two rig-ups. One that took Billy higher up and another that dropped him off the edge.

'You were like a kid wanting to play with a toy. You thought you were going up for a bit of superhuman jumping. Instead, you realised, at the very last second, that wasn't the direction you were going in. Over you went, screaming language that I'm not going to repeat.' He shook his head. 'That was the end of it. I put my foot down to it all. You have children.'

'I so badly wish I remembered.'

The happy, reflective look vanished from his face, but I wanted it back. It was reassuring. 'In all of the memories that have come back, you are in most of them. Either holding my hand or in the audience encouraging me. Thank you.'

He kissed me lightly and held me against him. After a few seconds, I pulled back. 'I remembered walking out of the villa and across the terrace under hundreds of twinkle lights, then down an aisle in a white dress.'

His face fell. 'You remember marrying me?' he asked hopefully.

'No,' I answered proudly. 'I'm halfway down the aisle, and when I look up, the memory fades. I'm assuming all the anxiety slipped away when I saw you there waiting for me.'

Kissing over the top of my hands, he whispered, 'I'm so sorry. I should never have let you both go off like that. You just looked so happy at the prospect of a bit of freedom, and...' He lifted his eyes to mine, his expression becoming a little sterner. 'You didn't tell me about the little selfie with a fan moment at the hotel.'

I blinked. I had forgotten all about the young girl outside the lift.

'She outed your location to the world, giving the leaches with cameras plenty of time to gather. I'm going to go fucking mental at Amanda for trying to grab at a bit of free press by not telling us.' Matt could scream at her all he wanted. She had put Isabella in danger, I was sacking her.

The door opened, and the same doctor as before walked in carrying an orange folder. 'All looks great,' he declared. 'I'm sorry to say that things are going to be jumbled for a while as it all comes back, but there is no reason to think your memory won't return in full.

Both Matt and I sighed with relief.

'When can I take her home?'

'Whenever Mrs Lord is ready. It is all about moderation. Take it easy, but try to live as normally as possible. It will encourage the memories.' He stopped and then, after a moment's thought, corrected his statement. 'Well, normal for you.' It was at this moment I realised that since arriving at the hospital, apart from Matt when we were alone, everyone, including Isabella at times, had been speaking in Italian.

Chapter Twenty-Seven

'Are you ready for this?' Matt's arms curled around my stomach, his head resting on my shoulder.

I sighed. Ahead of me, hanging on the wall of my wardrobe in the UK, was a floor-length, off-the-shoulder, beautiful sapphire blue dress made of satin with a label on the inside that said Oscar de la Renta. It was so perfect that I was scared to touch it.

'If you go commando in that, I'll make it worth your while,' Matt said, as a matter of fact. All the tension I was feeling about what would happen after I put the dress on dispersed.

No one could blame my anxiety. For the last two weeks, after we returned from another week of rest at the villa, the house had been buzzing with premiere excitement. On several occasions, Bastine had to stop me from crawling into the wardrobe with my rucksack.

Because memories had returned when I was thrown into the deep end, the general consensus was that should be the way forward. The protection wall Matt had built around me was forcefully pulled down. Bless him, he fought hard for that wall, but he was out-voiced, and on the second day back in the UK, I learnt who the 'general consensus' was.

One by one, or in little groups, people arrived and, seeing as most had spent years throwing me into uncomfortable situations for publicity purposes, I could, at the very least, put a face to a name. As daunting as this immersion was, it was reassuring to be amongst the familiar, beyond the touch of Matt or the smell of my children.

Ironically, the two people I was looking forward to meeting the most, were the only ones I didn't remember.

'Oiy butt-chin, you're going down on the tour.'

I stopped dead in the centre of the foyer. My attention grabbed equally by my main characters walking through the door and my blond-haired little angel facing off from the middle of the stairs.

'Pfft, dream on squirt,' William said while casting his cocky gaze over Jack.

Jack bristled like an assured boxer. With a raised eyebrow and his hands on his hips, he said, 'Bring it.' His chin raised at the end, and the size of my smile was actually hurting.

William huffed dismissively, and while walking towards me, he called out without looking back. 'Sharpen your sword milkybar, trouble's coming.' It would only be later, when my memories fully returned, that I would understand why that nickname grated Matt in particular.

Jack looked undeterred, but then Reena, who had glided in behind William, in a green and yellow catsuit, ended her call, and Jack caught her eye.

'Hey, little man,' she said, holding out her arms. Jack's whole demeanour softened, and he sped down the rest of the stairs, turning back into my little angel. From the last step, he launched, and she caught him, spinning him around to the sound of his giggles. 'You excited for the tour?' she asked, placing Jack on her hip. He nodded enthusiastically, and while I watched his head bob, I realised that was the second time the word 'tour' had been used.

The sliver of a bubble that still encased me exploded. I had a lot of memories of what happened after the last premiere. I just hadn't processed them yet. The main being there would be more than one premiere. I would be seeing a lot of airports. Second to that were the interviews, and I had a vague recollection of a documentary about how it all came to be. I had gotten off lightly so far, but there was not a doubt in my mind that it had come to an end.

'Mrs Lord, it is a pleasure to meet you,' William said, lowering into a flourishing bow. His dark, styled to perfection hair didn't move.

'Dude, all her stressed-out memories are back. I'm pretty sure she remembers you,' Reena said with a deep, dark laugh. A shiver ran up my back hearing it. Sarah was a slight character who was the polar opposite of intimidating, but I gave her the bellowing laugh of a heavy-set, male smoker.

William raised his head and assessed me cockily. With his, 'I own every room' presence and slender frame, I understood why bestowing my cherished characters onto them had not caused me any stress.

'Actually, I don't remember either of you. Which, I have to admit, for once, it's a relief to find a blacked-out memory there.'

Both of them raised their shoulders a little and looked at me with what could have been relief. With a shake to her breath, Reena slipped past William, and with Jack still glued to her side, she wrapped her spare arm around me. Jack made it a group hug while saying, 'Awww.'

'Thank you,' Reena said, stepping back. 'You fought for me to get the part. I really hope I've done justice to Sarah for you.'

'Me, on the other hand, let's face it, I am Lee,' William scoffed.

My gaze caught on the dimple in the middle of William's chin. Understanding Jack's nickname for him, I had to twist my face around to bury the giggle.

'Everyone is out back,' I said, trying to hide my humour.

Gathered around the patio table, with the sun pleasantly coating the courtyard outside my library, fifteen people chatted and planned.

I took my seat on Matt's right, next to Nicola, and William and Reena slipped in on Matt's left. Realising what he was entering,

Jack scampered off, declaring, 'I'm going to go throw beach balls at Issy in the pool.' He was braver than me.

'Even your sister could take you down,' William called after him in jest. Jack stuck his tongue out in response and ran off.

With a serious edge to his voice, Matt added, 'She's not far off being able to take me down.'

I beamed. Something Isabella had left out of her sugar-fuelled 'tell-all', was that her best friend's dad was a Krav Maga instructor. She already knew a hundred different ways to deter unwanted attention.

'Freya, we are going to throw around a lot of information, but if there is anything you would like clarifying, please just jump in.'

I scanned up to the end of the table to a woman so beautiful that if she stood still long enough, I could believe her to be a priceless statue. Tottering around six foot, she had the slender but curved figure, that no amount of gym time could give to the average woman. Her deep blue suit made the slate-black of her skin so striking that I almost said, *'Wow.'* Her eyes, which were only a couple of shades lighter, could have been selected from a colour palette in order to match her complexion.

'Thank you…' For a second, I thought I had her name, but then it was gone. I was though, fairly sure she was in charge of publicity for the production company. I had lots of memories of trying to get away from her.

'Demi,' she said with a sympathetic smile.

'Thank you, Demi. And, yes, I do have a question, actually.'

'Please,' she said, sitting back down. She seemed happy I was getting involved.

'Am I being kept out of the press tour after the premiere?' I thought I might as well get that answer early on.

'No,' she said nicely but with clearly no room for negotiation.

Matt straightened a little more next to me, and I heard him inhale deeply, but he remained quiet.

251

'Okay, thanks for clearing that up,' I said, sitting back, feeling fully put in my place.

'I get that you're nervous, Freya,' Sanjay said from next to Demi. Dressed in a three-piece linen suit and Panama hat, he was the picture of British, cool, calm, and collected. He also had something to do with publicity, but I thought he was part of my team and not representing the production company. 'When we first announced *Occurrences* was being turned into films, all the fans wanted to know was, were you on board? Were you actually going to be involved in production? If we don't show that you have not only backed this film, but are actively promoting it, the fans will lose faith. It was a risk keeping you out until now, but with how public the accident was, we'll get away with it until the premiere.'

I nodded slowly with a sigh, but he kept going. 'If your memories have not returned by then, every question will be staged, and at no point will you ever be interviewed alone. One of these lot,' he said, waving his hand out towards the main cast members and the director Paul Skelton, a bulk of a man, with a laugh that rivalled Reena's, 'will always be with you. We have also requested that all interviews are conducted by junior reporters. We're calling it an initiative to promote young talent, but it means you won't have met any of them before.'

'Okay,' I said more confidently. Matt took my hand and squeezed it lightly.

A moment of silence followed, but then they fell with ease into the planning.

I remembered the protocols from the last *Occurrences* premiere and the many others I had attended with Matt. I knew how to stand, smile, and walk, but because the flashing cameras in Florence had garbled my memories further, to be on the safe side, a red carpet was to be set up in my garden, with people hired to pretend to be snap-happy press lining the way. The word 'desensitise' was thrown around a lot.

Every minute detail was considered and reconsidered, but for most of it, I was a bystander. It felt like my being there was more out of courtesy. I would be given my instructions when they had all decided what they would be. It did though, give me a chance to zone in on each person, and with enough internal prompting, I was able to recall things about them and fundamentally, me that were previously forgotten.

Opposite me, discussing the press schedule for after the premiere with my agent Patricia, was Jeff Fielding, the producer. I recognised his bushy grey moustache and matching eyebrows from the snippet of a memory I had of walking into the first meeting to discuss turning *Occurrences* into films. He had a light-hearted nature and a soft appearance, but when he spoke, there was an assured, intelligent air to his demeanour that made you take note. Other things were starting to come back as I watched him play with the collar of his shirt and scrunch his nose up in disapproval of something said.

When he looked up and saw my broad smile directed straight at him, he returned it with a blush, lowering his head. He knew I was remembering the time he and I had played hooky, on the press tour for the last *Occurrences* film, in France. Thanks to his abysmal navigational skills, what was meant to be a one-hour round trip for some cheese, he had been going on about all week, turned into an eleven-hour, scenic drive, around the sparse French countryside.

Patricia might be a harsh, take no shit character, but she reminded me of Bastine. Her dark, cat-like eyes held the room to her will, and I was thankful she was my advocate. Every time someone suggested something I didn't like the sound of, she'd just say 'No,' and no one pushed. Most of my stressful work memories concluded with her giving me the tough love I needed to get over the nerves of being forced into the spotlight.

I was having similar flashbacks of Nicola, my blunt, quirky assistant, when something so unbelievable popped into my head that it made me gasp and turn towards her. She leant in next to me as if she had been expecting it.

'We never talk about it,' she said like she was simply telling me the time.

I could understand why, but if the full memory didn't return soon, she was going to have to explain why I had helped her extract a dead, naked, fat man from a sex swing.

After that revelation, I started to see the benefits of amnesia.

Pushing that disturbing image from my head, I gave my attention back to the table.

'They want you for the swimsuit edition,' Sanjay said to Reena and then lowered his eyes back to his notepad. From how fidgety he became, he could clearly feel the sharpness of her stare.

Reena was small, but she had an edge to her glare which made crossing her feel like a bad idea. A trait I had a lot of fun utilising with Sarah. I could see exactly why I fought for her.

'Offer me up, Sanj. I've got your back, Reen. They'll be so happy they won't question the shift.'

I looked around Matt to see William sitting back, arms outstretched with his foot resting on his knee. I chuckled under my breath, remembering what Matt had said about him in Florence.

As I moved back, I subtly looked Matt over, feeling a smile blush my cheeks. I had recently had some fun with Matt in swimwear. A light cough and shuffle in his seat told me Matt could see it replaying on my face. When I glanced up at him, a sultry look welcomed me, while his grip on my thigh tightened.

While the discussions around me blurred into white noise and the urge to pull Matt from the meeting intensified, I considered the hell I put Sarah and Lee through. As I was yet to read my books, I didn't know if I had ended their story the way I intended back in 2015.

I spent three books killing off an array of characters and throwing in every curveball I could think of to keep them apart. I just couldn't bring myself to make them happy. Misery likes company, after all. I remembered writing it in capitals across a notepad *SHE LEAVES IT ALL BEHIND*.

With my bitterness for life washed away, I thought about what I wanted to find on the last page. Didn't they, like I, deserve a happy ending? However it ended, I knew from reading the reviews that any happiness they found would only be 'happy for now'.

Killing off Bastine was just never an option.

The meeting ended with Patricia telling me she would email me an itinerary and Nicola running off before I could quiz her. Everyone was excited after all the hard work it had taken to make my imagination a reality, and bypassing all the attention it would bring, I couldn't wait to see what they had produced. The fact that I had very little memory of it being made was extremely reassuring.

On her way out, Patricia handed me a box of flashcards that I needed two hands to hold. It contained pictures of all the people attending the premiere that I should know. With the cards came detailed reports about how I knew them, how they were famous, and acceptable and non-acceptable things to say to them.

For the next fortnight, the kids thought it was great fun helping me with the flashcards. Jack and Isabella quizzed me, while Dylan and Charlotte reduced the pile for me by either eating them or throwing up on them.

Thankfully, they kept to their word about keeping me out of the press mix until after the premiere. Matt, my hero, was taking the brunt of that one. It had been worked that all interviews were to be done in London. It would seem everyone was happy to travel for a chat with Matt Lord. Every evening he had returned, kids long in bed, I'd ask how it had gone, but he'd shake his head, signalling he was all talked out, and instead, just pull my lips to his.

Whether it be on the kitchen table, my desk, or in the pool, he released all his tension, using his body and mine. His mouth and tongue were very much active, but I was the one making any noise at those times. My despair about the disappearance of my cheat sheet on him evaporated as I fell into the pleasurable task of re-searching for those happy spots. Matt didn't seem to mind in the slightest. If anything, he encouraged my exploration.

'I'll go commando if you do,' I said.

'Deal,' he said without hesitation.

I turned into him. 'Do you think you could be commando in the time it takes me to lock the door?'

He beamed. 'Absofuckinglutely,' he said with a cocky assurance.

Just as I turned the key in the door, from the other side, Jack yelled, 'Mummm, I'm hungry.'

'Go find Alex!' Matt shouted back.

'I can't find him.'

'Look harder.'

I heard Jack totter off, mumbling, and my chest swelled with love for both of them. I turned around and dropped my jeans to the floor. My t-shirt came off as I walked towards my naked husband. He wasn't the only one using our bodies as therapy.

When I reached him, he picked me up, and I wrapped my legs around his waist. Lifting me higher, he rested his tip against me. His mouth found my nipples, and he grazed each with his teeth while he lowered me onto him.

Exhaling all my tension, I arched my back, taking in all of him. He sat down on the flat sofa, and I brought my legs around, so I was kneeling over him. Slowly, I lowered, then drew back up, relishing in the pleasure of the rhythmic motion. His hands dug into my back, and his mouth caressed each breast. My core tightened, needing to deepen the pressure, and I increased the pace.

'You feel incredible,' he panted.

His mouth folded over mine as he pushed my hair from my face. I melted into him, pulling his chest tightly against me. Rocking my hips across him, his head fell into my neck.

'Fuck! Frey. Don't stop.'

Lost in the sensation of him, I moved faster, and he expanded inside me. Our hands slid over each other, hungrily claiming the other. Neither of us yet feeling like we had regained what had been lost.

In a practised move, Matt's hands lowered underneath my bum, lifting so only the end of him was inside me, then pulled me back down, hard. We both called out in absolute ecstasy, and he drew me up, repeating the motion over and over. As I fell into the abyss, he shuddered against me, and my convulsing orgasm intensified.

I opened my eyes, but before me was not the orgasm-saturated husband I expected to see.

I saw Matt in a café, looking at me in awe as I walked away from him.

I rounded the corner, and he caught up to me, electrifying me with static when he touched my shoulder. He looked so nervous and vulnerable. He started speaking, but my memory hadn't found the words yet. I held on tightly. I desperately wanted to remember this moment. Lights blurred around the image, and the memory came into focus.

'May I buy you a drink, Miss Patrick?' He looked over to the coffee counter and then back to me. 'One that comes with ice in a glass?'

I couldn't recall my response, only that I was apprehensive. *'They've all hurt you. This one could destroy you,'* rang through my head.

Like something had finally finished buffering, I saw the cluster of patrons huddling around steaming mugs, while trying to crane their necks to get a better look at the man waiting expectantly before me. I could smell the coffee and sweet pastries, even feel the sweat gathering on the back of my neck.

'I'm going to be blatantly honest with you.' I looked everywhere other than in his eyes. 'I have terrible taste in men. I mean absolutely bloody atrocious. So, for once in my life, I'm sorry, but I'm going to take a sidestep.' I squared my shoulders, feeling both proud and disgusted with myself. 'Why are you smiling?'

'All I heard was you're attracted to me.'

He looked so happy that I couldn't help laughing.

'Look,' he said, dropping the smile, and the conversation took a more serious tone. 'We're all arseholes, and I include women in that as well. You just haven't found the arsehole that can't live without you... yet. What you going to do, date men you're not attracted to?'

He didn't wait for me to reply before continuing. 'Obviously not, and if you're going to leave here and then go off and date another arsehole, that's not fair. I would like my chance, please.'

'If your acting career goes south, you'd make a great salesman.'

'That is true. I've been told before that I could sell ice to the Eskimos.'

'And how would you do that?'

'What?'

'Sell ice to the Eskimos.'

258

He pondered that for a couple of seconds and then said, 'Make it colourful. They have got to be sick of the sight of white.'

I was screwed, and I knew it. I wanted to both run from him and jump him. It was by far the most agonising decision I had ever contemplated.

While trying to steady my breathing, I looked away from him and saw a woman in the corner, possibly in her late forties holding a phone up towards us. I squinted, and then when I realised what she was doing, I ducked back, using Matt as a human shield between me and the camera.

Noticing my loss of attention, he scanned around and then back at me with a mischievous smile. Folding his arms across his chest, he looked cockily confident. I was now being distracted by the material of his jacket pulling against his arms and shoulders.

'You're not a big fan of being the centre of attention, are you?' There was humour in his voice, and I got the sense I was not going to like the direction this was going in.

'Can't say I am, no,' I replied cautiously.

Reaching into his pocket, he retrieved a pack of chewing gum, held it out in front of him, then purposely dropped it to the floor between us. The smile on his face grew, and he began to lower himself down.

'What are you doing?'

As if it was the most reasonable thing to say, he said, 'I'm going to go down on one knee and pick up my chewing gum.'

He lowered a little more, and I saw the woman with her phone still pointing at us. My face fell, and my body broke out into a cold sweat.

'You know, if we were to leave here now and say get a drink, I think the gum could stay down here.'

'And if we didn't?' I had no idea why I was practically daring him to do it, but there was something about him that bought out a wicked side in me.

He lowered a little more. 'Well, I am a gentleman, so while I'm on one knee, I am obviously going to reach up to offer you the gum.'

'You wouldn't.' I wanted to slap myself. Why did I keep daring him? My eyes darted around the room in a panic. There were only four people, but they all had phones pointing at us. 'I could just run away,' I quipped while folding my arms across my chest.

He scoffed. 'Yeah, jilting me while I'm on one knee that will get the attention off you.'

Further down he went until he was actually on one knee. His hand reached towards the gum.

'Okay. Okay. A drink.'

He raised his head, and I was presented with a 'winning' smile. 'Fantastic. Want some gum?' He held the packet out towards me on his palm while still on one knee.

Everyone in the room either softly squealed or squirmed excitedly around in their seat. Pursing my lips, I took the packet. 'Stay exactly where you are.'

'On my knees in front of you? No problem.'

So that all around me could see, I slowly slipped out a piece of gum and popped it into my mouth.

'Okay, let's go,' he said, jumping to his feet.

'Do you always get what you want?'

'Only when I really, really want it.' He drew in a deep breath and smiled broadly at me. A wave of nervous but excited energy flowed from him, and it was enough to make me feel lightheaded.

He leant around me to open the door, and I turned quickly to get away from the cameras.

'You're going to be trouble, aren't you?' I said with a little more fear in my voice than I had intended as I walked out of the door.

'I hope so.'

Cold air barrelled into me, and the image changed. Matt was holding Jack and Isabella, just born, against his naked chest in the nursery's rocking chair. Light gathered around them, and he looked up at me with tears in his eyes.

'Can we have more?' he asked quietly.

'Let's see if we can keep these two alive first, and then we'll talk about more.'

The amount of love pulsating through the nursery was enough to take my breath away. Matt was rocking gently and looking at me like I was a Goddess granting his every wish.

'I adore you. Thank you so much for pushing them out.'

I heard myself chuckle, but the light around my eyes flickered, and the scene before me morphed into Matt standing at an altar in a black tuxedo, surrounded by twinkle lights, waiting for me.

'Frey?' I heard my name, but it sounded far away.

I wanted to go to the voice, but I could see Matt in the pool at the villa. I was wrapped around him while cool water lapped at us, and he lazily floated us around.

'Marry me,' he said, lowering us further into the water.

It felt so out of the blue. I was trying to find the humour in his face, but all I saw was love, lust, and a little fear.

'Have a little spontaneous moment there, Lord?' I said with a nervous giggle.

His eyes never left my face as he answered, 'I bought the ring three weeks after I met you. You killed the spontaneity when you made me promise I wouldn't propose while you were pregnant.' I remained silent. This was the moment I realised with unquestionable certainty that we weren't together because of the kids. He was going to propose before we knew I was pregnant. 'I adore you. You are the love of my life. Will you marry me?'

'Yes.'

'Freya?' the voice rang out around me again.

I opened my eyes to see the man that I knew I would love with or without the memory of him. A tear ran down my cheek. 'Every piece of who I am loves you.' I kissed him lightly. 'I remember you,' I whispered.

He pulled back to take all of me in, shock radiating off him. 'Really?'

'I had never for a second forgotten that I love you, but now I remember how much you love me.'

'You have no fucking idea.' His lips crashed passionately into mine, and in one motion, he lifted me to lay us out across the sofa.

'Enough adult fun time, you two. Open this bloody door. You need to get ready. It's premiere time,' my boisterous agent called as the door handle rattled.

'Sod off,' Matt yelled back.

His attention fell back to me, and I couldn't resist saying, 'Hi.'

With the most devoted look of love I was yet to see, he replied, 'Welcome home.' His eyes remained on mine as his hips pushed my thighs wide, and he eased, ever so slowly into me. My back arched, and for the first time in weeks, Matt got to make love to his wife.

Chapter Twenty-Eight

Eventually, we opened the door, and I was pulled and pushed to and fro between different people. By the time they were finished with me, I had to admit, I was impressed. My hair was pinned back in loose curls, and the blue and grey blending of my eyeshadow highlighted the deep red of my glossed lips, but after finally remembering who I was, I no longer looked like me. In a desperate attempt not to lose what I had only just found, I focused on the golden tinges in my green eyes and the way the right side of my mouth lifted a fraction higher than the left when I smiled.

The room emptied, and for a few minutes, I was left alone. Standing in front of the mirror, I gently ran my hands over the crisp material. The dress fitted me perfectly, and in a way, it felt like a shield against what I was walking into.

'I've got to hand it to you, you look alright.'

'Wow, what a compliment.'

'You want a better one, eat a fucking calorie—You know why you could never kill me off, right?'

'Your charming personality?'

'No matter how bleak life got, no one could ever beat the strength out of you.'

'That's because you always made them look weak. You're not around, though, in the later memories coming back to me.'

'You don't have to be so strong when someone's got your back.'

'I think I married well this time.'

'You did, but if it goes tits up, and he turns into a prick, we'll deal with him like we did the last. For now, it's time you and I

said goodbye again. Be happy and stay out of trouble and oncoming traffic.'

I took a slow, deep breath. 'See you in the pages.'

'What are you doing? Let's go, go, go,' Patricia said, appearing in the open door. She too, had made an effort with a tailored black suit and a pair of dark green heels I was going to be asking about.

I scurried out behind her and was quickly ushered from the house and into the car. They were petrified one of the kids would get me with sticky fingerprints.

I climbed in next to Matt, who was wearing a tuxedo that reminded me of our wedding day. Running my hand along his thigh, I purred into his ear, 'Just so you know, I took you up on your commando deal.'

He raised an eyebrow at me, and for a second, I thought I was going over his shoulder, heading back to the house.

Patricia climbed in, and Matt sighed, letting his eyes wander over my dress. I drew my lips in tightly and shrugged.

My new publicist Hannah came in last, and we were ready to go. She was a battle axe of a woman who looked like a fairy, and I loved her. Amanda was sacked, without ceremony, on the same day she put my daughter in harm's way.

While we drove into London, they barked instructions. I tried to listen, but I was too absorbed watching the last seven years play out as each memory slotted back into the place it had been knocked from. Mostly, I watched as our families gathered for Christmas at our house. When the midwife passed me each of my children, screaming and covered in gunk. Then, a wedding that wasn't my own flashed before my eyes.

'Oh my God, Laura married Parker Jackson.'

Matt erupted into laughter at my audible shock. I couldn't believe it. Parker Jackson was the cocky, misfit actor that got away with doing whatever he wanted because he was so bloody charming.

'Oh, he chased her for years.'

I was still marvelling at my best friend marrying the actor, who played the main character from my favourite book growing up, when the car slowed, and the sound of the crowd outside pushed all other thoughts away.

The stars of the film, apart from the one in the car with me, were already walking the carpet, and all around us, camera flashes welcomed them. Patricia and Hannah got out before we reached the endpoint, so for a moment, Matt and I were left alone.

I was letting out a deep breath, trying to remember all my instructions, when Matt's fingers trailed over my jawline, drawing my attention to him. Resting on his palm was a red velvet box.

'Open it,' he said, kissing me on the cheek. 'It's time to let the cat out.'

I did as I was told and saw a round gold locket with seams of ivy running over it.

'It's exquisite.' I lifted it, and after running my fingers over the curved ridges, I clicked the locket open. Inside, there was a small picture of my little family all gathered in the garden on a green tartan blanket. On the other side was an inscription.

I belong to them

Printed in Great Britain
by Amazon

26110515R00158